Unforgettable You

Me, You, and Us Series: Book 2

by
Deanndra Hall

Unforgettable You
Me, You, and Us Series: Book 2

Celtic Muse Publishing, LLC
P.O. Box 3722
Paducah, KY 42002-3722

Copyright © 2015 Deanndra Hall
ISBN-13: 978-0692357866
ISBN-10: 0692357866
Print Edition

This book is a work of fiction.

Names of characters, places, and events are the construction of the author, except those locations that are well-known and of general knowledge, and all are used fictitiously. Any resemblance to persons living or dead is coincidental, and great care was taken to design places, locations, or businesses that fit into the regional landscape without actual identification; as such, resemblance to actual places, locations, or businesses is coincidental. Any mention of a branded item, artistic work, or well-known business establishment, is used for authenticity in the work of fiction and was chosen by the author because of personal preference, its high quality, or the authenticity it lends to the work of fiction; the author has received no remuneration, either monetary or in-kind, for use of said product names, artistic work, or business establishments, and mention is not intended as advertising, nor does it constitute an endorsement. The author is solely responsible for content.

Formatting by BB eBooks
Cover design by Novel Graphic Designs, used by permission of the artist

Disclaimer:

Material in this work of fiction is of a graphic sexual nature and is not intended for audiences under 18 years of age.

Dedication

To Heidi Ryan:

Sometimes when things get tough, I hear your voice:
"Don't you fucking quit, you hear me?"
Yes, I hear you. And I won't.
So thanks for that, and for all your support.
I'm proud to call you friend.

A word from the author . . .

This book's predecessor, *Adventurous Me*, was a surprise.

This book was not. And I have a lot of people to thank for that. I'll get to that in a minute.

After *Adventurous Me* came out, I decided that the characters were far too multi-dimensional and interesting to just walk away from them. Steffen, in particular, was someone I wanted to know more about. I have to admit: Every time I picture him, I see Alex Skarsgard. Sorry. That did make it impossible to leave him alone.

And so, here it is, Steffen's book. The impression you got from him in *Adventurous Me* may not be accurate. Sure, he seems like an ego-driven stud, but that's not who he is at all. Read on. You'll love him like I do, and along with heart-rending and sweet, it's just incredibly funny.

So here you go. Yes, there's sex. Yes, they spend time at Bliss. Yes, it's gritty and raw and nasty. And funny. And sexy. And tender. And family-oriented. But don't give it to your twelve-year-old – BIG mistake. Still, enjoy it. And we're not finished yet. You'll get to see into Dave's soul in the last book in this trilogy, and I promise you, it'll turn you inside-out just like these two have.

Thanks to Drue, Heidi, and the Construction Crew for their tireless efforts to get my name out there. And thanks to Sir, who said, "Of all your books, I love *Adventurous Me* the best." I heard you, baby.

Love and happy reading,
Deanndra

Visit my website and blog at:
www.deanndrahall.com

Connect with me on my:
Substance B page

Contact me at:
DeanndraHall@gmail.com

Join me on on Facebook at:
facebook.com/deanndra.hall

Catch me on Twitter at:
twitter.com/DeanndraHall

Write to me at:
P.O. Box 3722, Paducah, KY 42002-3722

More Titles from this Author

Love Under Construction Series

The Groundbreaking (Prequel)

The Groundbreaking is a preview of the main characters contained in all of the Love Under Construction Series books. Not intended as a work of erotic fiction, it is simply a way for the reader to get to know and love each character by discovering their backgrounds.

Laying a Foundation (Book 1) COMBO VOLUME includes The Groundbreaking (Prequel)

Sometimes death robs us of the life we thought we'd have; sometimes a relationship that just won't die can be almost as bad. And sometimes the universe aligns to take care of everything. When you've spent years alone, regardless the circumstances, getting back out there can be hard. But when you've finally opened up to love and it looks like you might lose it all, can love be enough to see you through?

Tearing Down Walls (Book 2)

Secrets – they can do more damage than the truth. Secrets have kept two people from realizing their full potential, but even worse, have kept them from forming lasting relationships and finding the love and acceptance they both desperately need. Can they finally let go of those secrets in time to find love – and maybe even to stay alive?

Renovating a Heart (Book 3)

Can a person's past really be so bad that they can never

recover from it? Sometimes it seems that way. One man hides the truth of a horrific loss in his teen years; one woman hides the truth of a broken, scarred life that took a wrong turn in her teens. Can they be honest with each other, or even with themselves, about their feelings? And will they be able to go that distance before one of them is lost forever?

Planning an Addition (Book 4)

When you think you're set for life and that life gets yanked out from under you, starting over is hard. One woman who's starting over finds herself in love with two men who've started over too, and she's forced to choose. Or is she? And when one of them is threatened by their past, everyone has choices to make. Can they make the right ones in time to save a life?

The Harper's Cove Series

Beginning with the flagship volume, *Karen and Brett at 326 Harper's Cove*, find out exactly what the neighbors of Harper's Cove are up to when they go inside and close their doors. According the Gloria, the drunken busy-body of the cove, they're all up to something perverse, and she's determined to find out their secrets. As she sneaks, peeks, pokes, and prods, her long-suffering husband, Russell, begs her to leave all of their nice neighbors alone. But could Gloria be right?

The Harper's Cove series books are fast, fun, nasty little reads priced just right to provide a quick, naughty romp. See if each of the couples of Harper's Cove shock you just enough to find out what the neighbors at the next address will do!

Karen and Brett at 326 Harper's Cove (Book 1)

Gloria wants more than anything to be invited to one of Karen and Brett Reynolds' parties, and she's very vocal about it. Karen and Brett, however, know full well that if Gloria were ever invited to one of their parties, she would be in a hurry to leave, and in an even bigger hurry to let everyone know they're the scourge of the neighborhood. Every Saturday night, Karen and Brett keep their secrets – all twelve of them.

Becca and Greg at 314 Harper's Cove (Book 2)

Even though they're quiet and stay to themselves, Becca and Greg Henderson seem pretty nice and average. They don't go out much or have many people over, except for that one couple who are probably relatives. But when that half-sister of Becca's moves in, it all seems a little fishy; she gets around pretty well for a person recovering from cancer. And where was Becca going all decked out in that weird outfit? The Henderson are tight-lipped, but Gloria hopes she can eventually get to the bottom of things. If she does, she'll get the biggest surprise of her life.

Donna and Connor at 228 Harper's Cove (Book 3)

Those nice people at 228, the Millicans? They're religious counselors, trying to help lovely couples who are having marital problems. Problem is, they're not counseling; training, maybe, but not counseling. But no matter what Donna says, Gloria still thinks the truck that delivered large crates to the Millicans' house in the wee hours of the morning two weeks after they'd moved in was pretty suspicious. Donna says it was exercise equipment that the moving company had lost, but Gloria's not so sure. Could it be that they're not as they appear?

Savannah and Martin at 219 Harper's Cove (Book 4)

Savannah and Martin McIntosh are new to the neighborhood, but that doesn't stop Gloria from trying her best to find out what they do on the second and fourth Friday nights of the month. Savannah insists they play cards, but Gloria's pretty sure it's more than that, considering the men she sees leaving the house in the wee hours of Saturday morning. But when she decides to get a little "up close and personal," she may get more than she bargained for.

And we're just getting started!

The Me, You, and Us Series

Adventurous Me (Book 1)

Boring, tiresome, predictable . . . all words Trish Stinson's soon-to-be ex-husband uses as excuses for why he's leaving after almost 30 years of marriage. But Trish's efforts to find adventure and prove him wrong land her in the lap of a man who leads her to an adventure she could've never predicted. And when that adventure throws her into a situation with a man who can't stand her, she's forced to decide between honor and her life.

Unforgettable You (Book 2)

Reeling from a relationship that didn't happen, Steffen Cothran stumbles upon a woman who may be the answer to his prayers, but Sheila Brewster has problems he couldn't have anticipated. They work hard to forge a relationship, only to have it destroyed by someone from Steffen's past – the one person he'd forgotten about. As Sheila, hurt and angry, walks out of his life, Steffen eventually gives up on love until that fateful night when curiosity takes him somewhere he never thought he'd be to see something he never dreamed he'd see.

Incredible Us (Book 3)

Dave Adams has just what he wants: Bliss, a well-respected BDSM club, all the subs a man could want, and a growing family who loves him. He expects his retirement years to be the best of his life – until he opens the club's back door and finds something, or someone, he could never have expected to find. He doesn't want to love Olivia Warren, over three decades his junior, but Dave is a natural protector, and he's never met anyone who needs protecting more than Olivia. Problem is, when her danger is over, he finds out that the relationship meant more than he ever dreamed.

The Celtic Fan (independent novel)

Journalist Steve Riley sets out to do the seemingly impossible: Find Nick Roberts, author of the bestselling book The Celtic Fan. When his traveling buddies lose interest, Steve continues on to a stolen address and finds someone who couldn't possibly be Roberts. As time goes by, Steve has to decide if he wants to break the story of a lifetime and break someone's heart, or give in to the feelings that promise him the love of a lifetime. Set in the beautiful Smoky Mountains of North Carolina, The Celtic Fan is both Steve's journey and excerpts from the original book written by Roberts about a young, wounded, WWII veteran and the forbidden love he finds.

Support your Indie authors!

Independent (Indie) authors are not a new phenomenon, but they are a hard-working one. As Indie authors, we write our books, have trouble finding anyone to beta read them for us, seldom have money to hire an editor, struggle with our cover art, find it nearly impossible to get a reviewer to even glance at our books, and do all of our own publicity, promotion, and marketing. This is not something that we do until we find someone to offer us a contract – this is a conscious decision we've made to do for ourselves that which we'd have to do regardless (especially promotion, which publishers rarely do anyway). We do it so big publishing doesn't take our money and give us nothing in return. We do it because we do not want to give up rights to something on which we've worked so hard. And we do it because we want to offer you a convenient, quality product for an excellent price.

Indie authors try to bring their readers something fresh, fun, and different. Please help your Indie authors:

- Buy our books! That makes it possible for us to continue to produce them;
- If you like them, please go back to the retailer from which you bought them and review them for us. That helps us more than you could know;

- If you like them, please tell your friends, relatives, nail tech, lawn care guy, anyone you can find, about our books. Recommend them, please;
- If you're in a book circle, always contact an Indie author to see if you can get free or discounted books to use in your circle. Many would love to help you out;
- If you see our books being pirated, please let us know. We worked weekends, holidays, and through vacations (if we even get one) to put these books out, so please report it if you see them being stolen.

More than anything else, we hope you enjoy our books and, if you do, please contact us in whatever manner we've provided as it suits you. Visit our blogs and websites, friend our Facebook sites, and follow us on Twitter. We'd love to get to know you!

Chapter One

"Hey, can we have lunch? I'd really like to talk to you, you know, clear the air and all that."

I want to sigh very loudly. It's bad enough that I put myself out there and got knocked down. Now the victor wants to rub it in? Not nice – not nice at all. It's been five weeks since the collaring ceremony following the pairing event, and I'm nowhere near past all of this.

For reasons I don't understand, I say, "Sure. Where do you want to go and when?" I want to scream, *No! I don't want to sit at a table with you!* But I'm not going to do that. I'm better than that.

Two hours later, he rises from the table as I walk up to it in the café down the street from the bank. "Steffen! It's good to see you!" His hand reaches out, and I take it and shake it.

"Clint. So what's this all about?"

"Let's order so we have a little bit of uninterrupted time, okay?" He motions for the server to come to the table, and we order quickly so she'll leave. "So, I just wanted to touch base with you. It's been five weeks and . . ."

"I know exactly how long it's been, thanks. What is it that you want, Clint?"

He gives me a sad look. "I want to know we're okay, that we're still friends. None of this was meant to hurt you, Steffen, you know that."

I sigh deeply. I know that in theory, but it still hurts. I'd been so sure when he and Trish had their problems that I'd be next in line. I wanted her; I'd had her when she first started coming to the club, and I was pretty sure we could have a good relationship if I just had some time with her. But that wouldn't be happening. Once again, good old Steffen gets passed over.

So I decide that it's not worth losing a long-term friendship over, and Clint and I have known each other for a long time. "I know. I realize that. I just don't know what to say. I don't want to feel this way, but I do. Remember, I was there with her when she was pretty sure you despised her. I just wanted a chance to see if we could have a relationship, you know? But she was gone. You snagged her."

Clint shakes his head and stares at the table. "I thought I'd lost her. You have no idea how that felt. I didn't think I could be more hurt than I was when Christi did what she did, but I was wrong. I don't know what the hell I was thinking, acting the way I did, but that will never, *never* happen again, never. She didn't deserve that and I'm so sorry about all of it. But I think we're going to be okay. Every day is a little better than the one before, and I'm really, really hopeful that it's all going to be fine." He finally looks up at me. "I'm sorry it all happened the way it did, Steffen. I hope we can still be friends."

I've never seen Clint Winstead look as sheepish as he does right now, and I feel bad that *he* feels so bad. He's had a rough time of it, and I'm glad he has someone like Trish now. His life has sucked so badly for so long. It's his time.

But what about my time? Will it ever come?

Thursday night is usually a slow night at the club. It's a crisp, early fall night when I stroll into the club and head to the locker room to find Gary, Austin, and a guy I haven't met talking about the ballgame the night before. It's weird, walking into a room and finding a bunch of bare-chested guys in leathers talking about football.

They all speak as I walk through and just keep talking about the game. I change and stalk back through the room; they say nothing as I pass. By the time I get to the bar, I'm in a better mood. And it doesn't hurt that Dave's standing back there, drawing beer and smiling at me. "Hey, Steffen! How ya doin'?"

"Pretty good, pretty good. Can I have a Lite?"

"Sure!" Dave draws the draft and sets it in front of me. "I'm glad you and Clint talked. He really values your friendship, you know."

I nod and smile. "And I value his. I'm glad we talked too. I've felt better ever since." And that's true. It's going on three months and we've barely seen each other, but that's because they aren't coming to the club much.

Instead, they're staying home and trying to get to know each other a lot better, and apparently it's working. A couple of people who've seen them said they seem really, really happy. I'm glad for that, truly glad. They both deserve to be happy.

"I have to tell you, I haven't seen Clint this happy in a long, long time, maybe never. Trish is so good for him. And the girls! She always wanted kids but that dickwad she was married to didn't, and now she's got two who adore her as much as she adores them. She's turned into an amazing mom and they're really attached to her already. It's a wonderful thing to see. Marrying her was the best thing he ever did."

Ouch. I want to yell, *Thanks for the reminder.* They got married last week on Labor Day, and I was invited, so I went, even though it was hard. I do want to stay friends with them. "So, when are you going to find yourself a permanent sub?" I ask with a grin for Dave from inside my beer mug.

"Me? Shit. I'm too old for that, too set in my ways. Who the hell would want me?"

That makes me laugh right out loud. "The women around here go wet when you walk through the door. They all think you're the hottest thing they've ever seen and you know it!"

He makes a face. "Well, I'm not the worst thing they've ever seen, I'm pretty sure."

"Aw, you're just an old stud, Adams. You can't help yourself!" Now I'm laughing so hard I'm snorting.

"I don't know about that, but so far none of them

have complained!" He's laughing too. I'd forgotten how much fun Dave can be.

"Find one, Dave. You need a woman."

"No, I need a housekeeper. I can get a woman any time I want one. I just can't keep 'em."

"One will come across your radar and you'll latch on. You just wait. She'll . . ."

"Whoa!" Dave stops me dead in my tracks. "Would you take a look at that!"

I turn to see what's gotten Dave stirred up and almost drop my beer mug. Clint and Trish have walked into the room and there's someone with them. I recognize her immediately: Sheila, Trish's best friend, last name, last name . . . Brewster. Yeah, that's it. I tried to talk to her at the wedding, but she was having none of that.

Her long, pumpkin-colored hair frames her face and makes her eyes look even bluer than they already are. She's taller than Trish, but not by much, and outweighs her by a good twenty pounds, every one of them voluptuous and sassy. Bigger tits, bigger hips, round and lush all over. Creamy skin. And freckles. I haven't seen that many freckles since Melinda Houser in second grade. And they're adorable.

They walk right up to me. "Steffen! How's it going?" Clint shakes my hand and slaps me on the shoulder with his left one.

"Doing quite well, thanks!" I turn toward Trish and ask, "Hey, sweetheart, how are you?" Instead of answering, Trish glances at Clint, he nods, and she hugs me. She feels incredible in my arms, and I think about asking Clint if the three of us can scene together, but I remember hearing him tell someone that he doesn't share. That would probably be a bad idea anyway.

When she turns loose and steps back, she smiles at me and my heart almost breaks. Then she says, "And I'd like you to meet someone. Sheila, this is Master Steffen. Steffen, this is my friend, Sheila. I think you two met last week at the wedding."

Her eyes are steady, and I like that. Confident. Strong. "It's a pleasure to meet you again! So is this the first time you've been to Bliss?"

She giggles, and it's a sound like chimes ringing. "It's the first time I've been to any club like this. I really don't know what to expect."

"Well, if you have any questions and they're not handy, ask me or Dave back here," I tell her, pointing at Dave, "and we'll try to answer them."

"Thanks. It's nice to meet you."

"Likewise. I hope to see you around again soon." And I mean that. I watch that beautiful ass sway as she walks away and god, I'd like to spank that. So would my cock. At least that's what it's telling me. Loudly.

"Wow." Dave's voice brings me back.

"Wow is right. That is one fine. Looking. Woman."

Dave nods. "Yes she is. I think that's one to watch."

"You want a run at her?"

Dave shakes his head. "Trish's friend? No. That would probably be a bad idea. I'm family."

I snicker. "And I'm not!"

The grin Dave gives me is full of mischief. "Well, you know what they say. He who hesitates is lost."

Trish and Sheila disappear into the locker room and all of a sudden, Clint's back. He grabs me by the upper arm and pulls me off the bar stool. "We need to talk."

My eyes have got to be the size of saucers. "What? Did I do something wrong?"

He drags me out the side door behind the bar and around the corner. When he stops and spins me around, he smiles. "Take it slow and easy. Remember that I said that. She's had the daylights scared out of her a time or two. Get it?"

I nod hard. "Got it."

"Okay. Slow and easy. She's really, really curious, so Trish and I are going to scene tonight, let her see something kind of tame before the hard stuff gets cranked up. I'm going to suggest that she sit over on one of the sofas with you so she'll have someone to answer her questions. That okay?"

I'm shaking with laughter. "Well, hell yeah! I haven't completely lost my mind! Sure. Works for me."

"Let's get back inside before they think we're up to something. Even though we are." Clint turns and strides back into the building. I'm taller and my legs are longer, but I'm having a little trouble keeping up.

We make it to the big room just in time to see Trish and Sheila come out of the locker room. Trish is her usual self, beautiful garter belt with a skirt attached, stockings snapped to it, stilettos, and nothing from the waist up. Sheila, unfortunately, is completely clothed.

Damn. But she still looks good. She's got on a beautiful silver and black corset with a sheer blouse over it and a pair of some kind of stretchy pants that look like water clinging to her curves. Double damn. What I'd give to be those pants.

They join us at the bar and Trish says, "Are you still planning to scene, Sir?"

Clint shoots Trish a smile that would melt steel. "Absolutely." He downs the rest of his soft drink and turns to Sheila. "Want to watch?"

She shrugs. "I guess. Is it going to be bad?"

Trish giggles. "Define bad!"

"No. Not bad at all. Easy stuff. Steffen can explain things to you if you'd like."

She turns and looks at me, and I can't read her face. "Sure." That's all she says.

"Well, then, come on over and have a seat!" I try to sound as cheerful as possible, but I'm getting the impression that she's really, really nervous, or maybe she doesn't like me at all. I can't tell. "Clint's been in the lifestyle for a good while. Everything will be fine."

"Yeah. Fine." Her face is still unreadable. I'd love to pick that brain, but I'm not going to push it per Clint. If I piss him off, I can forget this hook-up permanently. We find a sofa that's not occupied and have a seat. I fight the urge to put my hand across the back behind her. I want to, but I don't dare.

Clint and Trish move up into the performance area, and Clint puts a hand behind Trish's neck and pulls her up to him. He says something into her ear and she smiles up at him, then drops into presentation pose at his feet. I sneak a look at Sheila and she's watching so intently that she wouldn't notice if I looked her dead in the eye. In a moment or two, Clint says something else to Trish that we can't hear and she rises, then walks straight to the St. Andrew's cross near the wall. I watch Sheila's eyes go wide as she takes in the sight of Clint strapping Trish to the cross face-first.

When he pulls his flogger out of his bag, Sheila goes rigid. Her breathing quickens as Clint drags the familiar circle eight in the air with the falls of the flogger. As the first strike falls and Trish cries out, Sheila begins to pant.

Now I'm about to begin to pant. I take a good look down Sheila's chest, but with the corset it's impossible to see the state of her nipples. If I had to take a guess, I'd say they're rock hard. She licks her full, pouty lips and I almost see stars. Every strike of the flogger and every groan from Trish elicits some kind of response from Sheila, whether it's a wince, a squirm, or a gasp. She crosses and recrosses her legs over and over, and my balls feel like they're about to explode.

Clint stops and runs his hands over Trish's back, spreading the redness and warmth everywhere. He slips his finger between her legs and checks to see if she's ready. But when he's done that, Sheila turns and looks at me. "What's he doing?"

I raise my eyebrows and give her a small, placid smile. "He's checking to see if she's wet."

Her mouth drops open and she just stares at me. "Why would he do that?"

My answer? "To see if she needs any lube."

"For what?"

I grin. "For the fucking she's about to get."

Her jaw drops. "Wait. He's going to . . . they're going to have sex *here*? Right now? You're kidding."

"Not kidding. Not at all. Watch." I can't wait to see her face when they get started. Actually, it's me who gets the biggest surprise. Clint drags out a stand with a mounting point on it and finds a large phallic attachment to put on it. He unstraps Trish from the cross, points to the stand, and she positions herself above it on her knees, then slowly lowers herself onto it and stops. Clint binds her hands behind her back and moves back in front of her, unfastening his leathers as he goes. Once they're undone, he pulls his cock out, rubs the head back and forth over her lips a couple of times, then coaxes her mouth open and buries himself in her throat.

Trish lets loose with a deep moan and, as Clint keeps fucking into her throat, she's raising and lowering herself on the dildo. I sneak a glimpse at Sheila and see her staring, slack-jawed, and I wish my cock was between those pretty, open lips. Yeah. That would be awesome. Trish is moaning around Clint's dick, Clint's moaning with his head thrown back, and the glance I catch of Sheila makes me want to moan right out loud and tells me she's more turned on than appalled. And I'm pretty sure she'd never own up to that.

"Any other questions?" I can't help but ask. Yes, I'll admit it – I'm a smartass. I can't seem to help myself.

"No. I don't think so." I see something pass over her

face before she says, "Wait! Yeah."

"Yes?"

"Do they do this often?"

"Who? Members in general, or Clint and Trish specifically?"

"Clint and Trish."

"I wouldn't say often, but they do play here from time to time. I think they do most of their playing at home now. Clint doesn't share."

"Share what?"

"Trish."

Her mouth forms a surprised "O." "You mean sometimes they, more than, um . . ."

I nod, trying not to smirk. "Yeah. Occasionally. There are some people who enjoy that and welcome it."

She fixes me with a cold stare. "Do you share?"

I'm not going to lie to her. I really don't want to tell her the truth, but I won't lie. "Yeah, but not very often. Only if I'm invited. I never ask."

"No, I mean, do you share your woman?"

"Just depends." Her eyebrows shoot up. "I don't *have* a woman. We call them subs, short for submissives. If I did, no, I wouldn't be inclined to share a sub unless she wanted it. My utmost concern as a Dominant is her health and wellbeing, emotional, physical, and sexual. If that were something she really wanted, then yeah, I might pursue it, but only with someone we trusted completely."

She nods. "Trish has told me a little bit, but not a lot. I think she didn't want to scare me off before I had a chance to actually come and see."

"And now that you've seen?" I can't wait to hear the answer to this one.

"I really don't know what to think." She's still watching them intently. Trish is still riding the dildo, and Clint has begun a forceful ramming into her throat.

"Does it bother you that they're doing this right out in the open?"

She shakes her head, but says, "I'm not sure." She watches a few more seconds before she says, "It's like they're alone. It's like they've forgotten that we're sitting here."

"I assure you, they have. Right now, for the two of them, it's just a Dom and his sub enjoying the pleasures they can give themselves and each other. The fact that they're doing so in front of an audience is just icing on the cake for them."

"Huh." That's all she says. I wait, but she just watches silently. I'd love to know what's going on in that pretty head of hers. Clint says something to Trish that we can't hear, but I know exactly what it is, because I see her convulse with an orgasm just as Clint shoots into her throat. As he holds her head down over his cock, her hips continue to buck just a little until she's finally completely still and when she is, he backs out of her mouth and she takes a big, shuddering breath. There's saliva and cum all over her face and chest, running down those gorgeous breasts I'd love to touch just one more time, and he grabs a towel and cleans her up before wiping himself off. And when he finishes with that, he picks her up and carries her down the hallway. I'm getting ready to tell her about the private rooms when she asks, "Where are they going?"

"He's taking her to a private room for aftercare." Her eyes question. "She's on an endorphin high – we call it subspace. He'll put her on the bed in one of the rooms, cuddle her, give her something to drink, maybe a little bit of candy of some kind, just generally take care of her until she's back to normal. It's good for him, too. It helps them reconnect after something that intense, not to mention how vulnerable she felt there in the performance area, half naked, performing an act so intimate in front of a whole room full of people. They need to be able to feel good about what they did and reflect on it in private."

"How long will they be?"

I shrug. "Who knows? At least thirty minutes, I'd guess. Want something to drink?"

"Sure." I escort her to the bar and I get a soft drink because I've already had one beer; Sheila asks Dave for a beer. It's getting noisier, and there are a few more couples who've taken up residence in the performance areas around the room. "Can we watch someone else?"

I'm really surprised. "Of course. Which scene is of interest to you?"

"Um, that one?" She points at a couple who are just getting started. I'm not sure what they're about to do.

"If you like. Let's go get a seat." I escort her to a sofa in front of the performance area. We watch as the Dom lays the sub out on a bondage table and straps her down.

He readies her nipples, then puts a pair of clamps on. I catch a glimpse of Sheila out of the corner of my eye, and she's visibly wincing. "Any questions?"

"Yeah. Does she like that?"

"Yes, very much."

She makes a face. "You're kidding, right?"

I shake my head. "No, not at all. Some people find a degree of pain very stimulating." The look she gives me tells me she clearly thinks I've lost my mind. "Let me ask you something. Do you remember when you were a kid and they told you if your head was hurting you should do this?" I demonstrate by holding my right hand up, then pinching the area between my thumb and forefinger with the thumb and forefinger of the other hand. "You squeezed really hard and it was supposed to take away the headache pain?" She nods. "Well, that's kind of what discipline and punishment do. It's why submissives look for Dominants to meet that need. The pain they get from it increases the endorphins in their system and takes them higher, pretty much like a drug, takes their mind off anything else they've got on it. If you tried it, you might be surprised."

"Uh, no." That's all she says, but there's something going on behind those eyes that makes me want to know what she's really thinking.

We continue to watch as the Dom and sub who are scening work together. Once the clamps are on her nipples and she's been given an orgasm by manual stimulation, he helps her sit up, wraps her arms in a squared binder, and then takes her anally. I see Sheila wince out the corner of my eye and I fight the urge to laugh.

About the time they finish up, Clint and Trish come strolling out of the back, holding hands, a sight that makes *me* wince. "Everything okay out here?" Clint asks Sheila.

"Yes. Steffen has been very helpful." Now I feel like I'm about eighty years old.

"Good! I knew I could count on him. He's a very dependable kind of guy." Clint smiles broadly at me. Trish isn't smiling. She's still got that sleepy, half-gone look on her face. Yeah, he's definitely been working with her at home if she can slip into subspace that easily. Wow. Now I'm insanely jealous. He smiles at Sheila. "Want to come sit with us and talk? Maybe we can answer some questions for you."

"Sure." She looks at me expectantly. She can't see Clint when she looks at me, but I can, and he's shaking his head.

"Oh, I'd love to, but you probably need some time with Clint and Trish. I'll catch up with you later, okay?"

"Oh. Sure. Thanks, Steffen."

"You're quite welcome. It was a pleasure meeting you and I hope I see you again." I take her extended hand and kiss the back of it. Clint's fighting to keep his composure. Hey, I'm a gentleman. Suck on that.

"Same here. Bye." They stroll away in the direction of one of the larger sofas, and her beautiful ass calls to me as they go.

I watch her the rest of the evening. I'd like to say I

was covert about it, but it's hard to be inconspicuous when you're drooling everywhere. I'm not surprised when Dave poses the question, "What happened?"

"Clint told me to take it slow and easy. I'm just taking his advice." I take another sip of the diet drink I ordered. Only one alcoholic beverage. I keep hoping some sub with whom I can scene will suddenly appear.

"Ah! Wise. They know her pretty well, at least I know Trish does." He wipes down the bar in front of me. "She's a lovely woman. Do you have plans to . . ."

"Why, yes I do," I interrupt. I most definitely do.

"Well?"

"Well what?"

"Do you like her?"

"Clint, god, what's not to like? Beautiful tits, beautiful ass, beautiful legs, porcelain skin, that hair, those eyes. How could I not?"

"Forget about her looks. What about her?"

I snort – I can't help it. "Well, gee, it's really hard to get to know someone well on the first date, but . . ."

"Oh, cut the bullshit. What did you think?"

I'm looking for the right words. "Um, she seemed kind of, uh, repressed? And a bit scared maybe?"

"Fair assumption. She was engaged to a guy who went off on her one night and nearly beat her to death."

The words feel like they've punched holes in my gut. "Is he in jail?"

"Yes. For two more years. Everything was fine –

they'd been together for two or three years – and all of a sudden, everything just went south. He lied, said he was going to work, but he wasn't; he'd lost his job because he was skipping out to go to hotels with hookers, paying for the rooms with Sheila's credit cards. He raided every one of her accounts by forging her signature and almost bankrupted her. Gave her chlamydia; she was terrified he'd given her something worse. Used her credit card to buy a woman some expensive jewelry. And when she caught them together, he got mad at *her* and beat her until he put her in the hospital. So, as you can imagine, she's scared to death to get into another relationship. This is the first time she's even shown any interest in going out and doing anything; she usually just holes up in her house. But she's got a bullshit meter that's finely calibrated and a zero tolerance policy to go with it, so I'm hoping she'll be okay."

"Sweet lord, I would hope so. Bless her heart, that's horrible."

"Yeah. Trish doesn't know it, but I've made it my life's mission to find her a Dom, a good, responsible, respectable Dom, before that time is up so I know she's safe and cared for. She doesn't think he'll come after her when he gets out, but I'm not so sure."

"And so who are you thinking?"

"Well, who do you think? Are you at all interested?"

"Do I have functioning eyeballs? Yes, of course I'm interested. Very. But I don't know if she's interested in me."

Clint chuckles. "I'm about to take care of that. You

just play along and everything will be fine."

"I can definitely do that."

"Will you be at the club tonight?"

"If I need to be."

Clint snorts. "You need to be."

"Then I'll be there. No problem." Now my palms are starting to itch thinking of that ivory skin.

"So will we. See you then."

"Absolutely."

Now I've got to get myself psyched up for tonight. I don't know what he's got in mind, but I'm plenty willing to find out.

Chapter Two

The room is already buzzing with patrons when the three of them walk in, and I almost don't see them until I see Trish and Sheila's backs disappear into the locker room. That's when Clint walks up and slaps me on the back. "Hey, buddy!"

"Hey!" I take another swallow of beer. "Okay, so how about you tell me what's going on?"

"We've been talking, the three of us, explaining things to Sheila. And I think she wants to scene."

I know my eyes are the size of saucers. "Really? You're sure about this?"

"Yep. Pretty damn. Now listen, negotiate carefully. I think she wants to do it in private and with her clothes on, but it's a start, don't you think?"

"Well, hell yeah!" I want to jump up and down and cheer like she's a touchdown at a Seahawks game, but I keep my mouth shut.

"Okay, here they come. Act cool."

"Do I know another way to act?"

Clint slaps the back of my head. "Dork."

"Hey!" Before I can slap him back, the two of them

walk up. I try not to stare at Trish's nipples, but damn, they're fine. Another new garter belt with stockings and some rhinestone-studded platform pumps. Yeah, that's a beautiful package.

And this time, Sheila's tried. She's got on a corset with a ruffled skirt, fishnet hose, and a pair of black stiletto sandals. And her legs are smokin'. I can't help but smile at her, and she gives me a nervous little return grin. "My, you look nice tonight."

She giggles a little. "Thank you. Trish helped me pick it out."

I nod at Trish. "Very good work."

"Thank you, Sir," she replies, remembering her manners.

Sheila looks at Trish. "Am I supposed to . . ."

Trish nods. "Yes. It's a point of respect. He's a Dominant in this club, and a well-respected one at that."

I give her my best look of approval. "Why, thank you, subbie. I appreciate that."

"You're welcome, Sir. You deserve respect. You're quite the gentleman." She extends a hand to me and I take it and kiss it. That makes her giggle.

Clint wraps an arm around her waist. "So, Vännan, would you like to partake in some sins of the flesh tonight?"

"Yes, Master, I very much would."

"Would you please excuse us? I think there's a stage waiting for us." With that, he whisks her away and I'm left standing with Sheila.

"Well, hmmm. So would you like a drink? To sit

down?"

She smiles. "Yes and yes."

Dave pours us a couple of drinks and we head toward an empty sofa, but I turn to her and ask, "So which scene do you want to watch?"

A funny look passes over her face. "Could I talk to you about something?"

"Sure." I point to the sofa and sit. She joins me there, and she sits closer to me than she did the time before. "What's on your mind?"

"Um, Clint told me to ask you. I'm thinking I'd like to scene."

I nod, trying not to grin all over my face. "So, what would you like to do?"

"Just something very basic. No sex."

It's time to push the envelope. "I can reserve a stage."

"No!" Panic blooms across her cheeks. "No, I'd want to do it in private. Would that be possible?"

"Yes, absolutely. And now we have to negotiate the boundaries of this play. So," I ask as I level my gaze at her, "what exactly did you have in mind?"

"Well, Clint suggested that I learn to kneel. And then possibly to engage in some kind of, I don't know, making out, I guess you'd call it?"

"Okay, what do you want that to consist of?" I'm trying to get her to be specific.

"Well, maybe some kissing? Touching on top of my clothes maybe?" I nod but I don't say anything. I keep hoping she'll add more, and I'm not disappointed.

"Maybe aggressive touching?"

"Meaning what? Fondling through your clothes?" She nods. "Would you like to reach climax?" She nods again. *Hallelujah, it's my lucky day!,* I congratulate myself. "That's doable." I think about the first time I scened with Trish and how pissed Dave was at me. You can bet I won't make that mistake again. "You have a safeword, and it's red. If you use it, play stops. I'll honor it unless I don't hear you, and then just say it loud enough that I do. Understand?" She nods. "And don't nod anymore. I can't hear a nod."

"Okay."

"So if this is what you want to do, from this moment on you will address me as Sir. Understand?" She nods again, then verbally affirms. "Let me find out from Dave which rooms are available. Stay right here."

I scoot over to the bar and Dave's already looking straight at me. "Room three, Steffen."

"Wow. I didn't know you were psychic."

"Yep. Body language. It's breaking out all over her."

"Gotcha. Thanks." That makes me feel better. Dave can see that she's responding to me, and that means I have a good chance to make this work.

"Time to go." I reach for her hand when I make it back to the sofa, and she takes it and stands. Once we're in the room with the door closed, I turn to her and tell her, "Kneel on the floor. Ass on heels, knees as wide apart as you can get them. Head down, hands palm up on your thighs. Let's see how you look." I take her hand to help her kneel without falling, and then she assumes the position. "Nice. Hold your head up high." She follows my instruction. "Now, again, drop your head – not your neck, just your head." She tries again and succeeds beautifully. "Very good! You'll stay like that for a few minutes." I think for a few seconds. "Do you want to learn very generic positions, or the ones I like best?"

Her hesitation is only momentary. "Um, yours."

I can't hide my smile anymore. "Okay, keep that pose. It'll take you straight into mine. Put your arms behind you and grasp each elbow with the opposite hand." When she gets her arms situated, I add, "Now arch your back. More. More. There, right there. And adjust your head and neck again." When she's done, I step back and look.

There it is. Back arched and arms clasped behind her so her tits are on full, regal display. Knees apart; without the thong, I'd be able to see everything. "If I were your Dom, this is the pose you would use to greet me. It tells me that you're open to my use and waiting for me to appreciate that fact. How does it feel?"

She doesn't move when she answers, "Awkward, Sir."

"It gets easier with practice. Do you want more?"

"Yes, Sir. Please."

Aha. I like this, and better every minute. "Now, un-clasp your arms and bring them around in front of you. And pull your knees together. Put your hands on your thighs, palms up, and try to relax your arms. Straighten your back a little. There, that's it. Beautiful. This is the pose you would use to greet a Dom who is not *your*

Dominant. It says you're willing to serve without being open to their total use. That has to come with permission from your Dom." I take a good, long look at the beauty there in front of me.

And then it's time to practice some other positions. "Stand. Walk to the wall," I say and point to an empty space on one side of the room. She bobbles a little when she rises, so I add, "And practice kneeling and rising until you can do it gracefully."

"Yes, Sir." She moves to the wall there.

"Now, back up about two steps. Very good. Lean forward and put your hands on the wall, palms flat. Straighten your arms. Start backing out and walking your hands down the wall until you're bent perpendicular and your hands are straight out, even with your ears." She does exactly what I've told her and does it flawlessly. "Very nice. Arch your back. That's good. This is my second favorite position."

"What's your first?" I don't answer her. "Steffen?" I still don't answer. "Steffen?" She's trying to turn to catch my eye when it hits her. "Oh! Sir?"

"Much better. Straighten up. Go to the bed." She gives me a strange look and tries to comply, but she wobbles and has to put a hand out on the floor to keep from falling. "We're not going past what we negotiated, but I do want you to be comfortable."

"Yes, Sir. Help me up, Sir?"

I chuckle. "I know it seems awkward, but the more you do it, the easier it gets."

"Yes, Sir." I can't wait for this, and I point to the

bed. "Climb up, hands and knees." When she's done that and stopped, I bark, "Drop to your forearms, ass in the air." She does exactly that.

And that's when my Dominant kicks in. That ass is beautiful, and I want inside it so badly that I want to beg. Instead, I say, "And you will arch your back to make your pussy more accessible." I can tell what I just said makes her nervous. "Sub, you'll have to get used to that. Pussy, cunt, tits, cock, shaft, channel, asshole, rosette, pucker. You'll hear all of those and more around here. Just get used to it. Now, knees farther apart. Farther. Farther. Good, very good. I'll start by touching your nipples through your clothes. Is that acceptable?"

"Yes." I wait. "Oh, yes, Sir."

"Good." I think for a second and look at the straps peeking out. "Would it be okay with you if I did so on top of your bra but under your top?" Then I push a little. "Could you take your top off?" Before she can protest, I add, "It's no different than a swimsuit."

Relaxation softens the lines at the corners of her eyes. "I suppose so. May I take it off? Sir?" she adds as an afterthought.

"You may. I'll fold it and put it on the trunk over there."

"I'm going to need some help." The corset looks pretty tight, and I don't know exactly how this is going to work, but I get it unhooked and peel it off. The bra she has on underneath was obviously expensive. A bra under a corset. I can honestly say I've never seen that before. But once I have the corset folded on the trunk, I take a moment to take in what I've uncovered about this woman.

Holy shit. Those have to be the two most beautiful breasts I've ever, ever seen. I can feel my fingers twitching. I finally get myself back together enough to say, "Back into the position."

Dropping into position, her breasts swing down and forward and my cock tries to introduce itself to her in person. My mind yells out, *Down, boy!*, but it's no use. He's locked and loaded. and I reach up and under her. When my fingers find her buds she lets out a hiss of air.

Oh, my god, they're hard. And big. I have no problem making out their definition under that bra, no problem at all. I give each one a gentle pinch and she sucks in a breath. "Does it feel good?"

She answers with a squirm, "Yes, Sir." I ramp it up a little and she moans in earnest, so I don't stop. I can tell she's having trouble controlling herself.

"Does that feel good?" She nods. "No, you have to verbally speak. I might be in a spot where I can't see you, so you have to communicate with me."

"Yes, Sir. It feels good." I keep that up for about ten minutes. Now I know I've got her right where I want her. My abrupt stop startles her and I say, "This would be so much easier if you didn't have your little skirt on, just your panties. Would that be possible?"

"Well, I, um . . ."

I pretend I didn't see the thong earlier. "Oh! If you don't have on panties, then I understand." Squealing like a little girl crosses my mind, but I fight the urge.

"Oh, yeah, um, a thong." She blushes.

"That would be fine, wouldn't it?"

"Yes. I guess so, Sir."

"Great. I'll wait." I watch, my cock straining against my fly, as she peels off the skirt, which is more of a tutu than anything. Hot damn, her hips are luscious. My mind is racing and I try to rein it in. "Just lie down on the bed and I'll lie down beside you if that's okay." The fact that she complies tells me that she's ready. She settles in, and I settle in beside her. "You said you wanted to reach climax, so I can do that for you."

"Yes, Sir. Thank you, Sir."

She really is a fucking submissive. Oh, god, I want this to work out so badly. I can't screw this up. My hand is almost shaking as I reach out and touch the smoothness of her belly, so warm and soft. I want to kiss it, and I decide in that moment that I will. I lean forward and press my lips to her skin and, to my surprise, she moans softly. Kissing up her ribcage and between her breasts, I go on up her chest and her neck with my lips and tongue and, to my utter and complete delight, she throws her head back to give me access. When I kiss her chin, she pulls her face down and her lips meet mine.

I want to fuck her. Oh, god, I want to fuck her so bad I can't stand it, but I've got to hold it together. My tongue presses against her lips and they part, and next thing I know, her tongue is exploring the inside of my mouth and I groan into her. As we kiss, my hand wanders down and over the silkiness of her thong. I can feel her clit, hard and throbbing against my fingers, as I stroke the top of the fabric over and over. Ten minutes in, I feel her hand near mine and I realize she's moving the fabric out of the way. I break the kiss and look into her eyes. "Sub, this isn't the way we negotiated this. Is this really what you want?"

She gives me a breathless, "Uh-huh," followed with, "Sir."

Satiny fabric moved to the side, I drop my hand low and stroke up her slit. When I reach the wettest spot, I dip a finger in and test it. Deeper I don't know about, but the entrance to her pussy is good and tight, and she's dripping. I continue on until I find what I'm looking for. It's swollen and waiting, and I draw my finger ever-so-softy around it. That elicits a gasp from her and her back arches. I'm still kissing her, but I move back and say, "I want to look at you. Will that be okay?"

Her face burns red when she nods and I want to re-mind her to speak, but I don't want to discourage the direction she's taking, so I say nothing, sit up a little, and look down. Shaved smooth, I can plainly see her clit rising up out of its hood because it's so engorged. Then I nip her nipple through her bra and she cries out. I can feel her tensing. "Sheila, you're safe with me. Let go and come for me. Just let go. You're safe here."

She shrieks and her back arches, and I hang on for dear life. Her hips choose their own rhythm, and it's a beautiful thing, the way they thrust and buck. As her spasms start to slow down, I gradually slow my strokes. I finally stop, and I know she's wondering what comes next.

So I curl up against her and wrap my arms around her. To my surprise, she relaxes into my embrace and presses her forehead to my chest as we lie there on our sides, facing each other. I brush my fingers through that beautiful hair and hear her sigh, just a little sigh, but so important to me. It means I satisfied her, and that was my ultimate goal. Nothing else really mattered to me, doesn't really matter to me, that and her safety. Her tiny voice says, "Sir?"

"Yes, babe."

"Thank you."

"No, thank you for letting me experience that with you."

She looks down my torso. "What about you? What do you do about . . ."

"You don't worry about that. My responsibility."

"Would you like to, maybe, I don't know . . ."

"No. I said I'll worry about it. You just rest."

I can tell she's kind of shocked, and I know she's used to those selfish bastards who don't give a shit if anyone else is satisfied as long as they are. Those days are over for her – if she'll just stick with me.

In about an hour, I jostle her ever so softly. "Sheila? Sheila, you need to wake up."

"Oh!" She rubs her eyes and looks around. "Oh, what? Is everyone gone? What's wrong?"

I can't help but smile. "No, everyone's not gone, but we do need to get up and out of here. Someone else might want to use the room, not to mention that Clint and Trish might be ready to go."

"Oh, okay." She looks up into my face and doesn't smile, just says, "Thanks, Steffen. You're a good guy."

That almost makes me blush. "I try hard."

"It's working." She sits up, straightens what she's still wearing, and says, "Oh, no, I don't have any pants on." Then she starts to giggle, and that makes me laugh, and pretty soon we're laughing out loud together. "Will you, uh, you know . . ."

"Yeah, yeah, I'll look the other way." I turn with my back to her and hear her rustling around.

"I know that's kind of silly, since we, I mean, since you . . ."

"No, it's not. That was different. That was then; this is now. Don't worry about it – perfectly natural." I wait. "Dressed?"

"Yes. And now we walk out and everybody knows, um . . ."

"No, everybody thinks we did a lot more than we really did. But not one single person will judge. That's the beauty of a club like this. There may be members here for different reasons, but in the end, they all want the same thing."

Her brow furrows. "What's that?"

I shrug. "To be loved. Even if they don't realize it, that's really what they're looking for, love and acceptance. That's all. They're either looking for it, or looking to find a way to open up so they can accept it."

I can see the gears turning in her head, and she finally says, "I guess we'd better get out of here." She hesitates for a minute and her face turns red, but I can see she's trying to gather up her courage. "Would you want to, I mean, some other time, would you like to . . . oh, never mind."

My heart skips a couple of beats. "Play with you again?" She nods. "Oh, god, I hope you want to, because I most definitely do." That gets a shy smile out of her. "I'd be really hurt if you didn't."

"Master Steffen? Hurt?" she laughs.

I hope she can't see the sadness in my face when I say, "Yeah. Master Steffen gets hurt too, just like everybody else."

That kills the laughter and she gives me a sad smile back. "I'll remember that."

"Thanks." I stand and reach for her hand. "Come on, let's go. You just let me know when, where, and what, and I'm at your disposal." When she reaches for me and I feel her warmth and softness against my palm, for the first time in a long time, everything I am and know feels right.

Chapter Three

I want to see her. Hell, I think about her pretty much constantly. And I'm fairly certain that she's not thinking about me. At least that's what I thought, until Thursday night when she traipses into the club with Trish and Clint. When they step through the doorway, she gives me a tiny little wave and she and Trish disappear into the locker room. I'm standing in the men's locker room doorway and Clint heads straight for me. All he says as he passes me in the doorway is, "Come with me."

Once we're in the locker room, he starts stripping off and dressing out. And he turns to me, his eyes twinkling. "What the hell did you do to that woman?"

"What? Me?" I give him my "dunno" face. "I have no idea what you're talking about."

"Oh, shut the fuck up, Cothran. You know exactly what I'm talking about."

"I have no idea!" Now I'm really curious as to what's going on.

"Did you fuck her? Because I'm pretty sure you fucked her, and pretty well, I might add."

"No! I did *not* fuck her. Did she say I did? Because I didn't." Now I'm thinking I'm about to be chastised, and I didn't do a damn thing wrong. What the hell? We're grownups.

"No, she didn't say you did." Clint zips up his leathers and sits down on the bench, then motions for me to do the same. "I'm asking because I think she's fallen for you."

"Wha???? Me?"

"Yes, you, you middle-aged lothario you. Fallen. Hook, line, and sinker. Head over heels. In over her head. Yep. In deep. And I hope you have some kind of feelings for her, or I'm going to have a lot of explaining to do. At least some interest." He stops. "Well?"

I'm not really sure what to say – he's taken me completely by surprise. "Uh, um, I, uh . . ."

"Cothran, don't screw me over here, I mean it."

"No, no, no! I'm not! I'm just shocked."

"You look it. Why? Did you do your best 'cool and aloof' thing?"

"No! No, I'm really very interested in her too. Very." He gives me the evil eye. "I mean, I haven't thought about much else since the last time she was here. I mean anybody else. Fuck, you know what I mean." Now I'm blushing.

"Why, Cothran, you old dog! You've got it bad, don't you?"

"I don't know if I'd say that, but I do like her – a lot. *She* asked *me* if I'd be interested in playing with her again and I nearly had a heart attack. So yeah, I'm more than interested."

"Waking-up-thinking-about-her, beating-off-in-the-shower interested?"

"You don't have to be so fucking graphic, but yes, that interested."

He stands and slaps me on the shoulder. "Good. Personally, I think you should play with her a couple more times, and then ask her out on a date. A real date. Maybe say it's going to be a time to talk and negotiate. You know." He grins. "Looks like you've got a live one on the hook."

"Thank god. Finally. It's about time."

"Come on. They're waiting for us." We head out into the main room just in time for me to see Gary cozying up to Sheila, and Clint shoots me a look. I have no idea what to do at this point, so I just walk up to the bar, order a drink, and look over at her. When she spots me, a big, gorgeous grin spreads across those straight, white teeth, and I can feel my heart melting and running down into my boots.

I can tell she's trying to be nonchalant and casual when she says, "Steffen! Hi!" Gary's head swivels in my direction and he levels an I'd-like-to-kick-your-ass look at me.

"Hi, little subbie! How are you?"

"I'm great, um, Master Steffen." She winks and I see Gary bristle. *HAH!*, I want to yell. "Are you busy later?"

"No plans to be unless someone has something planned for me that I don't know about yet." I wink back. Now Gary looks really, really pissed off. She just grins. "Think I'm gonna go mingle. See you in a bit?"

Her smile is past sexy. "You know it." I walk away and wonder what's going to happen next. I've found a seat on one of the sofas just to turn and see Gary talking up a new sub over on the other side of the room and, next thing I know, I feel someone touch my shoulder and turn to see her looking down at me. "Is this seat taken, Sir?"

"Yes." She frowns. "By you. Sit down, please." The frown changes to a huge grin and she plops down beside me. "And work on your graceful approach to sitting, sub. You're too beautiful to just drop like a sack of potatoes."

"Oh, sorry. Um, Sir." I love the pink that spreads across her cheeks, and the way she bats those eyelashes almost makes me weak – almost. "I just never really thought about it."

"You'll start thinking about it eventually, about every move, every turn, every breath, and you'll think about how you look to everyone else. You'll be a reflection of your master, so you'll want to be at your absolute best at all times."

"I see." She sits for a few seconds like she's contem-plating something wide and deep, and then says, "So how do I go about getting a master?"

She's looking ahead. I think this may be a good sign. "Well, there are several ways. You could eventually wind up with someone you've played with quite often. Or you could wait until the annual pairing and try that."

"That's how Trish and Clint met, right?"

"Uh-huh. Or you could just approach someone, but

I wouldn't advise that. It's a great way to get a contract with someone you don't know very well." She makes a face, so I add, "Mind you, anyone you met here would be safe enough, but they might not be a good fit for you. You'd be living with this person. You want it to be a good fit."

She sits still for a few seconds, not saying anything. Then she blurts out, "So are you looking for a sub?"

I'm not going to lie to her. If there's anything I know about the lifestyle, it's that there has to be honesty or it just won't work. Ever. So I tell her the truth. "Actually, yes. I'm tired of being alone. If I don't find someone before then, I'm looking forward to next year's pairing." When I stop, I wonder if I've just stepped in it. I can't read her face.

Her next question is, "So, have you met anyone you'd consider?" She licks her lips and I feel my cock twitch.

No lies. "Matter of fact, I have." I wait while her eyes bore into me. "But enough of that. Do you want to play? You know, there's no better way for two people to get to know each other in the most intimate fashion." Most likely she's going to blush and turn away or turn me down cold.

Her gaze is steady and intense, and it blows all of my presupposed notions about her out the window when she answers with, "I'm ready. Shall we negotiate?"

Wow. Okay then. Strike while the iron is hot and all that. "Absolutely. You tell me what you have in mind."

"I thought that was up to the master." She licks her

lips again. I wish she'd quit doing that.

"It can be either party. In long-term relationships, it usually is the master. But I'm one of those Doms who just wants to meet my sub's needs. If you have a need, it's my job to see that it's satisfied." I'm not getting a response from her. "You've been watching scenes. Is there anything that interests you? Anything you'd like to try?"

Measuring me up, I'm sure, she eyes me out of the corner of her eye. "I want you to choose, Sir. I want to see how far you feel comfortable going."

That puts me in a precarious position. If I push too far, she'll run; if I don't go far enough, she'll interpret it as disinterest. I decide that if she runs, she runs. Dancing around something like this just isn't my style. "I'd like to start with restraining you, preferably with thigh restraints to which your wrists will be restrained as well." She nods. "Then a bit of sensation play."

She doesn't disappoint with her question. "What does that mean?"

I lift my eyebrows. "Well, it means blindfolded and subjected to different items that will cause different sensations on your skin."

"Like?"

"Like if I told you, it wouldn't be a surprise, now would it?" My best sexy smile pops out, and I can see she has an appreciation for it. "And after the sensation play, orgasm torture. Five orgasms or forty-five minutes, whichever comes first."

Her eyes jar open wide. "Five orgasms! I can't do

that!"

I just close my eyes and smile. "If you've never done that, it's because you've been with the wrong person." That look on her face tells me she's considering what I've said. "And?"

"I'm thinking. Then what?"

I look her dead in the eye. "Penetrative sex. Vaginally, not anally. I think we would need to know each other better and trust each other more for that. Oh, and interspersed with oral sex, both of us."

The blush that spreads across her cheeks tells me something very important: She's been thinking about this before she ever got here. That's why she wanted *me* to tell *her* what *I* wanted. She didn't want to be the one to ask for sex. And I get that, really, I do, so I've let her off the hook by telling her what I want. And I've never been one to be shy about asking for or initiating sex. Not a problem, by god.

I wait, and finally I say, "Well?"

She nods.

I wish I could say I was cool and detached, but I'm fighting a cheer and hoping she can't tell. Even if this doesn't work out in the long run, I'm pretty sure I'm going to remember tonight for the rest of my life. Being instantly attracted to someone never happens to me, but with this woman, that's pretty much what's happened. I manage to say, "Do you want any of this to take place in the public areas?"

She shakes her head violently. "Good god, no, Sir!" Her face is almost scarlet now. "I don't know if I'll ever be able to do that."

"At some point, a Dom may expect that from you." There's this look that I can't decipher on her face, and I'm wondering what's going through her head. I put a finger under her chin, tip her head up, and look into those beautiful eyes. "What's going on in that pretty head of yours? Tell me how you feel about that."

My throat closes when I see a tear in the corner of her eye. "Let's just say I don't feel very good about my body." And she stops dead. I wait until I can't wait anymore.

Now's my chance. "Sheila?" A tear trickles down her cheek, and my heart almost stops. "If you don't trust me, I can't work with you. What is it? It could be a trigger, so I need to know."

There's a shudder that comes over her before she finally speaks. "My, um, my ex used to tell me how ugly I am."

Oh god. That son of a bitch. I assumed he just slapped her around or something, but now my chest feels tight and I don't know what to do to make this better. Then I decide to do something I've never done. I stand and reach for her hand. "Come on. Let's go to a private room and talk."

Amazingly enough, she reaches for my hand so I can help her stand, and we head down the hallway. The door to one of the smaller rooms is open, and that's perfect. When the door closes behind us, I turn to her and say, "There's something you need to know about this place."

Her eyebrows shoot up so high that they almost disappear. "What?" I take her by the hand and lead her over to the bed. When we're seated on the side, I decide it's time to give her a little education in something very important.

"Listen, you may not have yet, but in time, if you hang around here, you're going to see all kinds of things. Amputees, people with burn scars, women who've had mastectomies, men with heart surgery scars, most anything you can think of. Some of the people who come in here are morbidly obese, and some are so thin they look like walking skeletons. They're coming in here to get their needs met, and no one – NO ONE – judges anyone else. There is absolutely nothing that would get gawking and stares from them. We have several transgendered people who are members here – you may have met a woman or two and you'd never know they were biologically men. And no one judges. So you've got nothing to be embarrassed or ashamed of. Understand?"

She nods sadly, so I repeat, "Tell me you understand."

"I do, Sir." Forlorn doesn't even describe the look she gives me, and it pushes the rage button in my core.

What comes out of my mouth next is gentle but firm. "You listen to me and listen good. Did I tell you I'd work with you?"

She shivers. "Yes, Sir."

As tenderly as I can manage, I take her chin in my hand and turn her face up to mine. "If you were a loser, I wouldn't have agreed to work with you. I've made a few bad choices in my life, but they taught me to make good ones. If I said I'd work with you, you've got more than a few redeeming qualities." And at this very moment, I decide this is one time in my life when I should say what I feel. "Sheila, you're a very beautiful woman. Anyone who would tell you differently is an idiot, plain and simple. I'm attracted to you in ways that I haven't been attracted to a woman for years now. You're absolutely luscious, and don't ever let anyone tell you anything different, you hear me?"

That's when I see it. There's something in her eyes that goes warm and soft, and her face almost glows. She's got to be the most exquisite thing I've ever seen when she looks into my eyes that way, and everything in my being is on overdrive. "Are you going to hold me after like you did the other night?" I realize then that she's about to cry.

"Honey, if you want, I'll hold you right now. If that's what you need, I will."

My heart breaks when she nods and starts to cry, and I'm no longer in control of myself – I pull her to me and just wrap my arms tight around her. When she bunches up against me and sobs, I just reach down, lift her legs, and pull them up and over my lap so I can sit there with her and let her cry. How could some bastard hurt her that way? Jail's too good for that motherfucker – he should be shot. I stroke that beautiful hair as her sobs start to slow, and I whisper to her, "You're hair is gorgeous, little one. It reminds me of a summer sunset, all fiery and glowing."

"Th-th-th-th-thank you," she manages to stutter out.

"Sir."

It's time for me to take control because I know it will make her more comfortable and confident. "You're welcome, little sub. Now, let's talk about what we came in here to do." She nods. "I want to amend it. No sensation play, and I don't want to do the orgasm torture, but I do want to give you one orgasm. I think it'll help you relax. If you want more, you can tell me. But everything else as we discussed. Agreeable?"

"Yes, Sir."

"Then the first thing for you to do is undress." She shoots me a look. "No. I don't undress you. You undress yourself. It's a willful baring of yourself to me. Most Doms will expect that from you. We're going to get into more of the formal issues later on, but tonight we'll just touch on some of them. But yes, you are expected to undress."

"Will you too, Sir?"

"Later, yes, but not initially. Balance of power. I'm in control and you have to acknowledge that or this won't work. Someone has to be in control. There's a secret I'll tell you later, but right now, you just need to learn to obey." I kiss her forehead and point to the center of the floor. "Up and undress for me." She stands and turns her back to me. "No. Face forward. I want to watch you as you undress." When she hesitates, I tell her, "You can do this. I know you can."

As I watch, she slips off her platform stilettos, then slips her black lace tee over her head and throws it on the floor. My first chance to direct her. "Sub, as you undress, you'll fold your clothes neatly and place them on the table over there," I say, pointing to a small table across the room. "One piece of clothing at a time." Expressionless, she picks up the shirt, takes it to the table, folds it neatly, and puts it there. Then she shimmies out of those tight faux leather pants she's wearing and does the same with them. She reaches back and unsnaps her bra, draws it down her arms, and, as she adds it to the other things she's already folded, she puts a hand on the table to steady herself as she pulls off her panties and adds them to the pile. That's when she turns to me.

Holy shit. I mean, really, holy shit. This girl, my god. It's been years since I've seen a body like this one, if I ever even have. Her breasts are full, but they're almost pubescent in their shape, with large, soft nipples a beautiful, pale rose color. Her waist is small and well-defined, and she's got curvy, ample hips that make me want to scream and shout. I'd been holding her while she cried, and that's not the sexiest thing in the world, but one look now and my cock is so hard that it feels like it's on fire. It's a fight to keep from unzipping my leathers and stroking myself. As she comes back toward me, I point to her shoes. "Put those back on. I like them and I want you to wear them."

I can tell I've surprised her. "You want me to wear them when we . . ." she trails off.

"Yes. I do. They're very sexy." Stepping into them, she makes her way back across the room to me and stands in front of me. Instead of giving in to my knee-jerk reaction to reach up and fondle her nipples, I point to the bed. "On the bed. On your back. Hands at your sides." While she climbs up into the middle of the bed, I go to the chest on the back wall and find the restraints. She lies very still while I fasten them around her thighs, then use the attached cuffs to secure her hands. I lie down on the bed beside her, then roll her onto her side until my chest is snugged up to her back. Slipping one arm under her, I roll us again until she's lying on top of me on her back. Arms wrapped around her waist, I give her a few seconds to get used to the position, her head back over my shoulder, her ear against mine. Then I drag my hands from her waist up her ribcage, up and under her breasts, and take a nipple in each hand. She cries out when I pinch them, so I ramp up the stimulation, a couple of pinches, then rolling them between my thumb and forefinger, followed by tugging upward. That really gets her going. She's moaning and squirming when I ask her, "Does this make you hot, subbie?"

"Yes, Sir, very hot, Sir."

I stifle the urge to snicker. "Good. I'm glad. So I'll keep it up for a few minutes." My fingers become more aggressive, pinching harder, twisting harder, pulling out farther, all the while listening to her cry out. I know she can feel my growing hardness right up the cleft of that beautiful ass, but I still do my best to let her know it's there and waiting. Ten minutes of that and I know she's ready.

My right hand wanders down her body ever so slowly, tracing little circles on her skin, and I feel her squirm against me as she realizes what's coming. When I slowly draw my knees up so my feet are flat on the bed, I make sure they part her legs on the way up and, by the time I've stopped, her legs are wide open, each one on the outside of mine. In this position, her legs actually drop down and away from her engorged little nub, leaving it high and prominently on display. Continuing to trace little patterns on her skin, I lift my head and look down the length of her body. Yep, I can see straight down to the cleft just below her mons and, before I drop my head back, I whisper in her ear, "Sub, you are so beautiful. Your body is a work of art." And it works; I feel her relax against me as my fingers continue their downward trek. Stroking her mound with three fingers brings out a moan, and I wait, trying to prolong the initial touch, but I just can't. That tiny, swollen bud calls to me and I can't say no.

My finger dips to her slit, drags from her introitus up through her engorged lips, and finds the prize. When I touch it, she cries out, and my left hand, still on her breast, pinches her nipple hard. The instant she cries out from the pinch, I go to work, tenderly circling the center of her arousal, feeling her squirm against me and go even wetter than she was. When I stop for a split second to grab the bottle of lube on the bedside table and pour a little on my right index finger, she whines until I'm finished and start in on her again. She wants it. I'm so damned excited I may just shoot off in my leathers.

She's escalating, growing more agitated, more excited, thrashing against the restraints, and I whisper into her ear, "At some point, I will own your orgasms. They'll be mine, and I'll give them to you whenever I please, even without touching you. But for now, I want you to come any time you're ready. Any time, sub."

I give her little nub about three more strokes and she explodes, wriggling and crying out, her hips bucking for all they're worth. I keep it up until I hear her cry out, "Nooooo! No more!" and, even though I don't want to, I stop. Once I've rolled us both to our sides, I scoot out from behind her, lay her flat, and take off the restraints. Instantly, her arms reach for me and, try as I may, I can't move away. I wrap my arms around her waist as hers encircle my neck and kiss her like a starving man looking for bread. Finally breaking away, I get up and stand by the bed, then unzip my leathers as she watches. I want to see her reaction when she sees this cock for the first time.

And there it is – her mouth forms an appropriate "O" and I almost laugh. It measures out at about nine and a half inches, and about seven and a half inches in circumference, long and meaty with a nicely-proportioned head. And it's got a very gentle upward curve that's great for g-spot stimulation. I've never met a woman who didn't love this dick. And did I mention that it's now rock-hard? Yeah. Hard as stone and throbbing. I can see my pulse in the veins up and down its length. I don't often admit this, but sometimes I just stare at it and can't believe it's mine. That sounds crazy, I know, but it's quite the point of pride for me, this fabulous tool. Okay, so maybe I'm exaggerating a bit, but hey, it's still pretty damn big. I can make a woman scream with it, so I don't mind showing it off when I get a chance.

And it's working. "Oh, god, Sir." That's all she says. I don't utter a word, just roll on a condom, climb back onto the bed with her, and wrap my arms around her with my gaze locked on hers.

"I intend to drive you insane. And I'm starting now." My lips meet hers and I make the kiss fierce, something to melt her. I take a hand down, grab my cock, line it up with the wettest spot on her body, and press forward.

How in the hell am I going to hold off for any length of time? Her back arches and her lips leave mine to cry out, "Oh my god! Damn, damn, damn!" I take my time, moving slowly inside her, relishing every little inch of her tightness and heat. Lost in it, she grips my shoulders and moans out, "Oh, damn. Oh, fuck. So good, so good. Don't stop, please, don't stop."

And that's exactly what I do, but before she has a chance to whine, I kiss down that remarkable body a little at a time, slide downward, let her fragrance soak into me. Lips trembling, I suck her clit between them and tug slightly. Her back arches again and she wraps her fingers in my hair and rasps out, "Oh, god, yes. That feels so good." That's not enough; I slip two fingers into her pussy and stroke slowly, feeling her body tense and coil. Just when I think she's about to give in and come, I stop again and begin to make my way back up that body, stopping to suck and tease her hard, huge, rosy nipples. When I get back up her neck to her mouth, I kiss her again and drive my cock home for the second round. She moans into my lips, and I return the favor.

I break away and look down into her face. "God, sub, your pussy's like heaven on earth. You have no idea what you're doing to me." A giggle drifts from her lips and then she kisses me, just as ferociously as I had her.

This is going quite well. Quite well indeed.

I repeat this whole process about eight times before my lips just brush hers and I tell her, "This is it. I want you to come with me. I'll hold off until you do, okay?" I feel like an explorer about to plant a flag on the top of the mountain he's just scaled, a claiming of the peak, and I feel her tense all over. About ten strokes in, I hear her voice escalate as she says, "Oh. Oh god. Oh god, oh god, oh god. Oh damn, oh god. Oh god, oh, oh, oh, OHHHHHH!!!" and she clamps down around my shaft – hard – as her hips thrust toward my pelvis. And that's it for me. On my final mission, I pump into her forcefully as my balls tighten and, in just a few seconds, I feel everything I have unload through the slit in the tip of my dick and fill my condom.

I don't want to pull out of her. Ever. I want to stay here, buried inside her, soaking in her heat, holding her softness against me. Once we've rolled to our sides, I just wrap my arms around her and kiss the top of her head. "Do all Doms treat their subs this well, Sir?"

This is that moment, the one where I decide if I want to be totally honest with this woman or just treat her like any other sub and hope something comes of it. And I hope the decision I make is the right one when I say, "No. Only if they care about them." I pull back so I can see her face, and what's written on it makes my heart flutter in my chest. "And I do care about you, Sheila. I want to see you satisfied, and I want to be satisfied too, but I'd die before I'd hurt you."

A tiny smile tugs the corner of her lips upward. "You really mean that, don't you?"

"A solid Dom/sub relationship is built on trust and communication. I can't be anything but honest with you or that's not accomplished." I follow that with, "If all relationships were built like a Dom/sub relationship, more couples would stay together."

She purses her lips and nods. "That's certainly true." I can practically see the gears turning, and then she adds, "I haven't lied to you about anything, Sir. Everything I've told you is one hundred percent true. And I'll never lie to you about anything, Steffen. You can count on that." At the sound of my name, my heart gives a little leap and I feel the greatest measure of hope that I have in a while.

"And I haven't lied to you about anything either, baby. I take this stuff seriously, and I don't mean just BDSM. I take relationships seriously. I have a lot of casual friends and acquaintances, but very few good, close friends. And I'd like to think that's what we're becoming."

"Me too, Sir. Me too." As she sighs and curls into my chest within the snugness of my arms, I hope she never finds out that I haven't entered into the sin of commission, just the sin of omission.

I haven't lied. I just haven't told the entire truth.

"Hey, babe, I think we probably need to get out of here." I've looked at my watch and we've been lying here for about an hour. "Want me to get dressed and get out of here so you can have some privacy?"

She screws up her face. "Why? We just had sex for an hour and a half. You've seen everything there is to see. I'm certainly okay with you watching me dress."

That prompts me to say, "You know, you're one of the easiest people to be around that I think I've ever met."

When she smiles and her face lights up, I feel like I've won the lottery. "You know, that's one of the nicest things anyone's said to me in a long, long time. Thanks for that."

"Well, it's true. You're a super-nice person. You must have a lot of friends."

Her face saddens. "Not so many. After what happened, it's hard to trust people." She's sitting up on the bed with the sheet pulled up and over her knees, and I reach over and take her hand as I lie there. I nod before I speak.

"Yeah. I can understand that. I hope I can convince you that you can trust me." Should I? Yep – I'm going to step out there. "You know, Sheila, it feels like maybe, I don't know, do you get the feeling that maybe we have something going on here that's worth exploring?"

My heart almost explodes when she nods. "Yeah. I think we might." Before I can say anything else, she adds, "Do you want to try? See where it goes?"

And there it is. My chance. I refuse to blow it. "Absolutely. So how about we start here: As long as we're working together as Dom and sub, I'll commit to not working with another sub. What do you think?"

I get a smile from that. "Yeah! I think that's good." Then she giggles. "I'm a little too shy to work with anyone else anyway. But I'm comfortable with you. You've been so, um, considerate. And patient. You're the first guy I've ever had sex with who seemed to actually be concerned about what I was getting out of it, not just using me as a big masturbator."

That makes me laugh. "Nope! I'm sure not going to do that! And I *am* concerned with your satisfaction, more so than with my own. You come first." Now I'm starting to feel bold, and I think about what Clint said. "So . . . would you like to maybe have dinner with me tomorrow night?"

Her eyes go wide. "You mean, like a date?"

I can feel my forehead wrinkling. "Yeah, like a date." Her next question surprises me.

"Isn't that against the rules?"

"What rules?"

"You know, the BDSM rules or something, I don't know."

Oh, how precious. She is absolutely the cutest thing I've ever seen. "The BDSM rules are the rules *we* make as a partnership. If we don't want a particular rule, we just don't make it. And no, Sheila, there are no rules against us having some kind of relationship. Remember what I told you: People enter into these agreements because they just want to be loved?" She nods. "Most people enter into a BDSM contract because they either love each other or they're capable of meeting each other's needs and want to do just that. And that, along with respect, are in their own ways love."

She nods. "True."

"So. Date? Dinner? Maybe a walk down to the pier?"

"Sure! What time?"

"Six?"

"That's good." She starts gathering up her clothes.

"And by the way, I don't even have your phone number."

She's drawing on her bra and I hate to see those gorgeous nipples disappear behind that fabric. "Oh, yeah! So let's get our phones out before we leave and exchange them. And you'll need my address to pick me up."

"That I will." Now I'm happier than I've been in a long, long time. Clint was right. I think this is a good idea. I'm having to suppress the desire to squeal like a little girl.

Tomorrow night, I've got a date.

I don't know where we're going. What should I wear?

The text surprises me a little, but it makes me smile too.

Reservations at Treadway's, so dressy casual. BTW, can't wait to see you.

I wait for a few minutes. Too strong? Then I smile.

Can't wait to see you too.

Ah. That's better.

I get home from work and scurry around to change and get ready to go. I don't think anyone can appreciate the position I'm in. As a regional manager, I've got eight branch banks under me. My office is in the biggest one. Within this system, we've got over one hundred employees, full-time and part-time, and about ninety-two percent of them are women. That means out of all of the women I know, about ninety-nine percent of them are involved in my business somehow, and I don't date within that pool. At all. Bad idea. That leaves me with pretty much no one except subs at the club and, up to this point, I've pretty well avoided that.

But Sheila's different. She's a friend of a friend, so that removes the work dimension. And I'm trying to handle this very carefully because I certainly don't want to lose Clint and Trish as friends. But I can't ignore the fact that I'm overwhelmingly attracted to this woman. If this goes nowhere, I'll be very disappointed.

Windswept Florists is right on my way, and I stop to pick up some colorful flowers that I think she'll like. I also ask for a single rose, and I leave it in its box in the back of the car so I can give it to them at the restaurant to bring to the table.

It's high school all over again when I ring her doorbell. My hands are sweating and my heart is racing. My first thought is, *Damn, Cothran, you've been out of the game too long.* But when she opens that door, I feel like my timing is just right.

She's got on this dress that hugs every curve and a pair of the sexiest shoes I've ever seen. The dress has this neckline that, I don't know what you call it, hell, I'm a guy, but it really, really shows off those amazing tits. And the shoes are sky-high and zip up the top like little short boots or something, but with designs cut out of them. Too, too hot. She's got her hair put up, and little tendrils are dripping from it in the back. My mind immediately goes back to last night and how she felt under me, and I'm fighting an erection the size of a loaf of French bread. "Well, well, well, aren't you beautiful?" is all I manage to squeak out.

"You clean up pretty good yourself. Although I think I like your birthday suit a lot better," she quips, and I want to strip off right there, knock her to the floor, and crawl up into her like a turtle in its shell.

"Well, thanks, but that's kind of apples and oranges if it applies to you. They don't make clothes that heavenly." She blushes. So I've won that round! *Attaboy, Cothran!* I pull the flowers out from behind me and when she sees them, I can see her soften even more.

"Oh, god, Sir, they're beautiful! Come on in." She holds the door open and I'm pleasantly surprised when I step inside. Tending to the flowers in the kitchen, her absence gives me a chance to look around. The house is lovely, nice contemporary colors and comfortable furniture, so different from my bachelor pad style, and it makes me want to grab the throw over the big double chair and sit in front of her fireplace with her in my lap. Snuggling. Popcorn in a bowl. An ice-cold Stella. Robert

Plant or Bad Company playing softly in the background. Oh, god, I've got it bad.

"Sheila?"

"Yeah?"

"Tonight, it's Steffen. We're just a guy and a girl on a date. Is that okay?" I ask, fingers invisibly crossed.

I have to admit, I'm totally unprepared for the smile she gives me when she turns. It's like she's lit up from the inside and it utterly blows me away. "I'd like that very much." Crossing the room toward me, she walks straight up to me and waits. It takes me a minute, and then I realize, *Damn, Cothran, it's HAS been too long since you've dated, obviously.* I take her hands, pull her to me, wrap my arms around her waist, and kiss her.

That's what she was waiting for. She coos into my mouth, and I cover her lips with mine, press them open with my tongue, and take a good, long drink of her, heart pounding and knees weak. If this is any indication of what the rest of the evening is going to be like, I'm a goner for sure. When I pull back, she follows me, nips my bottom lip, and then grins up at me. "Wow. That was delicious. Can we do that again?"

I grin back. "If we do it very many more times, we're going to be late for our reservations. But there's always after dinner."

"Why, yes, there is!" She picks up her bag and says, "Ready?"

Oh, hell yeah. I'm ready. I can't wait to see where this night goes.

Chapter Four

"So what's good here?" Sheila's looking over the menu like a detective searching for clues in a murder case.

"Well, their specialty is their broiled sea bass. It's supposed to be wonderful, but I usually opt for a steak."

She laughs. "Oh, so you're one of *those* guys?"

"Which guys would those be?" I ask her through my grin.

"The ones who want red meat. One of those manly men." She fakes pumping up her bicep and bursts into laughter.

"Just wait. You'll see. So what do you like?"

"Um, just about any kind of vegetable. And I like chicken a lot."

"That's easy. They have some chicken kabobs that are out of this world. And that would take care of your vegetables too. How's that sound?"

She shoots me a smile that makes my chest tighten. "That sounds wonderful."

Just then the waiter appears. When he asks, I look to Sheila. "The beautiful vision with me here will have a glass of pinot gris, and I'll have a merlot."

Boy, he was fast; we didn't have time to get a word in before he was back with the glasses and poured both right at the table. "What would the two of you like for dinner?"

"The lady will have the chicken kabobs and a garden salad, no onions," I say, and she nods, "and balsamic vinaigrette dressing. I'll have the T-bone, medium, with your grilled broccoli and a baked sweet potato, as well as the same salad the lady is having. And could you bring both of us a glass of water with our dinners, please?"

"Of course, sir! Thank you and your food will be out shortly." He stops, then looks back and forth at us. "May I ask, is this some sort of special occasion?"

Sheila and I both look at each other in surprise. I manage to stammer out, "Well, I guess you could say that. It's our first date."

He smiles warmly. "Well then, sir, the wine's unlimited and on the house. I hope Treadway's was the right choice for this momentous occasion!" With that, he spins and disappears.

Sheila was first to speak. "Wow. Just, um, wow."

I shake my head and grin. "A momentous occasion." As the words leave my lips, the hostess appears with a small bud vase and the long stem red rose I'd left at the front. Sheila smiles, then eyes me suspiciously.

"That brings me to a question." She doesn't sound mad or anything, but my heart almost stills. "Are you dating anyone else?"

I can't help it – I take her hand across the table, turn

it over, and trace little circles on her palm. She blushes and I know she's thinking about the little patterns I traced up and down her body the night before. "No. I don't date very much. Most of the women I know are somehow connected to my work, and I don't do that. You know, date women I work with. At all. Ever. One of Cothran's unbreakable policies."

"So where do you meet women?"

I laugh. "Apparently we're introduced by friends!"

Her face clouds over. "I'm being serious here, Steffen."

"So am I. I'm not kidding. I don't date the women I work with, and the only other place I ever seem to go is the club. And I've never been interested in dating a sub from there."

Now she gives me a hard stare. "Oh, they're good enough to have sex with, but not good enough to date?"

Most guys would think they're about to go down in flames, but I'm honest with her. "No, nothing like that. It's just that most of the women, not all, but most, want more than one guy, I mean, want to have sex with more than one guy. And I'm like Clint; I'm not that into sharing. So that's not going to happen. Even if they say that's not what they want, we've only got two subs at the club who haven't had sex with more than one guy there."

"Trish and who else?"

Uh-oh. *Gotta be honest, gotta be honest*, I hear playing in my head. "Well, actually, it's a sub who calls herself Babycakes and one named Katherine."

One eyebrow goes up. "Trish?"

"Nope."

"Who?"

I shake my head. "Now you know I can't tell you that."

"Yeah? Well, how do you know?"

I let out a big sigh. How did I know this was going to come up? "Because one of them was me."

For a second I think she's going to fall out of her chair. The voice that comes out is almost a squeak, and it's kinda loud. "You! Are you serious?"

"Shhhhh, shhhhhh, please! Yes, me. That was before she and Clint met. And everybody's fine with it, so don't make a big deal out of it. She was new, she needed some Doms who had some experience and could be trusted, and I was the first one who came across her radar. Dave gave me the nod – he trained her – so I scened with her." I can tell she's having a hard time with this. "Okay, so wait. Let me try to explain all of this."

She leans back in her chair and crosses her arms. "Go right ahead. This should be good."

Her snarl draws a chuckle out of me. "So we call it scening, and we call it that because we consider it more or less a theatrical performance."

"Even the sex?" Now she's leaning in toward me, elbows on the table, and I know I have her attention.

"Yes. Understand: A lot of clubs don't allow actual sex acts in the performance areas, just simulated or none at all. But Dave believes sex is an integral part of the BDSM performance, so he's always allowed it. Does that make sense?"

Something passes across her eyes and her face falls. "So everything you did with me was an act?"

Oh, god, this is going the wrong direction. "No, no, no! No, we just call pretty much everything scening because it's just how we talk, but no, that wasn't how I considered it at all. No, babe, that was as real as it gets. Didn't it feel real to you?"

Sweeping her hair back from her face, she nods. "Yes, it absolutely did."

"That's because it was. Every word I said to you last night, every touch, every kiss, that was real for me." This is it, and even though I know it's pretty damn stupid on my part, it's like I just can't stop, like I'm compelled to do it. "Sheila, I don't date. I don't take on new subs. And I don't tell women how I feel about them, but with you, I just can't help myself."

She shakes her head and grimaces. "Why does this sound like a really bad pickup line?"

"I don't know. I don't know anything about pickup lines. I go to the club and women approach *me*. I mean, I'm not being arrogant, but they do, they approach me because they want me to play with them. See, the club levels the playing field between men and women." She seems confused. "Hey, remember last night when I told you there was a secret I'd tell you later?"

"Yeah?"

"I guess now's a good time. Remember when I said I was in control; someone had to be in control?" She nods. "Well, believe it or not, you're the one in control. The sub has all the power."

Her brow furrows. "How?"

"Because you can stop play at any time. You have safety measures in place. That's why I told you to use the word red last night. You haven't chosen a safeword yet, but you can, and I'll have to abide by it. Last night, just a simple 'no' would've done the job. But if we keep going, you'll need a safeword, and if you decide you don't want to do something, or it's too painful, or you're tired, or whatever, and I do mean whatever, you can just call a halt to play. It's that simple." I see a light bulb go on in her head. "You hold the power in your hands. Me? I'm along for the ride. My job is to see that you're satisfied, and if I do my job well, my satisfaction is a by-product of your satisfaction."

"I have all the power?"

"Yes, ma'am. You sure do."

"Huh." I can see she's mulling it over.

"Yup. If a sub reports that she safeworded and the Dom or top didn't honor it, Dave does his own little version of an investigation and, ninety-nine times out of a hundred, the guy's out. That's it."

"Wow. I had no idea."

"Well, now you do." I take her hand again. "Look, I just want you to know that, regardless if you felt it or not, I feel some kind of connection to you. And I really want to explore it. I'm hoping it's not one-sided."

She gives me a tiny, shy smile. "It's not."

"Good. Then let's drink this free, unlimited wine and eat our dinner and have a good time." Our salads appear about that time, and we chat over them. "So, your family?"

"They're in Iowa."

That's kind of a surprise. "Iowa! Well, that's not exactly nearby."

"There were no jobs, so I left."

In that moment, I realize I have no idea what she does. "Where do you work?"

"I'm in research at the university hospital."

Oh my god. A smart woman. She'd never guess how thankful I am. "What kind of research?"

"Parkinson's, believe it or not, and some Alzheimer's. We've got a study going on right now, and I'm spending a lot of time on that." She takes another sip of wine and a bite of salad.

"That's fascinating. So you have a biology degree?"

"Doctorate in biological sciences." Holy shit – a doctor. I'm duly impressed. "I mean, it's not like being in practice somewhere, god knows I don't make *that* kind of money, but I feel like I'm contributing, making a difference, you know?"

"I know exactly what you mean."

The salad's good, super good, and the dressing has to be made there because it's too fresh and flavorful to have come from a bottle. While I'm chewing, she asks, "So Trish tells me you're in banking."

I nod, then manage to swallow the rest of the salad in my mouth. "Yes. I'm the regional manager for United Independent Bank, a name which I consider an oxymoron, but no one listens to a word I say." That gets a laugh out of her. "So I've got eight banks under me, about a hundred employees. When everything's running as it should, it's an easy job. When something goes wrong, it's a nightmare."

"Like?" she asks from inside her wine glass.

"Like last week when a teller put the proceeds of a home loan in the wrong account. We're still trying to figure out how she managed that. The numbers and names weren't even similar. Anyway, by the time we found it, the person who owned the account had spent about twenty-seven thousand dollars that wasn't his to spend."

Her eyebrows pop up. "Oh my god! How do you fix that?"

"Well, first, we have to cover it since it was our mistake. Second, we had to call the man who spent the money and talk to him. And when he basically told me to go screw myself because it was our mistake, I had to call the police."

"Oh no!"

"Oh yeah. It's a mess. I've spent almost two weeks now trying to fix this."

"And the teller?"

"If you're asking if she was fired, the answer is no. Everyone makes mistakes. She's been with us four years and we'd never had a problem with her. I sat down with her and found out they just diagnosed her little boy with leukemia, but she hadn't told a soul at work. We found her a job that's less stressful and she's staying with us. It should've been a pay cut, but I refused to cut her pay. Hell, if anything, she needs the money more now than she did before. I told them it was a temporary move so they should just leave her salary where it is."

Her eyes are steady. "And they listened?"

"Yes. I told them I had my reasons. The president of the bank called me, and I told him the same thing. He asked what was going on with her, and when I told him, he agreed with me. I would've been justified in firing her outright, but I didn't want to do that."

She looks like she's going to cry, and I'm shocked. This woman is far more tender-hearted than I imagined, and I find that incredibly sexy. Emotionless bitches do nothing for me and, trust me, I've had my share of experience with those. "That was absolutely, positively the right thing to do. You're very kind. A lot of bosses wouldn't have cared."

"Well, I'm not a lot of bosses. But I can tell you this: When I go to bed at night, I sleep well. I don't have a lot of regret. I try to treat my employees the way I'd want to be treated, and it's paid off. I have the lowest employee turnover in the whole of United Independent. I have a reputation for being a good person to work for, and I'm proud of that."

She nods. "And you should be. I bet your parents are proud."

"My mom is. My dad died about five years ago."

"Oh, I'm so sorry!"

"Yeah, sudden heart attack. So I watch what I eat very, very carefully and I make sure to get plenty of exercise in."

Apparently the kabobs are good because she's just

about devoured them. "Siblings?"

"Yeah, a sister who lives in Missouri, Cecilia. She's a teacher and her husband's a journalist."

"Older?"

"No, younger. Your siblings?"

"Three. Two older brothers and a younger sister. Robert's an attorney, Kenny's a surgeon, and my little sister, Maggie, is a dentist."

I shake my head. "A whole family of over-achievers!"

She laughs again – god, that's a beautiful sound. "Yeah! I guess we are." There's a pause, and she says, "Steffen, I'm having a really good time."

"Good, because I am too." My steak is beyond excellent. I can't remember red meat ever tasting this good before.

Once I've paid the server and we're outside, I turn toward the pier. "Want to walk?"

"Sure!" We head down and walk around hand in hand, watch the sun set, and get an ice cream cone apiece. On our walk back from the pier, I slip my arm around her waist and pull her close to me, and she does the same to me. We chatter all the way back to her house and when I pull in, she sits in the car for a minute without getting out.

"You okay?"

She nods. "Yeah. I'm fine." When she turns to me, I see all the emotion on her face and it blows me away. "Steffen, do you want to stay? Because I'd love it if you did."

This is yet another opportunity for me to drive home

the point that I see her as more than just a fuck. "Actually, I'd love to, but I don't do that. I'd want you to come to my house."

Those lines appear on her forehead again. "Why?"

I just smile. "Because I've heard women complain that they woke up and the guy they'd slept with the night before was gone. If you were to come to my house, I'd have nowhere to go. You wouldn't have to worry about that."

I can see her thinking that over, working it out, and trying to come to some kind of decision. "Huh."

Whoa! I think she's waiting for me to invite her to my house! I've never had this happen before, and I think it's hysterical in a way. She's polite, I'll give her that. I let her stew for about a half a minute before I ask, "So, would you like to come to my house?"

She folds her arms across her chest and glares at me. "Why are you teasing and tormenting me?"

I shoot her an evil grin. "Because it's so much fun." Then I drop my head and look up at her from under my brows. "So? Coming or not?"

She giggles. "Do you really want me to?"

That's it. I lean over to her, draw her face to mine, and kiss her. There's no doubt what she's thinking when I feel her lips touch mine. She wants me as much as I want her. "I think the question is, do you want to drive or shall I bring you home tomorrow?"

"You know, I think I want you to bring me home. I guess I should go in and get some clothes, huh?

I laugh. "Won't need 'em!"

She starts laughing too. "Well, okay, toothbrush and hairbrush. How 'bout that?"

"Oh, well, yeah, I'm not a fan of morning breath, so that sounds pretty good. Shall I sit out here?"

"No. Come on in." We're both still teasing each other and laughing as we head into the house.

It takes her all of ten minutes to throw some things in a bag. "Did you put extra panties in there?" I ask her.

"Yeah."

"Good. Those you'll need." I reach for her and draw her up against me, then kiss her again. She drops her bag and wraps those beautiful arms around my neck, and I swear I see stars and hear angels. Then I pull back and look down into those big blue eyes. "If we keep this up, we'll never get to my house."

"Come on then. Let's go." She grabs my hand and leads me out, locks the door, and pulls me down the steps to the car.

"Oh, god, Sir, oh god. Please? Please? I need to come."

Her hands are tied together with red shibari rope and then tied to the head of my bed. That naked body is gloriously on display, and there's a fire in my cock that I haven't felt in years. My spreader bar has come in handy too, and her ankles are secured to it while I administer a delicious level of torment. I work her right up to orgasm, only to let it subside before I start again. Six times so far. She's wound up like you wouldn't believe. "One more time, sub, and then I'll see what I can do about this."

"Oh, please, Sir!"

And now comes the part I want her to get. "Okay, listen to me. I'm going to tell you when you can come, and you have to hold off until then. Once I tell you that you can, it's all good."

"I'll try, Sir."

"No trying." I ramp up my finger motion, that swirling around her distended node, and she squirms with the effort of waiting. Finally, I tell her, "Sub, I want you to come for me." I stroke her clit extra hard and fast for a split second, and she comes hard, bucking and screaming. Making sure I let it go on long enough, I finally stop and bark out, "I'm flipping you over. On your knees, hands gripping the headboard." Shibari rope undone and dropped on the floor by the bed, I pick her up and roll her. Once she's on her stomach, I'm surprised at how fast she can scramble up and get into position. It's a joy to press my hands into her sides just under her arms and slide them down until they rest on those luscious hips. Wow. The girl is curvy in all the right places, and she brings my curve to life every time. My fingers grip into her flesh and I lean forward to kiss my way down her spine; the arch in her back tells me she loves it. There's something about this woman that makes me want to keep her happy and satisfy her. Something else floats through my mind, someone else I felt that way about, but I just let it keep going until it's gone – thank god. When I get to the base of her spine, I drag my tongue all the way back up just to hear her moan out, "Ahhhhhhhh."

"Good?"

"Awesome."

"I'm glad." I rise up on my knees behind her, roll on a condom, and then move into her, knowing she can feel my cock pressing against her ass. "I hope this is equally as good." I scoot my knees up and under her spread legs and press the head of my dick into her slick, hot opening. When I shove upward the first time, she lets out a little squeal. "You'll not come until I tell you it's all right. Understand?"

"Yes, Sir." My rhythm is vicious, and she falls right into it, pressing down against me as I rise up into her, moaning in a way that sets my blood boiling. God, her ass is a beautiful thing! So firm, so round, so satiny. Everything below my waist is knotting and tightening, and I need her so badly that I can barely breathe.

Before I even know I'm going to say it, I mutter out, "Girl, do you have any idea what you do to me?"

A breathless, "Oh, Sir," comes out of her lips and she groans loudly. Oh, god, I wish we knew each other well enough to just lose control, but I feel like I have to hold back so I don't push her or scare her. I don't want her nervous or afraid around me. She's been pushed around enough already. "Oh, Sir, please, may I come? Oh, god."

"Not yet, sub. Not yet. Hang in there with me and I promise you'll be rewarded." I'm almost there, teetering on the edge, and then I slap her ass with the palm of one hand and tell her, "Come with me, baby. Right now." Over the edge I go, and from the way her channel closes around me and pulses, I know she's there too. Her knuckles are white from gripping the headboard, and I give her about ten more good, hard thrusts, really push her hard. She's crying out and trembling, and I scoot back just a little, rise up straight, wrap my arms around her, and pull her up, her back against my chest.

Her head tips back against my shoulder, and I whisper in her ear, "You're incredible, do you know that? You're the woman every man dreams about."

There's a sleepy smile on her face. "Do you dream about me?"

The low rumble in my chest gives me away, my voice husky when I answer, "Since I met you? Every damn night. I don't dream about anything or anyone else."

"Oh, Steffen." She turns her head toward me and kisses my cheek, and I swear I think I'll be able to feel her lips there even next week. "I want to know you, really know you. You have a beautiful soul."

No one's ever said anything like that to me before. Everybody treats me like I'm some kind of ego-driven stud who wants one conquest after another. And I may put that face on at the club, act all cavalier and nonchalant, but it's just like I told her before: Everyone wants to be loved. Even me. It's eluded me all these years, and I'd like to think I've finally captured it. I want to hang on with both hands, dig my fingers into it, and never let go.

I cup one of her breasts in each hand, feel their weight, test the hardness of her nipples with my fingers, and listen to the sigh she blows out and onto my skin. She smells so sweet, like chocolate and cinnamon, and I can't get her close enough to me. I want to draw her in through my skin, swallow her down and put her inside me somehow, hold onto this moment for the next day, week, month. She turns and puts a hand on either side of my face, and her eyes are clear and bright when she speaks. "Do you want more? Because I do. I'm afraid, but I'm tired of being alone. I've had no one for so long. I'm so glad I'm here with you."

Just like she's holding my face, I hold hers and she presses her lips to mine. There's some kind of spark between us; I feel it almost pop and crackle as it travels along my spine, and when she shivers under my palms, I know she feels it too. Gasping for breath, I manage to pant out, "I'm glad I'm here with you too." The house is so quiet that I swear I can hear our hearts beating here in the low lamp light, that beautiful cayenne-colored hair shimmering, and I draw her down and into my arms. Lying there on our sides and facing each other, there's something about it all that feels so right, so comfortable and normal and relaxing.

Our lips meet, and then she draws back and looks straight into my eyes with those big baby blues. "Steffen, I need you again. Please?"

She needn't have asked. I'm already hard for her. It's a perpetual state of being for me if she's anywhere near. Snapping off the condom to roll another one on feels like second nature, and I shove her knees apart with mine, pull her legs up and around my waist, and slide into her waiting warmth.

It's like I've always been here with her, and she fits

so perfectly in my arms that I'm pretty sure she's been tailor-made for me. "Are you getting what you need? I just want you to get what you need," I whisper to her.

"You're more than enough, baby, more than enough." That voice, those words, those eyes – these overwhelmingly possessive feelings just take over, and I know we're supposed to be here together. We rock into each other quietly, exchanging little kisses, and some-times I just kiss her forehead. Holding her is like a drug, and I'm so damn high I don't ever want to come down. I hear her give a little tiny grunt and her pussy starts to pulse around my cock, and in less than a minute, I pour into my condom again.

We both still, her legs around my waist, my arms tight around her, and she presses her face to my chest and sighs. I've never felt so balanced and centered in my life. This woman belongs with me – I know that beyond a shadow of a doubt. To test the waters I say, "You sure there isn't somewhere you need to be in the morning?"

There's a gentle smile on her lips as she looks up at me. "There's no place I need to be that's more important than being here with you."

This is it. I make up my mind right then – I'm not letting go.

When I manage to pry one eye open, Sheila's sitting up in the bed, scratching her head through that tangled mane of hair. She sees me sneaking a peek at her and says, "Your morning wood is impressive."

I lift the sheet and look down. "Yeah, like that? It's all yours. You can build whatever you like with that."

"I want to build something that'll withstand the test of time." She leans down into my face and kisses me.

"What do you have in mind?" I clasp my hands behind my head to lift it so I can see her a little better, and she giggles.

"I don't know, silly! Oh, just something strong and sturdy and solid."

"And something silly?" With that, I grab her, throw her to the bed, climb on top of her, and start tickling her, and she shrieks with laughter. "Want something silly too, silly girl?"

"Yeah, yeah! Something silly!" I stop and look down into her face. "Steffen, you look good with stubble, you know?"

"Yeah? Think so?" I rub my jawline along her shoulder and she giggles again. "Like a scrub brush."

"Like a sexy scrub brush."

I roll my eyes. "Well, I can honestly say I've never been called a sexy scrub brush before. So thanks for that." She digs her fingers into my ribs to tickle me, and I growl back, "Okay, little girl, don't start something you can't finish!" and start tickling her again.

"I want to finish! I want to!" she shrieks. When we both calm, she says, "Uh-oh. Your morning wood is gone."

"Yeah. You tickled it right out of me."

"Sorry."

It's time to get up, I think, so I stumble off to the

bathroom. While I'm in there, I yell back out, "Want some breakfast?"

"Yeah. And I should probably go home."

"Why? Is your other boyfriend gonna miss you?" I laugh.

"Oh, yeah. He's missing me already. He's probably been wondering where I am." I can hear her giggling the whole time.

I come back and sit down in the bed, then draw her up against me and kiss her forehead. "Tell him I said back off 'cause there's a new sheriff in town, and he don't like being messed with, ya hear?"

"Yes, Sir! I'll tell him, Sir." She looks around the room and then turns back to me. "I love being here with you. Your house is amazing and so are you."

"Having you here is a joy, babe. I hope this is just the first time of many to come." I kiss her forehead again.

"Me too." She cranes her neck and gives me a peck on the lips. "Now I'm going to take a shower. And before you ask, no. I like to shower alone. Sorry. It's just a thing for me."

"Damn. And to think I actually had some wood I could get wet without the grain splitting." I'm grinning from ear to ear, thinking about last night. "Oh, well, go ahead. That's fine. I'll just wait out here and pout."

"You do that." She ruffles my hair as she gets up and laughs when I do my best to smooth it back down. That's impossible. I'm the king of bed head.

On the way back to her house, she asks, "So what are you doing today?"

"Well, looks like the very first thing I'll be doing is changing my sheets!" I wink at her. "And then I'm taking the car to the carwash. And then I'm going back home to finish a model I've been working on." She makes a face. "Plane. I have model planes. You know, the big ones that you fly? Remote control?"

"Oh! Yeah? I didn't see them."

"They're in the garage. Matter of fact, that's why the car's not in there right now. I've got one scattered out because I'm working on it. But when I get it finished, I'll be able to put the car back in there."

"How long have you been doing that?"

"Oh, for as long as I can remember. Since at least middle school, maybe before." I wait for a second, then ask, "Would you like to come next time I fly one of them?"

"I'd *love* that! Sounds like fun!"

"It is. I keep saying one of these days I'm going to learn to fly, but I just don't have time." I turn onto her street and I'm instantly sorry that in just a few minutes, this woman will be out of arm's reach for me. There's going to be a void at the house when I go back there, so I might as well prepare for it.

Once I'm parked, I turn to her. "Want me to walk you up?"

"Nah. I can do the walk of shame by myself." She laughs right out loud and I'm blown away by that smile, so natural and dazzling. Then she leans in and kisses me. "Thanks, Steffen. It was wonderful. See you soon?"

"Oh, baby, you can bet on that. I enjoyed it too." I

kiss her back. "Call you later?"

"Please!" She gets out and closes the door, then leans on the window opening. "I really do want to spend time with you if you want it too."

"I do. I'll give you a call later." Then I start to laugh. "Now get on in there and masturbate while you think of me. I know that's what you're going to do!"

"Wow. You've obviously got cameras in my house. I'll have to find those suckers and take them out of commission. Great. I'm not safe from prying eyes anywhere." She's still laughing and shaking her head when she gets to her front door, and she turns and waves at me before she goes inside and closes it behind her.

I knew it. It's like there's a huge hole on the other side of the car. I forgot my punch card for the car wash, so I head back home and I haven't more than walked in the door when my phone rings. And I know that ring-tone: The theme from *The Golden Girls*. "Yeah?"

"Well?"

"Well what?"

Clint sounds a little exasperated with me. "Well, how was it?"

"How was what?"

He growls out, "Cothran, damn it, you irritate the hell out of me sometimes. I know about the date. Sheila told Trish. How was it?"

I plop down on the sofa. "It was awesome, fantastic, amazing, incredible. She fucks like a pro."

"Wow. Information I didn't need."

"Well, you asked. And before you start chastising me for something I didn't do, I was very careful with her. We did a little restraint work, but that's all. And you know, I'm not sure I want to pursue BDSM with her."

Silence. Then, "Hello? I don't know who you are, but would you please put Steffen back on the phone?"

"Wise ass. You heard me."

"What the hell, Cothran?"

"I don't know, Winstead," I mock back. Then I get real with him. "Clint, there's just something about this girl. I want to be with her more than I've wanted anyone in a long, long time. She's just it, man. She's it."

"Hmmmm. Okay. Did you tell her that?"

"In so many words."

"Again, did you tell her that?"

"Yes, more or less."

"I still don't think you heard my question."

"Yes. Yes, I told her I wanted to be with her. She asked me if I was working with any other subs, and I told her that not only was I not, but I wasn't interested in pursuing that with anyone else. She just, I don't know, feels like she belongs in my arms, you know?"

There's a pause, and then Clint says in a tone low and warm, "I know exactly what you mean."

"Yeah. She's my Trish. I know that for sure."

I hear him snicker. "Are you her Clint?"

I'm trying not to laugh. "No. I'm even better."

"Oh? Zat so?" Now he's chuckling.

"Oh, yeah. So much better. You just can't imagine."

"That's not what my wife says."

"Well, your wife just didn't hang around long enough, that's all!" Now I'm almost screaming with laughter, and he is too.

"Listen, Steffen, if this is what you want, then I want it for you too. I want to see you happy. It's about damn time."

"Thanks. That means a lot to me." And it does. I don't have family around here except for my mother, and it's nice to have people who care about me, even if most of the time when I see them one of us is fucking somebody. There's camaraderie in that, I do believe.

"Seeing her again?"

"God, I hope so, but we didn't make any real plans, just made sure that the other knew we felt that way."

"Good. If I can help you in any way, just let me know. Good luck, my friend."

"Thanks, Clint. Give you a call in a couple of days?"

"You bet, buddy. Talk to you soon."

I pick up my car wash punch card and head back out the door. Maybe I'll stop at Mongolian Manor and pick up some stir-fry on the way home. That sounds good. I've worked up quite an appetite over the last twenty-four hours.

Chapter Five

"Hey!"

"Hi! What are you up to?"

I grin. "Calling you because I miss your voice."

"Awwww, that's sweet. I miss your smile."

Now I'm grinning so wide that my cheeks hurt. "I'm smiling right now because I'm talking to you. So, I was wondering, want to go to dinner tomorrow night? Something casual, pizza or something, since it's a work night, then back over here to watch a movie?"

"Oh, I can't." Uh-oh. Am I getting the brush-off so soon? If so, it's a record set. "We've got a visiting researcher coming in and I promised my supervisor that I'd help her get settled in her apartment. I'm going over to help her unpack boxes. I'll have to do that the next night too. But the night after that I'm finally free. If she's not done by then, she'll just have to get someone else to come and help her. I have a life too."

"Okay, so Wednesday night, pizza and then a movie over here?" My fingers are crossed.

"Yes! But let's not go out. Let's order the pizza in so we can stay there all evening." She waits. Then I finally get it.

"Oh! Yeah, okay, that's great. And you'll bring stuff so you can go to work from here the next morning, right?"

I hear her let out a tiny giggle. "If you want me to."

"Trust me, I want you to. I always want you to."

"Always is a pretty decisive word," she snickers.

"I've always been a pretty decisive guy," I counter. She stops snickering.

When I call her the next evening, the first thing she says is, "Hang on. Let me get my Bluetooth." I hear a lot of noise, and then she says, "Can you hear me?"

"Yeah. That's better."

"Yeah. I need my hands free." I hear paper rattling and then she says, "No, this is a box full of stuff that I think belongs in the bedroom." There's some more chatter in the background, and when it ends, she says in a voice so low that I can barely hear her, "Oh my god, this is a mess. I'm glad I only agreed to help for two nights. I couldn't do any more than that."

"Good. Because I miss you."

"I miss you too."

I'm trying hard not to laugh when I say, "And I want to fuck you."

"Oh, that's nice," she says, and I know the other person is somewhere near.

"Yeah, and I want to eat your pussy until you scream." I'm really working to not laugh.

"Well, same here."

"I don't have a pussy." Now I *am* laughing – I can't

help it.

"I know that, dear." She sounds a little put out, and I just laugh harder.

"Oh, now I'm 'dear?' Aren't we grumpy? Guess you get that way when you haven't had enough cock in the last twenty-four hours."

A little growl comes through the phone. "You are going to get me in so much trouble."

I'm laughing so loud that I can't believe the other person there can't hear me through the phone. "You know, I've been intending to talk to you about something. I think it's about time I took that pretty little ass of yours. I think I'd like to bury this big tool of mine in that beautiful little back door of yours, sweet cheeks. Whaddya say? A professional ass fucking will do you a world of good!"

"Steffen, you're incorrigible."

"Yeah, but I'm cute!" I'm also gasping for breath.

Her voice softens. "Yeah, you are. You're really, really cute." She pauses, and then she whispers fast and loudly, "And one helluva fuck. I'll talk to you later. Bye." And the phone goes dead.

I drop it on the sofa and double over, rolling around on the cushions. She's gonna kill me, I'm pretty sure, but that was a lot of fun. At ten thirty, my phone rings. "Yes, dear?"

"You think you're pretty funny, don't you?" She's trying to pretend she's mad, but I can hear her chuckling.

"A real riot. Oh, and I meant part of what I said."

"Which part?"

"Let's see . . . the parts about eating your pussy, *and* the part about ass fucking you."

"Oh, is that right?"

"Yeah, it absolutely is. Good thing you're not here." I'm still chuckling.

"Oh? And why is that?" Something sounds wrong. I can't figure out what it is, but it just doesn't sound right.

"Because if you were here, I'd do everything I said I was going to, and I'd do it to you right now." About that time, the doorbell rings. "Hang on. Door."

I look through the peep hole and then start to laugh. When I open the door, there she stands, phone in hand, and I realize the seemingly odd quality to the call was because I could also hear her outside the door and didn't realize it. "Can I come in?"

"I don't know. Do I want you to?" She's got on a short trench coat, and she opens the front.

She's fucking naked underneath.

Well, that cut my decision-making time drastically. "Yes. I absolutely want you to. Get in here." I yank her by the arm into the house, slam the door shut, and pin her against it, crushing her mouth with mine. She's mumbling into my lips and waving her arms around. "What?"

"Let me take off the coat!"

I shake my head. "No. I like it. Makes you look all mysterious, like a spy or something."

"I'm afraid we're about to ruin the lining."

"Yes, I think we probably are. I'll buy you a new one." I smash her against the door again, then lift her and wedge her between my body and the door so she can ratchet her legs around my waist like a vice. One arm under her ass, I manage to reach into my pocket and hand her a foil-wrapped condom with the other. "Here. Unwrap this while I release the animal." I undo my belt and fly, then push my boxer briefs down until my cock springs free. Once I get the condom rolled on, I bury myself in her with one swift stroke. She cries out as I take her rough and fast, and there's nothing in the world that I want to do more than fuck this girl, right here, right now. With my face pressed into her neck, I moan out, "God, Sheila, you're killing me. Your body's like a drug."

She takes my face in her hands, kisses me lightly, and snarls out, "Just fuck me."

And I do. I fuck her so hard I'm pretty sure her teeth are rattling. She bounces up and down from the force and occasionally mutters, "Oh god," or, "Damn, Steffen." With every stroke, her tits bounce a little, and occasionally I catch a nipple in my teeth and give it a nip, which makes her yell. I like that a lot. I'm banging her like a barn door in a tornado when she cries out, "Oh, damn, Steffen, I'm coming!" I don't try to tell her to wait or stop or anything, just let her go, and when she grips me, I come too. I swear, it was so hard and fast that I think I smell smoke.

"Good god, girl, this is what you get when you show up on my doorstep like that." I carry her to the sofa and let her perch her ass on the back, then pull out of her.

"That means I'll do it more often."

"Won't hurt my feelings at all." I lean down to her and kiss her, my hand wrapped around the back of her head. When I break away, I smile at her. "Hi there."

"Hi. Surprised?"

"Very. Pleasantly. Have you eaten?"

"Yes. Have you?"

"Yeah. About two hours ago. Unless you can think of a reason why I shouldn't, I'm taking you to the bed and fucking the hell out of you for the next two hours." I wait. "Gimme a reason why I shouldn't."

"Uh, I can't think of one," she sneers.

"Well, okay then. A fucking you'll get." I just pick her up and carry her, arms wrapped around my neck, down the hallway to the bedroom and climb up into the middle of the bed with her. Once I've deposited her there, I start stripping off my clothes until I don't have any more to strip off, and she's out of that coat and naked as the day she was born. My mouth waters. "And I meant what I said earlier."

To my amazement, she rolls over, draws her knees up, and plants her forearms on the mattress. "Fuck it. I'm ready." I can't move, I'm so shocked. "Well? It's waiting for you. It's tighter than my pussy and twice as hot."

That draws me out of my stupor. I manage, "Uh, uh, hang on," and reach for a condom, then grab a tube of gel lube and slather some on. This is foreign turf for me with her, and I open her cheeks and take a good look.

Beautiful. The perfect rosette. I squeeze some of the lube out and into her crack, then put the cap back on and start to work it into her hole. I run one finger in, then two, and I swear she's so tight that I think I hear it squeak. "Do this often?"

"Never."

I feel kind of lightheaded. "Whaaa???"

"Anal virgin. And I'm giving it to you. I hope you appreciate that."

Mind spinning, I reach between her legs. "Then you're going to come before I take it." I start flicking her clit and she lets out a scream. Three minutes later, she convulses, her whole body twitching, and I only let it go on for a few seconds. I'm in a hurry, dammit. This has never happened to me before, and I want to get to it. "Ready?"

"I have no idea how to be ready for this, so yeah, I guess so." I press two fingers in again and she doesn't make a sound. After a few minutes of working it, I press the head of my cock to her tiny sphincter. I start to work my way in and she calls out, "Oh, sonofabitch." Once I've managed to get through the initial barrier, I hit the second ring of muscles, and that's harder. She's panting and groaning, but I press on, literally, until I feel my shaft glide on through. That draws an, "Oh, damn!" out of her.

I finally stop. "I'm all the way in, baby. You sure you want this?"

She doesn't hesitate. "Yes. I absolutely do. Do it. I want to know what it's like."

"Okay, here we go." It's been at least a minute, so she should've gotten a chance to adjust to me a little. I draw back, then plow into her.

"Oh, shit! Oh. My. God. Damn."

"You okay?"

"Oh, yeah. Fuck me."

"I can stop if . . ."

"No, I meant that literally. Fuck me!"

Oh. She meant that literally. "Well, okay then, I'll do that."

I set about fucking her ass aggressively, and she's crying out and screaming, but every time I ask, "Do you want me to stop?" she yells back, "Fuck no! Give it to me!" I'm not sure what she's trying to do, but I'm wondering: Is this her anal version of ripping off a Band-Aid? I'm pretty sure it is. I try a couple of different angles and then just decide to go with whatever feels good to me because she's making so much noise that I can't gauge what she's enjoying and what she's not. It's a fair assumption that if she's not threatening to kill me, it must be okay.

She's fallen to just moaning, and I'm getting so close, so damn close, and I want her to come with me, but I'm pretty sure she's not going to. "Are you close, angel?"

"I have no idea," she pants back, "but this is good." That's a shock; I thought she was just tolerating it at best. All of a sudden, she comes out with, "Ohhhh, gawwwwd, ohhhhhhh, STEFFEN!" I'm pretty sure she just ripped my sheets, and her face is buried in the mattress as her body stiffens and shakes. Well, then; that must've been okay. About that time, I turn loose, and next thing I know, we're on our sides on the bed, my cock still buried in her ass.

And I manage a breathy, "What the hell?"

"God. Oh my god. Let's do that again."

Now I can't help it; I start to laugh. "You're going to have to work on your delivery, because I'm the most confused sonofabitch in the world right now. I thought you were hating this and then you just went crazy!"

"Would you *please* just wrap your arms around me, kiss the back of my neck, and be still and quiet for a second?" she growls out.

"Yeah, okay, arms, neck, quiet. Got it." I do exactly as she said, um, asked, and we both get still and quiet.

I wake up about an hour later, soft but still inside her, and she rouses a little when I pull out and head to the bathroom. I drop the condom in the trash can and take a leak. When I come back, she's rolled to face me. Even in the dim light, her eyes are bright as she looks back into mine. "You okay, baby?" I ask her, stroking her cheek.

"Yes. I'm excellent. You?"

I just grin. "I'm excellent too. You liked that?"

"I'll like it better when I'm more accustomed to it, but yes, I did. What I liked most was that I was doing it with you." She snuggles closer to me and whispers, "Steffen, I'm falling in love with you."

"I've already been there and bought season tickets," I whisper back.

"Good. I just wanted to know you'd be there with me."

I smile into her hair. "Always."

⟨◦◦◦⟩

About halfway through work the next day, I get a text and have to grin.

> *I'll be too late to do pizza this evening. BTW, I'm having trouble staying in one place because sitting is kind of uncomfortable. Is this normal?*

So I text back.

> *Yes. Especially if you've never before been fucked in the ass by a cock as big as mine. Which you haven't. Few have. Lucky you.*

I can just hear her laughing through the text. In about ten minutes, I get another one.

> *There's a conspicuous absence of your large cock in my asshole. Is this normal?*

I'm shaking with silent laughter when I text her back.

> *Only for those who can handle a cock as large as mine up in them. And apparently you can. You're doubly blessed.*

The next one comes in a minute later.

> *Fuck you, Steffen.*

I text back.

> *No, fuck you, Sheila. Hard. In the ass. Over and over.*

And this is the reply I get two minutes later.

Okay. Talk to you later, baby.

I just smile as I text back. God, she's amazing.

Yeah, angel, talk to you later. xoxoxoxoxoxo

Hers?

Mwah!

I send her a text that evening at eight.

Hey, are you still working or can you talk?

When I don't hear anything, I try again.

Are you okay?

And I get this reply.

I'M TRYING TO DRIVE. I'm on my way. Just hang on.

Good. I'm pretty happy about that.

Ten minutes later, I hear her car alarm chirp and I go to the door and open it. She marches up the steps with two huge bags in her hands. When I give her a weird look, she says, "German food. Bratwursts, Reubens, all kinds of German food. I'm hungry."

"Me too!" We unpack the sacks and boxes and get some plates. While she's plating the food, I get some drinks and silverware. Food on the table, we sit down and take up forks. It's absolutely delicious. I'm stunned and grateful.

I feel her hand on mine and I look up. There's this sincerity there when she says, "You know, I didn't even ask you if you wanted me here or if you were doing something else. That was really rude of me. I can go if you want."

I'm sure my smile is sad when I look at her. "No. I don't want you to go. There's nothing I could be doing that would be more important than spending time with you."

"Wow. Thanks. You just made my day." She takes another big bite of the brat that she's cut up.

"Thanks. You made my day by being here." The Reuben is excellent, and I've got about half of one down. "What made you think of German food?"

"Because I was looking up your name on the internet today to see where it came from, and it's German."

"That's because all of my grandparents were. They immigrated to this country when my parents were both small."

"Both families?"

"Yup. Both families. But they didn't wind up in the same neighborhood until my parents were in their teens. They started dating in high school and never dated anyone else. It was just the two of them until he died."

"Oh my god." Every ounce of sadness in the world seems to be on her face. "That's so sweet and so sad."

"Yeah." I swallow hard. "We were close. He and I used to go to ball games all the time. I really miss him. So does my mom. Both of your parents still alive?"

"Yeah."

Then I realize something. "You know, I have no idea how old you are. I know Trish is late forties, early fifties."

"I'm forty-two." She takes another big bite of schnitzel.

"I'm forty-five. And I think we both look damn good for our ages."

"Me too."

"Hey, want to go to the club tomorrow night?"

A big smile spreads across her face. "Yes! Let's! I'd love that. I have some new stuff to wear too."

I shoot her a look. "I'm your Dom. I should approve it before you wear it."

"You're my Dom?" She grins.

"Yes. I'm your Dom." Then I level my gaze at her. "Don't be a brat. I don't want to have to spank you, but I will if it's necessary."

She shakes her head. "Wow. That would be a shame."

"Yes, wouldn't it?" I'm giving it my best effort as I try hard not to laugh, but it's impossible to suppress it. "Do you have any idea how much fun you are?"

"In bed or out?" she smirks.

"Yes."

"Awwwww, thanks! How sweet!" As she moves some food around on her plate, she says, "You're getting a blow job tonight." I drop my head and start to laugh. "What? What's so funny?"

"You." Our eyes meet and I hope she can see in mine all the feelings I have for her, bouncing around and careening off each other inside me. "The conversations we have are priceless. No one would believe some of them if I told them."

"I know. So eat your dinner. You had one more sausage than I did, so I want yours to make up for it." She grins and winks at me.

I'm laughing so hard that tears are almost rolling down my face. When I finally pull myself together enough to speak, I say, "I'd rather spend time with you than to do anything else on earth, no matter what we're doing."

Her smile is soft and shy. "I love you, Steffen. It's like we were made to be together."

"I know. It's like we've always known each other." I take another bite and realize she's staring at me. "What?"

There's a shrug followed by, "Oh, nothing," as she picks up her fork and makes short work of the potato salad on her plate. I watch her and realize I'm the luckiest guy I know. Well, okay, maybe Clint's got me beat, but not by much. This woman is amazing.

The clock catches my eye. "Damn! I've got to finish this and get it cleaned up. I want to watch the news. There was a big bank robbery this afternoon at a bank downtown and I want to see if they've caught the guy." I'm gobbling up my food as fast as I can. The food is gone but before I can pick up my plate, she puts a hand on mine. "What?"

She tosses her head in the direction of the living room. "Go. I'll clean up."

"But are you sure you . . ."

"Go!" she demands and points toward the living room. I kiss her forehead and head that way.

They're still talking about the robbery when she joins me on the sofa. "What happened?"

"Oh, some asshat walked into the Fidelity Bank and held them up at gunpoint. Didn't hurt anybody, but they're pretty sure it's the same guy who robbed another one of their branches last week and a Citizens Savings Bank the week before."

"At gunpoint?"

"Yeah. I don't ever want any of my people exposed to that." It worries me. Seems like our banks are the only local ones this guy hasn't hit. "I'm calling my boss tomorrow to ask for more security at all our locations until this guy is caught."

"Good idea." Now they're talking about some balloon launch in France, and Sheila drops to her knees in front of me. The care she's putting into unbuckling my belt and unbuttoning and unzipping my pants is making me want her so much more; it's like torture, a sweet torture. God, those pouty pink lips and big blue eyes are so fucking gorgeous and unbelievably sexy. Her small, soft hands around my dick harden it until I hurt, and she starts pumping up and down slowly, dragging out every movement. "You're so hard, baby. Aching?"

I drop my head onto the back of the sofa. "Um-hum. Throbbing."

"Dark too. Look at that. So big and hard." She nibbles at the tip, runs her tongue into the slit, nibbles all the way down one side, around and underneath the base, and then up the other side. I know I'm moaning out loud, but I don't care. It's too damn good not to.

"Babe, take me in your mouth. Please. I can't stand it anymore." I see those luscious lips open wide and then my cock vanishes into her throat. It's a beautiful sight, my manhood buried in that heat, her tongue trailing up and down its length. "You ever had your face fucked?" She nods. "Tolerate it?" There's the sensation of her grinning around my shaft, and she nods again. "Then that's what I'm about to do. I'll let you work for a little while, but then I'm taking over." She works it, letting her lips slide down, down, down, until I feel the head of my cock hit the back of her throat and her lips almost seat themselves at its base. Boy oh boy, this woman knows what she's doing.

My takeover never happens. I just get lost in what she's doing, how it feels, how she looks, and I know my eyes must be glazed over, but I really don't care. It's like magic, watching my dick disappear and reappear like a cuckoo in a clock, her eyes watering and nose running as she takes it down again and again, never stopping more than a few seconds. I realize I'm gripping the piping on the edges of the sofa cushions with my hands, and I start to shake all over. She's got me, controlling me, owning me with that rosy mouth of hers, and I'm trying so hard to keep from coming, trying to make it last, and I don't know how long I can. "Sweet lord, baby, you're tormenting me, know that? It's torture, girl."

What she does next surprises me. As she keeps up the steady rhythm, she stands and works while she's bent over. I'm trying to figure out what she's doing, and then it's clear: She's undressing. That's a neat trick. She's got on a blouse that buttons up the front – how convenient. When she's completely bare, she reaches for the waistband of my pants and I raise my ass up just enough for her to pull them down. In the meantime, I yank my tee shirt over my head and try to throw it on the floor, but she grabs it instead.

All of that activity has distracted me a bit, but not much, and I'm peaking all over again. She's shifting somehow, and then I hear that familiar sound of foil ripping. Next thing I know, she's up, rolls a condom onto my stony shaft, and proceeds to mount me. Once she's fully seated on my cock, she puts my tee shirt to her face, blows her nose, wipes her face, and then leans in and kisses me. Sultry describes it to the letter when those big, hard nipples brush my chest. I just stay reclined against the back of the sofa while she braces herself, hands on my shoulders, and lifts and falls, those ripe tits bouncing just a little each time she hits bottom. I can't say a word; I'm too wrapped up in the way her body is undulating. The flush that spreads across her chest, up her neck, onto her cheeks and down to the tops of her tits lights me up like a Christmas tree. Everything about her says sex, and it's overwhelming.

Without warning, I come. I was trying so hard not to, but when I do, she slams up and down on me a half dozen times and trembles with her own orgasm. Finally falling forward on my chest, she wraps her arms around my waist and I do the same with her. My kiss applied to the top of her head makes her purr. "Girl, you are just full of surprises."

I hear a little giggle. "I know. I've always been like that. My friends call me Captain Random because you never know what I'm going to do next."

"That's fun!"

"Not always." Pressing her hands into my chest, she pushes herself upright, my dick still buried in her. "It can be annoying. Like deciding on the spur of the moment to pick up German food."

"No, that's charming."

"As long as you're not busy, especially as long as you're not busy with someone else."

That takes me by surprise. "Sheila, I told you, there is no one else."

"I know you said that, but . . ."

"But what?"

She shakes her head. "Look at you. You're like a Norse god. Every woman in the restaurant the other night was eyeing you, and about seventy-five percent of them were drooling too." There's a long pause, and then she asks, "Steffen, are you . . ."

"No. Again, I'm telling you, there's. No. One. Else. I've never made it a habit to date more than one woman at a time. It gets too complicated, and it also gets in the way of growing a relationship. So no, there isn't and won't be until such time as you no longer want to see me."

"That's not going to happen." She grins like a jack-o-lantern.

I tip my head toward the hallway. "Good. Now, shall we continue this in the bedroom?" An odd look crosses her face. "What?"

"Nothing."

"Girl, that's the second time you've said that to me tonight. Now, what is it?"

She shrugs. "It's just that I'm exhausted. All I really want to do is sleep. Would that be okay?"

I can't help it – I throw my head back and laugh. "You just took me on a wild ride and you're afraid I'll be mad because you just want to sleep? Go get cleaned up and climb in the bed. I'll lock up and be there in a few minutes."

There's that one hundred megawatt smile. "Okay. I just want to cuddle with you." She leans in again and kisses me.

That beautiful face. I'll never grow tired of that beautiful face. Her smile is like sunshine and lights up the room. I take that face in my hands and tenderly kiss her back. "I want to cuddle with you too." I slap her thigh. "Go! Get ready for bed." She gives me another peck on the lips, disengages herself from my worn-out cock, and heads down the hall.

I lock the door, pick up my clothes, look around to see if anything else is necessary, and make the trip down the hall to the bedroom. There, I'm greeted with the sight of her angelic face on my pillow, eyes closed and breathing softly. Disturbed as I scoot into the bed, she rolls up against me and curls up, her face to my chest. My arms can't hold her tight enough, my lips can't kiss her sweetly enough. I want this woman to be mine. And for the first time in forever, I feel like I just might have a chance at that.

———— ◆◇◆ ————

Clint forks up a mouthful of Caesar salad. "So, how are you guys doing?"

"I think we're doing pretty good. You were right."

"How so?"

"I've fallen for her."

He grins from ear to ear. "I knew it!"

"The good news is that she's fallen for me too."

"Excellent! My goal is closer than I thought."

I take a sip of my water. "So, what's going on with her asshole ex?"

"He's up for parole. I don't think he'll get it. From what we hear, he's been in a dozen or more fights since he got there." Clint pushes his empty salad plate away and props his elbows on the table. "He's just trouble all the way around. Trish says he wasn't always like this. Sheila thinks he got involved in drugs."

"That'll do it for sure." I've finished my salad too and I'm really hungry for that chicken piccata. "We're going to the club tonight. You guys?"

"Nah. Can't. McKenna's got some school program we're going to." He sits and fiddles with his fork for a second or two and then tears down my whole world with one question. "Have you told Sheila about you know who?"

I'm really confused at first. "Who are you talking about?"

"You know, She Who Shall Not Be Named."

And it hits me. Oh, god, no. I don't want to talk

about her, think about her, hear her name, consider the fact that she's on the same planet with me. "No. I have not. I don't want to either."

"Does that mean you finally got the divorce finalized?"

A sense of dread like a tidal wave sweeps over me. "No. They've never found her."

"Don't you think you should tell Sheila?"

"Why? That has nothing to do with my life now." I'm starting to feel panicky. I feel that way any time this subject comes up. It's like I'm being choked by an unseen hand, my chest tightening, breathing shallow, stomach churning.

Clint lowers his head and looks up at me from under his brows. "Steffen, technically you're still married."

That pisses me off. "No, I'm not."

He gives me The Look. "Okay, if you decided you wanted to get married tomorrow . . ."

"Which I won't," I'm quick to counter.

"Okay, but if you did, could you? Legally, I mean?" He gives me The Other Look.

A big sigh escapes my lips. "No. Legally, I couldn't."

"Then you should tell Sheila. Didn't she ask you if you'd ever been married?"

"No."

"Have you discussed past relationships?"

"No. She didn't want to because of her ex, and I don't want to either. I think she's afraid of knowing about all the subs I've worked with too."

Now he's getting kind of pissed, I can tell. "I told

you how she's wired. She won't tolerate lying of any kind, and you've as good as lied to her. Why didn't you just tell her?"

"Because," I offer and shrug, "because, honestly, I just forgot. Until now. So thanks for reminding me," I add with a snarl.

Now it's his turn to sigh and drop back into his chair. "I've tried to forget too. That was a mess. I don't ever want to relive that."

"Me neither."

I decide right then that I'm saying nothing to Sheila. But I have a phone call to make.

Damn Clint for making me think about this stuff. After I've dealt with the heightened security at the bank, I make the call to Michael Riley. He's not in, but when he calls me back, he knows exactly what I want.

"Mr. Cothran?"

"Yes! Any luck?"

"No, sir. The investigators haven't been able to find her." He hesitates, then asks me, "Is there a particular reason you're trying to find her? You know, besides the obvious?"

"Yes, actually, there is. If I get to a point that I have to find her to move forward and can't, is there anything I can do?"

"Oh, yes. You can just petition the court and have it taken care of. It won't be that easy, and it'll probably take several months for them to confirm that she can't be found but, after that, it'll go on through. No judge in the land would leave you dangling like that if he knows you've exhausted all channels." Relief washes over me just hearing that. "Would you like for me to start that process now?"

I think for a minute. "How long are we talking here?"

"It could be a few weeks, and it could be a few months. No way of knowing. But I can't imagine it could take a year."

"Yeah. Do it. Let me know what I need to do, if I need to appear, whatever. But set it in motion."

"Will do, sir."

"Thanks, Mr. Riley. I appreciate it. Let me know."

"I'll keep you informed, sir."

There – done. Maybe in a few months that horrible part of my life will be over, thank god. And Sheila will never have to know, at least until our relationship is pretty well settled.

Chapter Six

"Let's see." Various articles of not-quite-clothing are spread out on the bed for me to look over. "What are you thinking? In the way of putting it together, I mean."

Sheila's fingers skim over the lace. "Well, I thought I'd wear the bra, the thong, the garter belt and hose, and the tutu."

A chuckle makes its way out before I can stop it. "You know I love the tutu."

"You're just saying that. Are you being sarcastic?"

"No, I'm not! I really do love it. Put it all on. Shoes?" She picks up a pair of low cut stiletto-heeled boots. "I love those. Really. Do it. Put it all on and let me see."

"Leave then."

I laugh. "I've seen you naked and fucking me in the living room and now you're shy?"

"No! I want you to be surprised when you see the whole thing." Off comes her top while she's talking.

"Okay, okay! I'll go. Let me know when I can come in."

"I will." I give her a little peck of a kiss as I walk out

of the room and up the hallway. Before I can even sit down on her sofa with the paper, she calls out, "You can come back."

"Good, because I . . . holy shit." The sight that greets me takes my breath away. Those long legs look longer, those full tits look fuller, and that high, firm ass is breathtaking. "Wow! I don't think I should let you wear that to the club." She frowns, and I laugh. "I'll wind up getting my ass kicked by a dozen guys who want you to themselves."

"They'll just be disappointed. See, I'm going there with this guy who's amazing and sexy and smart and funny and . . ." She marches right up to me and kisses me, and I almost melt.

I break the kiss and grin. "Don't forget lucky. Very lucky."

"Oh, yeah! Lucky." She starts stripping everything off. "How late are we staying? And what are we going to do?"

"We'll figure all of that out when we get there."

The club is packed, busier than I've seen it in a good while. After disappearing into the locker room, Sheila comes back out toward the bar where I'm sitting, and I hear Dave mutter under his breath, "Holy shit."

"Yeah, I had the same reaction when she tried it on for me earlier."

"That's one fine-looking woman. You're a lucky man." I love the way he's looking at her, like he could eat her up.

"Yes, I am. And yes, she is. She's beautiful in every

way. Hey, baby!" She wraps an arm around my shoulders.

"Hi, Dave!"

"Hey, sweetie! Don't you look like a vision!"

"Thanks! So, babe, what's up?"

I level my gaze with hers. "From this point on, you'll address me as Sir. Walk right over there and get that big pillow. And walk slowly so I can watch your delicious ass."

"Yes, Sir." She grins as she walks away.

"Clint told me what you talked about."

I turn to Dave. "Not you too? I don't want to talk about that."

Dave shakes his head slowly. "Steffen, you need to tell her."

I give my head a shake. "It'll be taken care of before she needs to know. And then she'll never need to know."

"She'll *always* need to know if the man she's involved with is already married." About that time, Sheila comes back, pillow in hand.

I point to the floor. "Drop it and kneel."

"Yes, Sir." She does exactly that, and fairly gracefully too.

I chat with Dave for about ten more minutes, and she rests her head against my thigh as I stroke that long hair, copper-penny bright and glowing. Randomly and out of nowhere, I suddenly wonder if any kids she might have would have hair that color, and then I realize that she's at an age where if she's going to have a kid, it has to be soon. Has she ever thought about that? Would she even want that? I'd only thought about it once before, and that was a long time ago. What the hell am I doing thinking about this? I'd better get my shit together. Nobody's having a baby anytime soon. I must've had an odd look on my face because Dave asks, "You okay?"

"Yeah. Just had something on my mind. Guess we'd better get to it if we're going to scene. Sub, rise for me." I take her hand to steady her and she comes up, proving to me that she's been practicing by the ease she displays. We stroll across the room, take in the scenes going on, and find a seat on a sofa. "So, what do you have in mind tonight?"

The wheels are turning, based on the look on her face. Finally, she says, "Um, I like restraint." But her lip trembles just a little when she asks, "And what about flogging?"

"You've never been flogged. Sure that's what you want?" She nods. "On the St. Andrew's?" She nods again. "No top, just your garter belt, hose, and heels. Just move your thong to the side." I know how hard it is to get a thong off when you're wearing a garter belt. It requires undressing and redressing. No need for that. Then something shifts, but I don't know what. "What's wrong? Sheila, talk to me." Her eyes have gotten red and it appears she's about to cry.

"Will it hurt a lot?"

Even though I don't know the details, I have a good idea of what went on with her ex, and a wave of love and pride rushes through me. She trusts me enough to experiment with something that terrifies her, and I will not take that for granted, so I shake my head fervently. "No. It'll make your skin warm, though." I take her face in my hands. "Angel, are you sure you want to do this?" She just nods and bites her lip. "Okay. But you stop me if you need to, promise? I don't want you going on just to please me. I don't want you scared or hurt, understand?" She nods again. "And then we'll do something else. What do you want that to be?"

There's an almost imperceptible shiver that runs through her before she says, "I don't know. Can we have sex?"

"Out here?" Now I'm shocked.

"Yeah. I want to get used to doing that."

I almost fall off the sofa. "You're sure?"

She nods. "Trish does it."

"That's not a good reason to do anything, just because someone you know does it. It needs to be something *you* want to do. Are you absolutely, positively sure?" She nods again. "Well, okay then. Maybe anally while you're still on the cross for time and simplicity?" She nods again. That really surprises me. We've only had anal sex once, and I never dreamed she'd be interested in doing that in front of others. "Is that all? Then off to the private room?"

"Um . . . could you find someone to use the giant vibrator on me while you're doing that?"

"You mean while I'm ass fucking you?" Now I'm pretty sure I'm here with a woman I've never met before.

"Yeah."

"Wow, well, uh, yeah, I'm pretty sure I could do that.

If you're sure." She nods again. "Okay, then, well, um, would you be agreeable to possibly performing some kind of act to satisfy that person, if that's what they want in exchange for the favor?"

For a second, I think she'll back out, and then, very cautiously, she says, "Uh, yeah, if it's someone you know and trust."

"I'll see if I can find someone, but understand: When they come over to negotiate, that's my negotiation, not yours. I'm your Dom, and you'll do as I arrange. Understood?" She nods.

Now I'm certain I don't know her at all. Then I get an idea. "Hang on just a second. Stay right here."

I head across the room to the bar, and Dave looks up as I approach. "You scening?"

"Yeah, but I may need your help. You game?"

He grins. "With that girl? Oh, yeah. You just tell me what you need and I'll do it."

I knew I could count on Dave. Once I've explained, I ask him, "What would you like in return?"

He just smiles. "Let your sub decide that. Anything. Nothing. Whatever she's comfortable with. Doesn't matter. I'll help regardless."

And that's why I love Dave.

He asks one of the other guys to take over for him at the bar and follows me back to the sofa. "Master Adams has agreed to help us. Your safeword is red, and you use it anytime you need to. If you call yellow, we'll reevaluate and see what we need to change. Got it?" She nods. "You need to say it out loud. I may not always be able to see you nod, so I need to hear your voice. Remember?"

"Yes, Sir."

I look her directly in the eyes. "Because there will be two of us in this scene with you, Master Adams is Sir. And from this point on, you'll address me as Master. Do you understand?"

"Yes, Sss . . . Master."

"Very good. And we need to come up with a hand signal, something easy for you to do and easy to remember, in case at some point you have a gag in your mouth or something."

There's that shiver again. "The 'or something' scares me a little."

I smile. "I just said that because I couldn't think of an 'or something.'"

"Oh, okay." She sits and thinks for a minute, then says, "How about this?" Holding up her fist, she makes a knocking type of movement up and down. "Will that work?"

"Yeah! That's perfect! So, got it? Red for stop, yellow for reevaluate, the hand signal if you can't speak, but otherwise, speak out loud, don't nod. Got all that?"

"Yes, Sss . . . Master." There's a little hesitation in her voice, and then she motions for me to come closer, so I bend down and she leans up to my ear. "What does he want?"

This will be a good lesson for her – very good. "He and I talked about it, and he wants you to decide. Ask him. And it's your call."

Her eyelashes flutter as she looks up at Dave, and I

know what she's thinking. He's a good-looking man, and I'm guessing there's a war going on inside her right now between what she wants and what she thinks I'd want her to do. "Um, Sir, what would be your pleasure?"

Wow. Hearing her say that makes *me* hard. I can't imagine what it's doing to Dave.

Dave's voice is liquid gold when he says, "Little sub, your call: Blow job, hand job, or fuck. Or nothing if all of the previous makes you too uncomfortable."

She looks to me, so I tell her point-blank, "Your choice, angel. Up to you. None of those acts will make me upset or uncomfortable. Any of those choices is fair, but totally your call." But I know what I'm hoping she'll say.

Her eyes roam up and down Dave. "Um . . . blow job?"

That was *not* what I was hoping for.

Dave nods. "Works for me." He gives her a casual smile, and I see her relax.

Then she looks to me, but I make sure my facial expression doesn't give away the fact that I was hoping she'd decline every option he'd offered. I really don't want to share her, but this was her choice, and I'll accept it. "Good. Got that worked out. There's a performance area opening up over there. Ready?"

"Yes, Master." She seems confident now that it's settled between her, Dave, and me. She waits for me to escort her; I haven't yet explained to her about walking a respectful distance behind me. That will come. I'm not overly concerned with protocol yet. I just want her to get into the mindset and enjoy it at the same time. I think everything else will work itself out eventually, especially as much time as she and Trish like to spend together.

We mount the steps with Dave waiting at the bottom and to the side, and then I point to the floor. "Present yourself." She drops and manages to be in an almost perfect presentation stance, plenty good enough for me anyway. "Very good. Now, rise and go to the cross." Crossing the room, she steps up onto the foot rests and waits while I strap her in. I rummage around through the equipment in the corner and find the things I'm looking for. One is a nice suede flogger, and I swish it around to make sure it's as supple as I like. Perfect. I step up beside her, and she looks a little rattled. "Your safeword?"

"Red, Master."

"Very good. I'll begin by giving you ten lashes on each cheek with the flogger and see how that goes. Is that agreeable?"

"Yes, Master."

I lay my hand on her shoulder blade. "Baby girl, relax. Try to enjoy the sensations. Just let them wash over you. Most of the time I'd have you count, but I'll keep the count tonight. You just worry about getting what you need, okay? They won't be hard strikes, so it should be fine."

She nods, followed by, "Oh, I'm sorry. Yes, Sir. I mean, Master."

"It's okay. You're under stress, but you remembered. That's good. Okay, here we go."

I announce to the audience what we'll be doing, then

return to her and announce in a strong voice, "Prepare yourself, submissive. The discipline will begin."

The initial contact is easy enough, but after the first six blows, she's panting a little. I bark to her, "Sub, concentrate on the sensations."

She responds immediately with, "Yes, Master." Good – she's still with me.

The rest of the lashes go pretty well. Her ass is a beautiful shade of rose when I'm done, and she's panting soundly. Returning to her head, I look into her face from behind the cross. She's fine; a little flushed, but otherwise fine. "Holding up?"

"Yes, Master," she says, her voice a little shaky but still okay.

I motion to Dave to join us, and he takes the vibrator I hand to him. He knows how this works – he'll be looking to me for his cue. Moving back behind her, I move the string from the thong to the side. The lube I brought into the scene with me is my favorite, so I coat her hole thoroughly, then unzip my leathers, roll the latex down, and slather the lube up and down my cock. "Submissive, prepare yourself to be entered." She tenses almost immediately, and I remind her, "Relax. This will go much better if you do." It's work to get the head of my cock into her rosette, but it finally slips through the first ring of muscles and stops at the second, and I push harder to get it through that barrier. Once I do, I hear her whimper. "Sub, your color."

"Green, Master."

"Very good." I continue to push in until I'm all the

way there, then I get very, very still so her body can grow accustomed to my shaft. After one minute, I lean into her shoulder and tell her, under my breath, "I'm going to fuck you now, angel. Don't be afraid to let me know how it feels. You can cry out, scream, whatever you want. Ready?"

Breathlessly, she calls back to me, "Yes, Master." I draw out and then shove back in, and she squeals a little. The second time, I get the same reaction, but the third time, she just moans loudly. Talk about something that'll get you hard – that'll do it. I've managed to get in eight or nine strokes when I look at Dave and signal him with a nod. He kneels in front of her, then directs a gentle smile into her eyes as he hits the switch.

A scream is the best way I can describe what shoots from her lips, although it's more like tires on pavement. I'm pretty sure most of it is surprise; she knew it was coming, she just didn't know when. The vibrations are so strong that I can feel them in my dick, and I know it's driving her crazy. She's trying to squirm, but the bindings won't let her, and she's crying out and panting and making a *lot* of noise. I'm tall enough and my legs are long enough that I'm having to stand with my feet far, far apart to make me short enough. There's a lot of tensing going on in her lower body, and I remind her, "Sub, you will not come until I tell you that you can." Good time to practice orgasm control, especially with Dave at the helm. He's a pro.

"Yes, Master," she manages to huff out. That vibrator is bound to be driving her mad, but she's hanging in there. In a few more minutes she groans out, "Oh my god, Master, please, may I come?"

"You needn't ask. I'll tell you when to come, sub." I'm laying it on thick, but I won't have to for long. Even though I can't see from my vantage point, I can hear the variations in the sounds the vibrator's making, and I know Dave's manipulating it in such a way that she's having to work to control herself. And unless I miss my guess, he's also fondling her nipples with his free hand to add to her challenge. He didn't ask me about that; he knows that I'd expect it, so he wouldn't hesitate.

I can feel my own climax growing deep in my gut, my balls tightening, the muscles in my ass bunching, and I know I'm really, really close. I close my eyes and try to think about changing the oil in my car. That always helps to take my mind off sex. And it works – for about a minute and a half. Then I go right back to thinking about that hot little ass my fingers are digging into, and I'm almost ready again.

After I've managed to stave it off once more by thinking about cleaning out the refrigerator, I decide it's time to give in. I'm really, really surprised that she hasn't called her safeword, but it hasn't happened.

It's all building and climbing inside me, and I lean into Sheila's shoulder and whisper in her ear, "I'm almost ready. Are you?"

"Yes, Sir," she groans back. "Oh, god, please, Sir, please?" She's so crazed that she forgets what she's supposed to call me, but I can understand that. It's no big deal.

"Okay." I take about six more strokes, then say loud-ly enough for the crowd to hear me, "Sub, come with your master." As soon as the words are out, I give one of those creamy, delicate shoulders a hard nip.

And that's it for me. I unload into the condom and when I do, I feel her tighten down on me like a clamp on a hose and she starts to scream. The vibrator's still humming like mad, and I'm pretty sure she's about to blow apart. As soon as I pull out of her, I signal Dave and he shuts off the vibrator.

Her chest is heaving, her tits rising and falling as she sucks in air. I check; yeah, she's almost in subspace, her eyes half closed and lips slightly parted. Leathers zipped up, I trail the fingers of both hands from her shoulders all the way down her back and down her ass, and she arches her back and whimpers. It only takes a few seconds to release her from the bindings and she's in my arms, cuddled close while I carry her to the back.

I kick the door to the private room closed and climb up into the middle of the bed with her, then draw her up tight against me. I want to just lie there and hold her, but she owes Dave a courtesy before we can just relax and before she leaves subspace. He's already opened the door and is standing in the doorway, leaning against the facing, so I motion for him to sit on the edge of the bed. "Submissive, your Sir has an expectation born of a promise you made to him. I expect you to fulfill that obligation. On your knees in front of him."

I help her stand from the bed and she kneels in front of Dave. He waits, and I sit down beside him. "Undo his leathers for him as a courtesy." Her hands are shaking as she does so, and when the laces are loosened and his fly is open, she reaches a hesitant hand in and brings out his cock. I'd forgotten how big, thick, and hard his is, not to mention that he's uncircumcised, and I notice her looking at it strangely. Then I realize: She's probably never seen an uncircumcised penis before in her life. I glance at Dave and point to his cock, and he almost laughs.

"Ever seen one like this before?" he asks. She shakes her head, and he chuckles. "Here. Let me help you." Once he's retracted his foreskin, he takes his cock in one hand and puts the other hand behind her head. "Open wide, darlin'. I expect you to take it all."

I watch as she hesitates for only a second, then opens her mouth and lets him guide her head down over his cock. Something in my chest aches watching his length disappear in between those beautiful lips, but I have to accept it, and I know it won't change the way we feel about each other. Being involved in the lifestyle for so many years and having shared dozens of subs, I'm unprepared to feel this way, though. It's a surprise for me, and it just reinforces what I believe about the way I feel about her.

She's so high and out of it that I watch Dave stand and actually face fuck her. I don't think she's even capable of doing it herself at this point, and her hands rest lightly on his thighs as he strokes into her mouth and moans. Sitting beside where he's standing, I have almost the same view he does, and I'm hard just watching her suck him. He's moving slowly but still forcing his cock deep into her throat, and she's struggling with each stroke but not giving up. "Stop fighting the gag, darlin', and just let it go. Drop your jaw and open your throat – like you're yawning. There ya go! You've got it! Oh, baby, that's good. That's so good."

It goes on and on – I'd forgotten what a master of control Dave is, not to mention a spectacular teacher – and I watch her go from struggling and almost panicked to relaxed and letting him use her as he pleases. "Okay, now, I'm about to finish up. I'm going to speed up and I want you to just let it happen, okay? Don't panic. And when I finish, I'm going to hold you down on it for a little bit. You won't be able to breathe, but don't get upset or fight it. I know how long you can take it, and I won't hurt you or hold you on me too long, okay? So here we go. I'll let you know when, darlin'."

He starts to stroke into her faster and more forceful-ly, and I reach out and stroke her hair as he does. That seems to help her relax, and he grunts a little with each strike. Finally, he moans out, "Here it comes, darlin'. In three, two, one . . ."

There's a momentary look of fear on her face as he pumps a bucket load of cum into her throat and mouth, and she rolls her eyes up to look at both of us, but I smile back at her as Dave pants out, "Hold still." He pulls her head down on him one last time and holds it there. Her eyes tear up and water as he grows perfectly still, and her face reddens. There's no doubt in my mind that he's counting the seconds, and I'm guessing thirty.

That's a little extreme for a new sub, but still a good teaching opportunity. She makes a couple of choking sounds, but she doesn't use her hand signal, so I wait. At the end of his count, he uses her hair to pull her off his dick and she gulps in a lungful of air.

There's already a towel in my hand and I set to work wiping her face off and cleaning her up as Dave strokes her hair to calm her. When I've got her all tidied up, I scoot back on the bed as Dave helps her from the floor and up beside me. I roll her away from me, her back to my chest, and Dave scoots up in front of her so we can both wrap our arms around her. She reaches out to Dave, and he helps her wrap her arms around his neck, then kisses her lips gently. I kiss her neck and ear and tighten my grip around her.

We lie like that for a good while. I know Dave is looking into her face and stroking her cheek, making sure she feels appreciated and calm. I can't imagine what it would be like without him around here. He's the single greatest stabilizing factor in the whole community, and he's become my dad since mine passed away, not to mention that my dad was never a kinkster, so I could never talk to him about things like this. Finally, he whispers to her, "You're turning out to be a wonderful submissive, darlin'. I know Master Steffen is very, very proud of you."

In a tiny, wavering voice, I hear her whisper, "Master Steffen, are you proud of me?"

"Oh, baby," I whisper back, "I'm so, so proud of you. You were beautiful and you did so well. There's no

Dom in this club who's as proud of their sub as I am of you."

Dave leans in and drops a kiss on her forehead. "I'm going back out to the bar, baby. You stay here with your Dom and come back to us, okay? You're a precious thing. Get some rest." With that, he stands, laces his leathers back up, and strides out of the room but, before he goes through the doorway, he turns back, smiles at me, and gives me a tiny salute.

The black satin sheets are cool as I roll her back and forth to pull the covers back, and she shivers when her skin touches them. Drawing her close, I whisper to her, "God, you were amazing, baby, just amazing. I'm so proud of you. You did so well. Just relax and rest. You're here with me and we're safe." Once she's snuggled in, I pull the covers over both of us. It's our little cocoon, a little quiet place where we can just be together and not think about anything except what we just did and how we feel about it.

I finally decide it's time she's back in the world with me. "Sheila? You with me, baby?"

"Yes, Sir," she manages to whisper. It's so sweet and small that I kiss her forehead. No need to lie – I've fallen in love with this woman. Her softness and warmth in my arms feeds something inside me that's been hungry for a long time.

We both drift off and when I open my eyes and look at the clock, it's about a quarter after nine. She's still lying just like she was before, curled into me like a fern into moss. "Hey, baby, wake up. Sheila? Come on, wake up. We're going to have to go soon."

"Um-hmmmm," she groans out.

"No, really, baby. Wake up. Come on, wake up." I shake her a little, and that gets her eyes open.

"Hey." She kisses my chin before she asks, "Everything okay?" There's a sleepy smile on her face that melts my heart.

"Of course! Why wouldn't it be?"

She shrugs. "I don't want you to be mad at me because of, you know, Dave. I wanted to be fair with him."

"Did you enjoy pleasing him?"

"Yes."

"How did that make you feel, pleasing him with me right there?"

She's quiet for a minute. "At first it was weird, but then it was hot. The way he was looking at me while I did it, the way you were looking at me. It made me feel very, um, I don't know how to describe it . . ."

"Did it make you horny?"

Her face turns bright red. "Um, yeah. Yeah, it did. It really, really made me want you. That's strange, but I liked it. I liked being out there in front of everybody too, especially when you, you know."

"Say it, Sheila. You've got to learn to use the terms. How else will you ever be able to ask for what you need?"

There's a struggle going on in her head, and she finally says, "When you ass fucked me." She stops. "I really liked it when you fucked my ass in front of everybody."

"I'm so glad. I'd do anything for you. I hope you know that. It's my job to give you whatever you need, and I'll always do that gladly."

She nods. "I love you, Steffen. I'd rather be with you than anywhere else with anybody else."

"I'd rather be with you too, angel. Always. Come on. Let's get up and get dressed. Ready?"

She nods again and rubs her eyes. "Yeah, sure. I'm ready." We walk, arms around each other's waists, to the doorway of the ladies locker room, where I drop her off and head to the men's. I come out and stroll to the bar, where Dave stands smirking at me.

"What?"

Dave shakes his head. "Man, that girl's . . . Clint says you're in deep."

It's true, so why deny it? "I am. Really, really deep. I'm totally wrapped up in her."

"Good. It's time you had someone to care for who cares about you back."

"Thanks." I feel her presence at my side and turn to wrap my arms around her. "Ready to go, beautiful?"

"Yeah. Night, Dave. Thank you."

"No, thank you, little one. You're turning into an amazing submissive."

She gives him a little red-faced smile and a wave as we walk away.

"I guess I'm dropping you at your place?" I ask once we're in the car.

"Or you can stay with me. We haven't stayed at my house."

I grin at her in the dark. "You've never asked me."

She giggles. "Well?"

"Sure! I'll have to get up early and go home to shower and dress because I don't have anything with me. Do you have an extra toothbrush?"

Her finger points out the window. "Stop right there. Drugstore. Go in and get a cheap one." That sounds like a really good idea, and I do exactly that.

The house is dark when we get there, and she flips on the lights and says, "Hope you like my bed."

"Will you be in it?"

She laughs. "Of course!"

My arms slip around her waist and I rub my nose against hers. "Then I'm sure I'll love it." Our lips meet for a scorching kiss, and my hands roam her back, then pull her close and tight. Everything about her is right, everything. I want this woman. Forever.

Chapter Seven

W e've been seeing each other for a few weeks now, so I think it's time. And the holidays are just around the corner. Everyone needs to know each other or things will be awkward.

"Do I look okay?"

I give her a wide smile. "You look perfect. She's going to love you."

"Are you sure? Oh, god, is my hair sticking up on this side?" She points to the side of her head, then rakes in her hair.

"No. Your hair is not sticking up. You don't have anything in your teeth. And your pants do not make your ass look fat. So I think all the bases are covered."

She laughs and looks at me cross-eyed. "Oh, haha-ha."

"I know. I'm a real scream." Striding across the porch, I open the door for her and sweep my arm toward it so she'll enter. Then I call out, "Mom! We're here! Where are you?"

I hear some rustling around and then she shoots through the kitchen doorway. "Here! I'm right here! Oh, son, it's so good to see you!" She kisses me on both cheeks and I realize how long it's been since I've come over to see her and how much I love being around her. I don't care if she *is* my mom – she's so cute. "And who is this lovely lady?"

"Mom, this is Sheila Brewster. Sheila, this is my mother, Maggie Cothran." My nose goes into high gear. "God, it smells good in here! What in the world are you cooking?"

"Stuffed peppers and roasted cauliflower. I've got a nice salad too, and we've got Black Forest cake for dessert! I hope you came hungry, dear," she directs at Sheila.

"Yes ma'am, Mrs. Cothran, I did."

"That's Maggie to you, dear. Well, come on, both of you! Sit down and tell me what's been going on."

We chit-chat for twenty minutes, and Sheila volunteers to help Mom in the kitchen while I go out to check her car. It's been making a funny sound for a week, and she's just now mentioning it. I get in, start it, and check a few things, then turn the steering wheel. Ah, I know that sound well: Power steering pump. It's going out.

When I get back inside, the meal is on the table, the places set, and it's time to eat. We make more small talk during dinner, then sit in the living room while my mother entertains Sheila with tales from my childhood, much to my mortification. When it's time to go, she insists that we take cake home with us. For once, I don't argue with my mother. On this issue, she's obviously right.

We wave and drive away, and I drive two blocks, then whip into a parking space and shut off the car. I can't stand it anymore. She looks surprised when I turn to her. "So? What did you think?"

She shrugs. "I think the more important question is, what did she think about me?"

"She liked you. A lot. I think it's all good. Besides, if she didn't, we just wouldn't go around her."

"You mean you'd pass on seeing your mother for a woman?" I can tell she doesn't believe me.

"I absolutely would. If it were someone I felt I had a future with, I'd pass in a heartbeat."

"Really?"

I nod. "Really." Her hand slips into mine, and I feel that connection I always feel with her. "I'd just have to do that. But I'd never have to worry about that. My mother is all for anyone who makes me happy."

Her eyes are bright. "Do I make you happy?"

"Baby, you make me *very* happy. I can't remember ever being this happy."

"Good! Because I love you, Steffen. I only want you to be happy."

"And I want you to be happy too. Are you?"

She nods and smiles. "Yeah. Yeah, I am. Very happy."

"Good." Even then, there's something in her face and her voice that give me pause. What is it? I can't quite figure it out. I pull back out into traffic and continue on toward her house. "Oh, I meant to ask: What are you doing about Christmas? I mean, with your family in

Iowa."

"I'm kinda hoping to go and see them. I want to anyway."

"Oh." Does that mean I'm going to be here alone for the holidays like always? "When are you leaving and when will you be back?"

"I was planning to leave on the Tuesday before and come back the day after."

"Okay." Yep. I'm going to be alone.

"Unless you can't get off work then, and I'll just go whenever you can."

I wonder if I heard right. "You want me to come with you?"

She snorts. "Well, of course! I want them to meet you and you to meet them. I think you'll all get along. I've got one brother who can be a pain sometimes, but everyone else is very laid back and easy to get along with."

I just got asked to spend the Christmas holidays in the home of a woman's family. I'm not sure if I should be excited or terrified. "So, how do they feel about you inviting me to their house?"

"My mother asked if you were coming. She seemed excited when I told her I was going to ask you. So yeah, I think they're fine with it." She's grinning at me.

"Cool."

"Yeah, just don't tell them that you tie me up and fuck me. I don't think they'd understand that."

"Oh, that was the very first thing I was planning to tell them. 'Hi. I'm so glad to meet you. I'm Steffen and I tie your daughter up and fuck her senseless.' Yeah. That was going to be my conversation starter!" I'm laughing and she's laughing and I try to imagine what that would be like. I envision a couple like in the painting "American Gothic," horrified looks on their faces as I tell them that piece of good news. Then I wait a couple more minutes before I ask, "So, what would you like for Christmas?" *Other than a ring,* I think. Isn't that what all unmarried women want? Frankly, I've been thinking about it myself. For her, I mean, not for me.

"Oh, I don't know. I've needed a new blow dryer for awhile, and I really need a new coat. There's a bag that I just fell in love with at Macy's. I could use a French cookbook. Oh, and any kind of music or books, except history. I hate those." After a moment's hesitation, she asks, "What about you? What would you like?"

"Hmmmm. Well, I guess I could use a new alarm clock."

"Yours is kinda ancient."

"Yeah, I know, but I know how to work it." That makes her giggle. "I saw a pair of boots at the Harley-Davidson store that I really like. Tickets to the opera or the symphony – I'd like those. Or a new camera, since mine bit the dust."

"Good. Those give me something to work with." She's quiet, watching out the window as we roll by a donut shop, a car dealership, and a veterinarian's office. "Oh, by the way, Trish and Clint invited us over for dinner Friday night. Can we go?"

"I don't see why not. I hadn't made any plans for us.

Tell them we'd love to."

"Great." We pull into her driveway. "Are you coming in?"

I turn off the car and sit back in the seat. "That brings me to something I've been wanting to talk to you about."

"Oh? What's that?"

I take a big, deep breath. This is a major step for me, regardless how easily it comes to other people. "We spend most of our off-work time together. Why don't you move in with me? I'm not suggesting that you get rid of your house yet. I just think it would simplify things."

"But if you wanted to get away from me, there'd be nowhere for you to go."

I lean toward her and nibble on her earlobe. "Away from you is the last place on earth I want to be." At that, she turns her face toward me and I kiss her, one of those lovely kisses that binds two people together in the most intimate of ways. "I want to be with you every minute of every day. Don't you know that?"

There's a weird look on her face when she says, "Sometimes I wonder."

That catches me off guard. "I don't understand . . ."

"Never mind. It's just me. Don't worry about it. So yeah, I could do that. I'd like to do that. When?"

"Whenever you want to. We can wait until after the holidays to decide if we need to shuffle furniture around, that kind of thing. That way I've met your family and we know if everyone's on the same page."

"Sounds like a plan. Now, as I asked before, are you

coming in?"

I laugh out loud. "Well, hell yeah, I'm coming in! Just try to keep me out!"

Once we get inside, she looks through the mail from the day while I go to the kitchen for a beer, and I hear her gasp. When I round the corner from the kitchen, she's pale and shaking. "Babe, what's wrong? Sheila?" Her eyes are wet and round. "Hey, what's going on?"

"Notice of his parole hearing." Her hand is trembling as she hands me the paper. I look it over; yep, sure enough, there it is, the date. Five days before Christmas. Well, happy holidays to us. "What am I going to do if he gets out?"

"He's not going to get out. Clint told me he's been in all kinds of trouble in there, right?"

"I have no idea." Apparently she hasn't been tipped off that Clint's watching the situation. Thank god for Trish.

"Well, he's not going to get out. And if he does, we'll deal with it then. But you don't have to be afraid, Sheila. As long as I'm around, he's not going to hurt you. And if he does manage to, god help him." I throw the paper onto the table and reach for her. Sobbing, she falls into my arms and I hold her tight. "No one's going to hurt you, angel. You're safe." She's shakes so hard her teeth almost chatter, and it's clear she's terrified. That guy must've really worked her over. I haven't asked, and I don't think I'm going to. I'm pretty sure I don't want to know.

"Can I move in with you tomorrow?"

That makes me smile because it means that she trusts me, and I'm so glad. "Yes. You absolutely may. I'd love that. Now, let's get some sleep. You'll feel better in the morning, you'll see." We walk arm in arm to the bedroom, get ready for bed, and climb in. Her eyes search my face, and I kiss her, then pull her in tight and really kiss her, like I mean it, like it's my dying act and I want to make it count.

Finding the top edge of her panties, I slip my fingers into the waistband and pull them down and off, then slip my boxer briefs off. My growing hardness moves against her belly, and she moans into my mouth and grinds her mound against me. Her voice is breathy and hoarse with want. "Steffen, how do you want me? You can have me any way you want. I'll do anything you ask. I love you. I want you so much."

"I want you too, angel. Let's just let it happen. I just want to fall into you." With that, I slip inside her as we lie there on our sides, and rock gently into her. She presses back as my cock retreats, and we set up an easy rhythm, sweet and simple and satisfying. After a few minutes I feel her reach down between us and start to stroke herself, and I kiss her again.

She murmurs, "Tell me when you're about to come and I'll come too."

"Yes, baby," I whisper back through her lips. "Yes."

I know I'll remember this evening with total clarity. There's no rope, no cuffs, no spreader bar or flogger or blindfold, just me and her and this warmth and familiarity that I've never had with another woman, and it fills her bedroom like fog over the bay. Her moans and sighs light a fire inside me that I know I'll never be able to put out, and I'm overwhelmed with love and thankfulness that she's here with me and has chosen to love me. It's a gift I never expected to get, and it's the most precious thing she could've ever given me. When I whisper to her, "I'm there, baby. Let go," she flicks herself a couple of times and convulses in my arms as I pour myself into her. We lie together there in a fragment of the glow from the street light out front, our arms encircling each other, legs intertwined, and I feel a peace I can't ever remember feeling before. I kiss her sweet lips again, then press mine to her forehead. "I've never felt this way about anyone before. Thanks for loving me, precious."

"Thanks for letting me," she sighs back to me. We cuddle, our bodies fitted together like puzzle pieces, and for the first time in a long time, I hear the clicking sound as every tile falls into place.

"Look what I brought!" Sheila calls out as soon as we get in the front door on Friday evening. "I know how Clint loves my scalloped potatoes!"

Trish laughs from the kitchen. "Yes, he does. You're putting me to shame, you know that? Why don't you just make them for your own man and leave mine alone?"

I frown. "She does, babe. Maybe a little too much," Listening to the two of them is like listening to some kind of goofy sitcom, and I lean down and kiss the side of Sheila's neck.

"Oh, Sir, do it again," she whispers, so I give that tender flesh a little nip.

A faux stern look passes across Trish's face. "You two leave the play until you get home. Kids, remember?"

"I know. What a shame too. I'm past ready," I snarl into Sheila's ear and she lets out a gasp that only I can hear.

"So, how are the two of you really doing?" Boy, Clint doesn't waste any time – no time at all. We've retreated into the living room while the girls put away leftovers and whisper about something. God only knows what. I don't think I want to know. When two or more women are whispering together, something bad's about to happen, or at least that's been my experience.

"We're fine – good, in fact. She doesn't know it yet, but I think I'm going to ask for exclusivity. I mean, it's obvious we're already exclusive, but I want it to kinda be official, you know?"

Clint gives me a knowing nod. "I know exactly what you mean. If I could do anything over with Trish, other than, well, you know, it would be that setup I did with Gary at the grocery. I think about that and I hate myself. I mean, it taught her a valuable lesson, but I really wish I hadn't shared her. It haunts me sometimes."

"Let it go. We all have regrets." I speak from experience here. I have a whopper of a regret and nothing I can do about it, at least right now. "Trish loves you and you love her. You're both very lucky. And I'm hoping my luck's changed."

"She seems to be crazy about you," Clint says as he

kicks off his shoes.

"And I'm crazy about her."

"Marriage crazy?"

I shrug. "I dunno. I think it's kinda early for that, don't you?"

Clint shakes his head. "Nope. Not at all. Not if you know for sure she's the one." He waits, an expectant look in his eyes. "You know, you're not getting any younger."

I let out a hard sigh and, in a voice loaded with sarcasm, reply, "Wow. What a confidence boost. Thanks so much for that reminder, my friend." He has a point, but I'm not about to concede that.

"I didn't mean it that way."

"Yes, you did."

Clint smirks at me. "Yeah, maybe I did! But really, why wait? If you're sure, I mean." He stops again. "You are sure, right?"

I nod. "Yeah. I'm sure. I don't know if she is, but I am."

"Have you asked her?"

"To marry me?"

"No, idiot. How she feels about you." He just shakes his head at me. "Try to keep up, wouldja?"

Now it's my turn to glare. I've missed this, Clint and me, sparring as always. "No, I haven't had to. She's been very clear about what she feels for me, and I find that very encouraging."

"Babe, you guys want some pie?" I hear Trish call out from the kitchen.

"Yes, dear," I yell back. Out of nowhere, a pillow slams me in the face and I hear Clint laugh. "Hey!"

"Calling my wife 'dear.' I oughta take your girlfriend down the hall and show her what a real man's like." Now Clint's laughing right out loud.

I start to laugh too. "Oh yeah? Is that right? And how exactly do you expect to do that?"

About that time, McKenna comes running into the room. "Mr. Steffen, look! Look what I made at school!" It's some misshapen clay thing, and I look to Clint, pleading with my eyes for him to help me out, but he just shrugs and laughs silently.

I try to look and sound excited. "Wow! That's really nice! What are you going to do with it?"

"Oh, I dunno." She looks at it, then her face brightens and her eyes meet mine. "I think I'll save it for Christmas and give it to Daddy! You'd like it, wouldn't you, Daddy?" Now it's *my* turn to shoot *him* that look that says he'd better answer this right or he'll never get past it.

"Sure, sweet cheeks! I'd love it! Did you get your homework done?"

Her previously bright, chubby little face falls and her shoulders drop. "Not yet. But almost." He shoots her the evil eye and she repeats, "Almost."

"It's okay, but you really need to get back to work on it. If you're not finished when Mr. Steffen and Miss Sheila get ready to leave, I'll come and get you so you can say goodbye, okay?"

"Okay, Daddy." Her eyes are sad when she looks at

me. Homework dodge foiled. She crosses to where he sits and whispers something into his ear in a child's typical cupped-hand fashion.

"If you want to," he replies, "and if it's okay with him."

Now she's grinning when she comes back to me. "Mr. Steffen, is it okay if I call you Uncle Steffen? Please?"

I wasn't expecting that, but I know the right answer. "Yes, ma'am. You certainly may. I'd like that a lot."

"Hailee! Hailee! We've got an uncle!" she screams down the hall as she runs back toward their bedroom.

It takes so little to make a child happy. I think back to when I was that age and I'm not sure I would've ever guessed the path I'd take. I'm reflecting on that when Sheila glides through the door, two plates and forks with pie included, one in each hand. "Here you go, babe. Homemade chess pie, Trish's specialty."

"Oh, god. It's so good," Clint manages to moan out as Trish comes strolling in, her offering identical to Sheila's.

One bite – that's all it takes. "Honey, can you bake like this?"

Sheila starts to laugh. "Oh, I can definitely bake like that. I can astound you with my baking skills. Like cupcakes?"

"Love 'em!" Clint calls out to her.

I nod vigorously. "Yep, I'm with him."

"Good. You're getting some cupcakes." She leans over and kisses me, the sweetness of the pie eclipsed by the honey that is her lips. "Does it matter what kind?"

I shake my head. "No. Not at all."

And it doesn't. The idea of a woman baking *anything* for me, well, any woman other than my mother, is a foreign concept. My mind hums as I try to imagine her in my kitchen, mixer running full speed, oven preheating, pans banging together, and me across the room, trying desperately to get those little cupcake papers apart so I can put them in the tins for her. She's singing along with the radio, and the sun's shining through the window. For the first time in my life, I dare to believe that it might really happen. I mean, why couldn't it? I want it so badly. Maybe my ship's finally come in.

Christmas is coming. I could be wrong, but I'm guessing this will be my best Christmas ever.

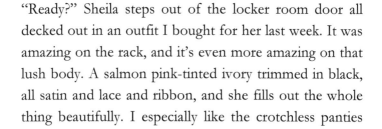

"Ready?" Sheila steps out of the locker room door all decked out in an outfit I bought for her last week. It was amazing on the rack, and it's even more amazing on that lush body. A salmon pink-tinted ivory trimmed in black, all satin and lace and ribbon, and she fills out the whole thing beautifully. I especially like the crotchless panties and the open-tip bra. Very nice and very, very convenient.

"So, what are we negotiating?" She licks her lips as we take a seat on the sofa in the commons room, and I almost come undone.

"I don't want to negotiate tonight. I just want to play. Is that okay?" Her eyes have a hint of worry in them. "Do you trust me enough to do that?"

I wait and watch as she considers it. Finally, after what seems like an hour, she says, "Yes. I do."

"What's your safeword?"

"Red."

"And your hand signal?" She holds up both fists and bobs them up and down in a knocking motion. "Very good. Now, we're going to start with you on the bondage table, face down."

"Okay. And then what?" There's trepidation in her voice that a complete stranger could easily pick up on.

"That's for me to decide, but I want it to be something you'll remember."

She frowns. "In a bad way?"

I have to laugh at her. "Of course not! In a very good way. But it's going to be something you've never experienced before. So, are you ready?"

"As ready as I'll ever be, I guess," she replies as she stands. We'd had a talk on the way and as I walk toward the performance area, she walks about three steps behind me.

Once I mount the steps, I turn to take her hand as she climbs up, then drop my head to look her in the eyes. "Presentation pose." She demonstrates it just exactly as I taught her, and I can see the looks of approval and even envy on the faces of the guys standing around the stage. I turn to the group gathered there. "Tonight I decided on something a little more, um, colorful, I guess you'd say." Turning back to her, I order, "To the bondage table, face down." Once she's prone, I bind her to the table, wrists and ankles. I kneel in front of her. "You okay? Neck? Head? Breathing?"

She whispers back, "Yes, Sir. Not forever, but I'll be okay for a good while."

"Great. Now the fun begins." I stand and turn back to the audience. "I'll start with some flogging to warm her skin and then move into something far more interesting."

Of course, she's still wondering what this far more interesting thing is, but she'll just have to wait. I begin with the flogger, laying repeated, mildly strong lashes across her back from one side and then moving to the other to repeat the process. Her skin is pinking up and looks delicious. After twenty lashes from each side, I lean down and kiss the right side of her ribcage and I hear her suck in a deep breath. That means I'm ramping up her sensitivity, so I start again with the flogger and put down twenty more lashes on each side. By the time I'm done, her skin is a warm, rosy red – no marks, just red.

As I promised, the fun begins now. I told her before she came out of the locker room to put her hair up, and she did a really good job. The hooks on her bra come apart easily, and once it's out of the way, I place a rolled-up towel down each side of her body, then reach down under the table where I've left a bottle of almond oil. After pouring just a little in my palm, I rub my palms together and begin to stroke the oil onto her back, still red from the flogging and fiery to my touch. She groans softly as the oil begins to add to her relaxation, and I can't help but smile. I make sure it's all over her upper and lower back, and down both of her sides to the top of the towels. Completely covered, her skin glistens as I snap the bottle closed and return it to its place under the edge of the table.

Before I straighten up, I move my hand over and find the plate, a big old odd dinner plate I had lying around the house from my college days – I'd slipped it inside my gig bag. On it are three candles in pink, blue, and purple. The murmur coming from the crowd tells me they know what's about to happen and want it. Sheila's head is turned toward them, and she can't see what I'm doing or what I have in my hands. There's a lighter on the plate also, but before I light a candle, I lean down to her ear. "You remember your safeword, correct?"

"Yes, Sir. Red."

"Very good. This may hurt a little at first, but if you give it a chance, it can come to feel good." With that, I turn my attention back to the audience. "This is one of my favorite things to perform with a sub. I find it relaxing and creative, and they tell me it's very pleasurable, especially since I work hard to make sure the skin is properly prepared. Which color first? Does anyone have a preference?"

"Purple," a guy named Felix calls out, and I nod and smile.

"Purple it is!" Lighting the candle as it lies on the plate, I wait until it begins to liquefy. I hold the plate over Sheila's back, and when I have the candle where I want to start, I draw the plate away.

The first drip catches her by surprise, and she squeals a little. I whisper to her, "Concentrate on the sensation. Nothing else." I see her nod as more drips begin to fall on her skin, and I draw the candle back and forth, up and down, and in a circular pattern, above her back. After about ten minutes of that, I blow out the purple candle and take a couple of minutes to stroke her hair and talk to her. I round the table, squat beside it, and look into her eyes. "You okay, little subbie?"

"Yes, Sir," she moans back.

"Your safeword?"

"Red, Sir."

"Very good. You're doing quite well, and you're beautiful too." With that, I rise, go back around to the back of the table, and start with the blue candle. She's moaning a little and squirming a lot. This is kind of a surprise to me; I'd about halfway expected her to safeword after the first five drips, but she's hanging in there. Her skin is still rosy from the flogging, and I know that's making the heat more intense. When I'm finished with the blue candle, I blow it out and return to look into her face. "You sure you're doing okay?"

She nods, then moans out, "Yes, Sir."

"Okay then. We're almost finished." Once I start with the pink candle, I concentrate on any area where there is no wax, and it drips down her sides and onto the towels. It occurs to me that she's being amazingly still. Once the pink candle is blown out, I pick up my phone from a side table where I've left it and take a picture of her back. Angled in such a way that her face doesn't show, I try to get the best shot I can because I want to be able to show her later what it looked like. I also get closer to get some of the detail in. She'll want to see this, I'm sure. As soon as I've got the shots, I start loosening the restraints so she can reposition herself and, when she's free, I tell her, "Sub, hands and knees."

She complies instantly, so fast, in fact, that I'm shocked. The wax holds and the towels drop away as she rises, and her bra falls away, leaving her breasts hanging free and beautifully pendulous. Once she's on her hands and knees, I move to stand in front of the table. In this position and at that height, her face is directly in line with my cock, and I know what she's thinking. She'd be absolutely right – that's *exactly* what I'm about to do.

Leathers unzipped, my rock-hard shaft falls out and right in front of her mouth. I look down into her face, expecting her to give me a go-to-hell look, and instead, what I find there is pure lust. Any hardness I hadn't experienced to that point appears immediately and, to my surprise, her mouth drops wide open and she waits. "Sub, your safeword."

"Red, Sir," she responds with a lick of her lips. God, that lip-licking thing pushes all of my horny buttons.

"Do you need to use it?"

"No, Sir, I. Do. Not." No one in that room could miss the emphasis behind those words.

"I made you recite something earlier. Say it back to me now, sub."

"You and me and no one else, Sir."

"Say it again."

"You and me and no one else, Sir."

"Very good. Until we finish here, in this room there is no one but you and me. No. One. Else. Remember that."

"Yes, Sir. You and me and no one else, Sir."

Slipping into the air, those words are replaced by my dick, and I do believe it's harder than it's ever been in my life. I let her suck on it for a few minutes, lick it, just generally have a little fun, but then I grasp her head on either side and look down at her. Our blue eyes meet, and I say loudly enough for everyone to hear, "I fuck your face now." There's no fear, no hesitation, no shame on that face, just trust and love, and I draw back and press in forcefully the first time.

Her gag reflex kicks in and she chokes, but I draw back and press back in again, only for her to choke once again. "Sub, you and me and no one else." And that does it. On the next stroke inward, her jaw drops, her throat opens, and I feel the head of my cock hit the soft back of her tight passage. She times her breathing with my strokes, and I can't help but be proud of her. My sub. My woman. This one is a keeper.

The tensing begins and I know I'm almost there. I want desperately to come in her throat, but I'll save that for later. Right now, we're scening, and we've got quite an audience. I pull out to a "pop" from her lips and order, "Drop to your forearms." Rounding to the back of the table, I step up into the split in it, then rest a knee on it as I roll on a condom and stroke myself a few times. At the same time, I run a finger into her pussy.

Yep, soaked, exactly as I suspected. She hasn't made a sound, so I say in a forceful voice, "I'll fuck you now. Please feel free to let me hear how you feel about the fucking you're getting, sub."

Before she can answer me, I ram into her slick channel, and she cries out, "Oh, god, Sir!" The rhythm I take up really works her over, and she's crying out with every stroke. After just a couple of minutes, she calls out, "Oh, god, fuck me, Sir! Fuck me hard!" I'm just about to turn loose when she calls out, "I want it, Sir! Fuck me, Sir – FUCK ME HARD!"

This is just too good. It's beyond anything I could've expected, so I slide her ever-so-slightly forward, climb up onto the table behind her on my knees, and, sitting back on my heels, slide partially underneath her and start to stroke upward into her. It's deeper and harder than she was counting on, I'm sure, because in just a few strokes she cries out, "Oh my god, Sir! Fuck, fuck, fuck! Oh, shit, Sir! Oh, fuck, Sir! Oh, god . . ." Ten more strokes and she cries out, "Oh, god, Sir, may I come? Please, please, may I come?"

"No, sub. You'll hold that orgasm until I tell you that you may release it. Do you understand?"

She nods and groans out, "Yes, Sir. Oh, please, Sir, I need to come! Please? Please let me come, Sir?"

Begging like that falling from those beautiful lips I fucked just minutes before does something to me, and I know I only have a scant minute before I'm at the point of no return. The pressure builds, my balls feel like they're full of smoldering coals, and I slap her ass as I tell her, "Come whenever you're ready, sub. Come with me!"

When I let go and come, I swear I can see sparkles in the air, and I'm fucking up into her so hard that I'm lifting her knees off the table. She screams out, "Oh, god, Sir, OH GAWWDDD . . ." and the ripples in her pussy begin, starting a trembling in her body that travels through my cock and into my own body. "Oh, god, Sir, fuck me, oh, fuck me, fuck me, fuck me . . ." she groans and trails off, leaving me to grind into her depths, my hands on her ass, pressing her down into me as I finish off and her spasms slow.

I lean down over her and wrap my arms around her waist, then pull her upward until she's sitting on my cock, the wax on her back pressing into my chest, and I kiss her neck under her left ear. That elicits another groan from her, and she turns her head until her lips meet mine.

There has never in the history of mankind been a kiss that sweet before. Never. Everything I already knew about her, about me, about us, is all reinforced in that brief moment when the world disappears into a haze and it's just the two of us. When she breaks the kiss, I murmur into her ear, "Baby, I've never felt like this before in my life. There's never been anyone else like you, and there never will be. You're it, Sheila; you're the other half of my whole." Arms tightening around her, I can feel her body relax against mine, and I realize no other woman has ever satisfied me the way she does. If there was any doubt in my mind, it just flew out the window. This is it.

My search is over. She's the one.

There's no easy way to get us apart and off the table, at least no graceful way that I can find, so I whisper to her, "Can you get up?"

"I'll try." She manages to get back down onto her knees, and I zip my leathers and climb off the table, then take her hand to help her stand. Instead of letting her walk back to a private room, I pick her up, and her hands wind around my neck, her fingers finding their way into my hair. The way she strokes my scalp gets me hard all over again, and by the time we reach the private room, I'm right back to aching for her.

Once the door is closed, I lay her on the bed, then climb in beside her and whisper softly, "Do you have any idea what you do to me, girl?"

There's that sleepy smile when she answers, "I don't know what I've done before, but I hope I've given you another hard-on, because I really want you to fuck me again."

I try hard not to laugh. "Again? Didn't I do a good enough job before?"

"Nope. I want more." Before I can say anything else, she grabs my face in both hands and kisses me, running her tongue all over mine and down my throat, and my cock starts to absolutely throb. "Will you fuck me again? Please? Sir?" she asks, her eyes searching mine once she's broken the kiss.

"No. I won't fuck you again." That answer meets with a frown of disappointment until I add, "But I'll gladly make love to you, and I'll do it all night if you want."

"I do." She kisses me again, and then I hear her mutter, "I guess that's as close as I'll ever get."

Now I'm confused. "As close as you'll ever get to what?"

"Oh, never mind. Just kiss me again." She tries to pin my lips to hers, but I'm having none of that until she answers my question.

"What did you mean? As close as you'll ever get to what?"

Out comes a long sigh. "I said never mind. If you keep talking, you'll go limp, and then you'll be of no use to me." She lets out a giggle with the last part of that sentence, and I know it's to deflect my question, but I also know she's right. This line of conversation will waste a perfectly good erection, and I know it won't be too many years before I'll wish I had this boner back, so I'd better get busy.

"You're exasperating, know that?" I snicker as I slide my steely length into her wetness. God, she's decadent.

"I know, but you know what they say." My puzzled look makes her finish with, "Practice makes perfect."

"You're already perfect, baby. There's not one thing I'd change about you." I reach up and move a couple of strands of hair out of her face. "Not one thing."

Chapter Eight

The restaurant isn't crowded at all for a Friday night, but then, Christmas was three days ago and people aren't having their New Year's parties yet, so it's kind of dead everywhere. Decorations are still all over the place, and theirs are particularly impressive – deep reds, golds, and copper. I made reservations and told them I wanted something kind of private, and it couldn't be more so. They've given us a two-person booth midway back with a small serving space and curtains around it. Perfect. I owe somebody a big, fat tip.

Once we're seated, I order a nice wine and try to relax a little. I'm forty-five years old and this is a conversation I've never had, so I hope I do it right. If I mess this up . . . well, I can't. I'm not sure how anything can go wrong as long as I'm honest, but I guess anything's possible.

I'm so nervous I feel like I'm going to throw up. "So, I thought Christmas went pretty well."

"Yeah, me too! You and Kenny really seemed to get along." Her youngest brother and I have a lot in common, and we really hit it off. He's a fun guy.

"I like him a lot. I like your whole family a lot."

"Well, just so you know, they liked *you* a lot too." She grins and I feel my chest start to warm. "And I really enjoyed Thanksgiving at your mom's. She's such a lovely person. I'd love to spend more time with her."

"I'm sure we can do that. She's asked me to set a regular dinner time weekly, but I've always been too busy. Maybe I should make time though."

"I'd say you should." She took another sip from her wine glass. "They finally caught that bank robber guy, so he's no threat anymore. I was so worried about you."

"And that was good news from the parole board, right?"

Relief is painted all over her. "Oh, absolutely! I don't think he's going anywhere."

Good. This is all going to be okay.

Our server, Armand, brings our appetizer, a beautiful crostino. I can tell Sheila's impressed, but that wasn't my intent. I wanted her to be relaxed and happy. I hope she'll be happy at the end of the evening too. We devour that, our salads, the entrée – she wanted filet mignon, and I want her to have whatever she wants – and when it's dessert time, I order the most disgustingly decadent, elaborate, complicated thing they have. I want it to take a while to make it to the table so I can talk to her.

"Sheila?"

"Yeah?"

"I have something I need to say to you." My stomach is churning and I'm pretty sure I'm sweating.

Her eyes pop open and she looks a little afraid.

That's not a good sign. "Yeah?"

I reach across the table for her hand, and when she drops it in mine, she visibly relaxes. That's *exactly* what I was hoping for. "Baby, I've wanted to talk to you for a couple of weeks, but I had to be sure I was ready."

I see a tiny little smile form in one corner of her mouth. "And?"

I take a deep breath, straighten my spine, and look directly into those incredible eyes. *Here goes, Cothran. Sink or swim time.* "Sheila . . . babe . . . I just want you to know that this isn't some fun thing that I'm going to want until I'm tired of you. You're not just some toy for me. You're not just another submissive."

She drops her eyes, bats her eyelashes, and responds with, "And I wouldn't do the things I do with you with anybody else. Ever." She turns those eyes up to me and says, "I trust you, Steffen. Completely. I've never trusted anybody this much."

My heart almost bursts. It's so right. This is all so right, and I can't even slow down. "That's all I needed to hear. Because I want you to know, this isn't just some game for me. Sheila . . ." I only hesitate for a second. "I've fallen for you. I didn't mean for it to happen, and I never dreamed it would, but it's true and it's not going away. And I only hope that someday you can . . ."

She shoots me a grin, puts her finger to my lips to shush me, and quietly says, "Steffen, shut up. I love you too. Just kiss me, please?" And I do something I never thought I'd do.

I get up, fall to my knees beside her chair, wrap my

arms around her waist, and kiss her. And I feel it. It's like some kind of agreement has been reached, and it's accompanied by that sure sensation that tells me it's not fading away or petering out. She drops into the kiss like a skydiver out of a plane, and for the first time in my life, I realize I'm in a real relationship, not some Dom/sub thing that's all about play and nothing about real life.

I'm in love with a woman who's in love with me.

Hot damn. Cothran finally made it. Took me long enough. I guess it's true; it's never too late. When I finally break away from her, I look up into her face with a grin I can't seem to control. "Glad we got that settled."

Her smile is huge and genuine. "Me too. I've wanted to say that to you for weeks and couldn't work up the nerve."

"Glad I could be of service!" When I pull the box out of my pocket, I see her eyes light up. She can tell from the shape that it's not a ring. I'm pretty sure I'm not ready for that yet, but even so, when I hand it to her and she opens it to lift the bracelet out, she's beaming. It took me forever to pick it out. I was at the jewelry store all afternoon – so long, in fact, that my poor secretary, Bridget, thought something horrible had happened to me. It's platinum with alternating blue sapphires and blue tourmalines, and I think it's just about the most striking piece of jewelry I've ever seen.

"Put it on me, please?" My hands are shaking, so I take a deep breath to calm myself, then manage to get it fastened around her arm.

"Like it?"

"Oh, Steffen, I love it! It's beautiful. Thank you."

I kiss the back of her hand. "Just think of it as a 'going steady' gift, I suppose." I take my seat again just as the dessert shows up. When the server leaves, I grin over at her. "Come over here and sit in my lap. Let me feed this to you." She doesn't say a word, just gets up, settles herself on my lap, and opens her mouth when I spoon up a huge bite. Then I take my napkin and wipe the chocolate from the corners of her mouth before I take a bite myself. And now I'm absolutely, positively sure that this is the best night of my life. There's an angel sitting on my lap, and I can't wait to get her home and lay her across it.

I'm being a real smart ass when we get back to the house. "You are staying, right? Please, god, tell me you are?" We're both laughing like teenagers.

"Do I have to do the walk of shame tomorrow morning at nine?" she laughs back.

"No. I'll let you sneak out at eight if it'll make it easier!" I give her my best fake smirk.

"Wow. Thanks for that." She play-slaps me on the arm as I unlock the door. "I swear, I'm taking two days off next week so I can get moved in here. I haven't had time for anything."

"Glass of wine? Because I'm definitely having one." I pull down two glasses.

"You know it. I want to toast us." As I pull out the bottle of Dom Pérignon, she reaches for one of the glasses, then turns and gets a look at the bottle. "Champagne! Did you already have this planned?"

From under my brows, I grin at her. "Maaayyybeeee . . . let's just say I was hoping." I pour, hand one off, then lean toward her and hold out my glass. "To us. May this thing between us grow until we think it can't grow any more, and then may it grow even more."

"To us. Ditto." We clink and she drinks a little. "I know I'm not just your submissive, but I still like to play. So, do you want to . . ."

"Oh, absolutely! You, my dear, are the best sub I've ever had in my life. No way am I giving that up unless you just don't want it anymore."

"Oh, no. Not gonna happen. I want it. God, yeah, I want it, babe. Actually," she says, rising and taking my glass out of my hand to set it on the counter, "I want it right now."

Moving to trap my ass against the edge of the countertop, her pelvis presses against mine to pin me, and I reach up to grasp her chin. "Right now, huh?"

"Yes," she hisses. "Right now."

"I think I can make that happen. In the bedroom. Now. Everything off. I'll be right there." I watch her ass sway as she heads down the hall, a little extra "oomph" in it for my benefit. Umm-mmm-mmmm. My cock is tenting my slacks as I go back to make sure the door is locked and I turn off lights on my way out of the room, grabbing the bottle and the glasses as I go by.

And yeah, she's naked and on my bed. Which is now

our bed, and maybe someday soon will be permanently. I never thought marrying would be appealing to me, but damn, this girl makes me want to bind myself to her and never turn loose. "Elbows and knees." She scrambles up and I take the restraints from the hook in the closet. The larger end I fasten around her ankle; the shorter, around her wrist. It leaves her face down on the bed and helpless, head turned slightly, and that headful of lustrous hair fanned out everywhere. One look at that glistening pussy and I'm so hard that I feel kind of dizzy. She's so damn beautiful, and I can't understand what a woman like this wants with me, but I'm sure glad she's here. Then she says something that makes my heart leap. It's breathy and low, but I hear her loud and clear.

"Oh, god, Master, please. Take me. Please?"

I can't wait. I roll the condom on as fast as I can and bury myself in her so far that I may not be able to get back out. Her cry and the way she presses herself back onto me makes my heart race out of control, and my hands are shaking as I grip the soft, ivory globes of her ass. My god, she's amazing, and she's all mine, all five feet and six inches of her. "Angel, I want to hear your pleasure. Make all the noise you'd like; you'll only make me fuck you harder and longer, and I know that's what you want."

"Yes, Master. Please. Oh, please . . ." When her voice trails off, I slam into her twice with considerable force and she cries out, "Oh, god! Oh, oh, fuck me, please! Harder!"

All my temperance falls away. Everything in my body

and my mind and my soul is dead-set on watching her come apart. I lean in and reach under her to stroke her clit and she cries out, "Oh, Master, oh fuck. Fuck, fuck, fuck!"

I nibble her ribcage and growl, "I want you, Sheila. I need you so much. Come for me, baby."

Before I can take three more strokes, she cries out, "Oh, god, Steffen, I love you too! Fuck me so hard, baby!" That makes me ramp up my stroking of her bud, and in seconds I feel her tighten just before she screams out, "Oh, god! I'm coming! Oh, Steffen, I'm, I'm . . ."

Her pussy chokes down hard on my cock and I almost see stars as she contracts around me, but I keep stroking, wanting to give her everything she needs. When she's finally reduced to moaning, "Oh, god, oh, please, oh, god, oh, please," I stop.

"Get ready. You're gonna fly, angel. Spread those wings."

I tear into her like a maniac, and she's right there with me. Within minutes, she cries out, "Oh, oh, oh, oh, oh god, oh god, oh, I'm coming, oh, OH GOD!" and her whole body shakes. I wring it out of her, every bit, and keep going. My cock's so hard that I really think the tip will probably blow off like a bullet out of a gun, but I don't even slow and she's winding up again. Five minutes later she shrieks out, "Oh, god, Steffen, oh, god, oh god, oh god, FUCK!!! OH GOD, FUCK YEAH!" and she totally loses control. And that's it for me. My balls draw up hard until I think they're going to choke me and I shoot off like fireworks on the Fourth of July.

Grinding into her, I listen to her moaning and crying out until I'm done, then practically fall onto the bed.

She's still trembling. I tip her over and pull her back into my chest, reaching around her to take off the restraints. When they're off, she rolls to me, still shaking, and buries her face in my chest. I hold her; I hold her so tight that I'm not sure she can breathe, but I just want to hold her forever. I whisper to her, "Baby, you're such a damn good fuck. You're the most important thing in my whole world. I want to be with you forever."

She turns her tear-stained face up to mine. "I love you too, Steffen. I never want you to let me go." I lean down and kiss her nose first, then her lips, and I feel her yield to me, uninhibited and unreserved. "I'm all yours for as long as you'll have me."

"Forever?"

She nods against my chest. "Forever."

"Then my life is complete." She sighs against me and, for the first time ever, I know I have a real good shot at happiness. This girl is now the center of my universe, and I'll make sure I'm the same for her. We're an us. And that's everything to me.

We sleep until morning, tangled around each other like honeysuckle vines. "Hey, sleepyhead!" I kiss her forehead when I find her looking up at me with one eye. "Do you know how beautiful you are when you're asleep?"

"No. Why don't you tell me?" She grins and rims one of my nipples with her fingertip.

"You are. You're gorgeous when you're sleeping." I

snicker. "You're also not bratty. And I like that very much."

"Oh, when I'm awake I'm bratty, huh?" she laughs and tweaks one of my nipples.

Now I'm laughing outright. "Yeah, if your eyes are open and you're breathing, you're pretty much being a brat." I kiss her lips lightly and add, "But my little brat is adorable. Now turn me loose. I'm going to the bathroom." When I take my arms from around her, there's a definite sense of loss in my chest. I want to stay here with her forever.

I barely get a good stream going when I hear her call out, "Hey, somebody's at the door. Are you expecting anyone?"

"No. Get it, wouldja? I'm in no position to!" I hear her shuffle out of the bedroom. But when I come out of the bathroom, I hear her voice call back, "Steffen?" And it's got a weird edge to it. Commando's faster, so I slip on my jeans and stride up the hall.

Nothing could've prepared me for what I see there. Sheila's holding the door, an odd, lost look on her face, like her whole world's disintegrated. And standing there in my doorway was the one person I never thought I'd see.

Adele. The one name that can blow my world apart and send it to hell in a split second.

"What the fuck? What are you doing here?"

The bitch shoots me that wicked grin. "Why wouldn't I be here? I'm your *WIFE.*" She spits the last word at me, and I know I go pale. Now I match Sheila's coloring. There's not a drop of blood left in my face, I'm sure.

"Wife?" Sheila's voice interrupts my thoughts. "Wife. Steffen, is this woman your wife?"

And just like that, my whole world comes crashing down around me. "Sheila, it's complicated. I need to explain to you . . ."

She shakes her head, her face still blank, and she refuses to meet my gaze. "Oh, no. No explanation needed. I'll just get out of your way and let the two of you talk."

I reach out to take her arm, but she jerks away from me, and there's a ripping sensation in my chest. "Sheila, don't. Just don't. We need to . . ."

"Nope. Nothing to talk about." She disappears down the hallway.

When I turn back to Adele, I know she can see the fury on my face. "You've got some explaining to do. How *dare* you show up here like this! You get your sorry ass off my property and . . ."

"Steffen Cothran! Is that any way to talk in front of your son?"

Her words stop me dead in my tracks. For the first time, I notice that there's a little boy with her. He can't be more than six or seven, and there's something in his face that looks familiar to me, but I can't put a finger on it. He smiles up at me, his angelic little cheeks glowing.

"Adele, what kind of trick is . . ."

"No trick. I was pregnant with him when I left. Now do your fatherly duty and say hello to your son." She's grinning malevolently and then thrusts the boy toward me.

"You're my daddy?" he asks in innocence.

"I'm not sure about that."

"Mommy says you are. Right, Mommy?" He looks up at Adele.

She gives him a sickening smile. "Yes, Morris, he is. Right, Daddy?"

Now I'm getting really pissed but, before I can say anything else, Sheila breezes past us. "Sheila! Baby, wait! Stop!" She throws a hand up and keeps walking. "I'll take you home!"

"Not necessary," she calls back.

"But baby! Wait! Please!" She just ignores me, and I watch my whole future stalk off down the street, all the while punching numbers into her smartphone. Unable to hold it anymore, I turn my rage on Adele.

"What do you want? I've been looking for you for seven years. All I wanted was for you to sign the papers and get this over with, and you've been hiding out. Then you pick now, of all times, to show up?"

"Of course! I've been watching you. I knew you were almost happy. Almost. Nice try, Cothran. Are you going to let me and your son in, or are we going to have to stand out here all day?"

I open the door wider and let them pass into the house. Before I can stop her, she plants Morris on the sofa and heads down the hallway herself. She disappears into the bedroom, then sticks her head out and smirks. "Well, I see your kink hasn't changed at all. Good submissive?"

"Fuck off, Adele."

"Kid, Cothran."

I look at Morris. "Sorry. Bad words. Do you need a drink?" I hear Adele flushing the toilet in my bathroom and my stomach turns. I'll have to go and buy a new toilet seat, because I'll never be able to sit on that one again.

"Do you have soda?"

"Yes, I have lemon-lime and regular. What would you like?"

"Lemon-lime, please." To be Adele's kid, he's surprisingly polite. Wonder who taught him that? You can bet your bottom dollar it wasn't her.

"That little bit of business has been dismissed. Now we need to have a little chat." She marches back into the room and sits down, then looks at Morris and pulls something out of her bag. "Little man, why don't you take this and go right out there? That's the den. There's a TV out there and you can sit back there and play video games." Aha. It's one of those portable video game things. I have no idea what they're called. So she babysits him with video games. Wow.

"Okay! Thanks, Mommy!" He snatches the unit out of her hands and heads for the den.

She smiles as he walks away. "He's a lovely child, don't you think?"

The anger boiling inside me refuses to stay to a low, gentle roll and comes bubbling out all over. "I'm tired of this bullshit. What the hell do you want? Why are you here?"

"I think we should start over."

I stare at her as I feel my eyebrows disappearing into my hairline. "Start over? I'm not starting a damn thing with you!" I cross the living room to my little desk there and pull out an envelope. Thrusting it toward her, I rasp out, "Sign these papers and it'll be over."

"I don't want it to be over." She pretends to be sad, but I see right through her act.

Teeth gritted tight, I snarl out, "Sign the damn papers, bitch. That kid's not mine and you know it."

"Are you sure about that? I know you recognized him as soon as you saw him." There's a wicked glint in her eyes, and I'm not sure what that's about. "I'm not signing anything until I get what I want."

"And what exactly is that?"

"You. On a silver platter. Back child support. A place to live. A car to drive. Childcare. Whatever it takes to raise your kid."

"My attorney's name is Michael Riley. Call him. He'll tell you exactly which corner of hell to visit for all of that. Now sign the damn papers." I throw them at her. For a fleeting second, I see something that actually looks like remorse on her face, but it's quickly replaced by sheer meanness. "We've been looking for you for years, so you're getting nothing."

"We'll see about that." She stands and looks around. "You know, I'd forgotten how much I love this house. I'll enjoy living in it again. Morris, come along! We're going to get a kid's meal and go to the park." He stomps back into the living room and hands her the video game.

Squatting down to his level, I try to get a good look into the little boy's eyes. "So, Morris, where do you go to school?" For a split second, I could swear I see panic in Adele's eyes.

Fear and abandonment register on his face. "I don't go to school. Mommy says I don't have to. I'm too smart."

Oh my god. She's not even sending him to school. All of a sudden, I'm not scared anymore. If she's not even sending him to school, what else is she *not* doing as a parent? "Well, that's a shame. School can be fun. Okay, run along and I'll see you again soon, okay? Have fun at the park."

Adele composes herself quickly and says, "I'll be in touch."

"Oh, so will I, bitch, so will I." As soon as she clears the door, I start to slam it shut, but Morris turns around and watches me in sadness as she drags him down the steps and out the walk. In that brief glimpse, I recognize the eyes, and I know who his father is.

It's Clint Winstead.

My hand is shaking as I take my cell out and dial Sheila's number. No answer, so I leave a message. "Baby, please call me. There's so much you don't understand, that I don't even understand, but please let me explain. Please? Please call me." I hit END and sit down on the sofa.

My whole world has just dissolved, but all I'm really concerned about right at this moment is how confused and hurt Sheila must be. I've got to talk to her, and I'm not sure how I'm going to get her to let me, but I've got to try. Then I decide I'd better make another call.

"Steffen, what the fuck is going on?"

Uh-oh. "So you heard?"

He sounds really, really pissed. "Hell, yeah, I heard. I'm still hearing. I'll be hearing for the next couple of years if this doesn't get straightened out. Trish is furious with you, and I can't even begin to gauge how Sheila is feeling. You still hadn't told her about Adele?"

Something slaps me in the face with those words. "Yeah, I told her about Adele like you told Trish about Christi."

"Oh, that's really, really low, Steffen. Really low. I can't believe you'd go there . . ."

"Look, you can be mad at me later, but right now, you and I have a bigger problem."

His laughter is sarcastic, and it's not wasted on me. "Oh, yeah? I don't have a problem right now *except* you."

"That's not true. I need to talk to you, and I need to talk to you *alone*. When I tell you what I have to tell you, you'll be glad Trish isn't with you."

There's a deep pause on the other end before he responds, "Steffen, Trish and I don't have any secrets. If there's something you need to tell me, then she needs to know too."

"I think that's a huge mistake."

"You let me be the judge of that. How soon do I need to know about this?"

"Right now. Give me fifteen to shower and then head over here. And whatever you do, *don't* bring the girls. Hear me? Please?" I'm getting desperate now. If Adele shows up over there before I get a chance to tell Clint, it'll ruin his relationship with Trish, and I can't bear the thought of that happening. "Hurry. It's really important."

He doesn't sound quite so angry when he says, "Okay then. We'll be there as fast as we can get there. But this had better be important, Steffen."

"Oh, it is. Trust me. It's very, very important."

"See you in, oh, probably thirty?"

"See you then." I hit END again, then dial Sheila once more. "Baby, please, I really, really need to talk to you. It's important that you understand what's going on here. It's not at all like you think. Not at all. Please, please, call me." Once I end the call, I wait and stare at my phone, but she doesn't call back. After five minutes, I dash off to the shower.

On my trip through the bedroom, I look at the bed. The restraints are still lying there, the bed sheets all rumpled, and I pick up a pillow and sniff. Sheila. I can smell her perfume on it where she slept last night, and I hug it to me and bury my face in it. When I finally look up, I glance over at the dresser and there, on its dark surface, is the bracelet, dropped and abandoned. That's all I can take, and I do something I haven't done in over twenty years.

I cry.

"God, Cothran, you look like you've seen a ghost." Clint stares at me when I open the door, and when Trish turns and looks at me, she mirrors his expression.

"I have. And you're about to too." I move out of the doorway to let them in. "Have a seat. This won't take long unless we need the paramedics."

"What the fuck?" Clint sits down and pulls Trish down next to him. "Okay, so what's this big emergency?"

"You know that Adele showed up."

"Yeah. I got that part. You never got that taken care of?"

"How could I? We couldn't find her. But I got my attorney to set the final dissolution into motion a while back and I was just waiting to hear from him. I wanted to finalize it. I really thought I could get it done without Sheila ever having to know."

Trish shakes her head. "You weren't planning to *ever* tell her? Because, I've gotta tell ya, I don't like that one bit."

"Oh, I was planning to eventually tell her, just not yet."

Clint eyes me. "Didn't she ask you if you'd been married before?"

I shake my head. "No. Honest to god, it never came up. She did ask me if I'd ever been divorced, and I said no."

Clint rolls his eyes and sighs deeply. "Semantics. You as good as lied to her, Steffen. What the fuck were you thinking?"

"That the situation would be very difficult to explain, and I needed her to trust me totally before I even tried that. Adele is hard to explain. Actually, that one time she asked was the only time we even got close to a situation where I could talk about it, and that was just a short time ago, not early on. I haven't considered myself married in a very long time. You know that."

"Yeah, but legally . . ."

I interrupt him. "We've got much, much bigger fish to fry, my friend." I look at Trish. "I hope you love him, because I'm about to tell you something that's going to be pretty hard to take."

"I do." Trish reaches for the hand of a very confused Clint. "Do your worst."

"Okay." I turn all my attention to Clint, and now I have his. "When Trish got that call from Sheila and you guys started talking about this, did you think to tell her about all the times you scened with me and Adele?"

Now his face is turning a deep crimson. "No. Didn't cross my mind. That was a long time ago." I see Trish's mouth drop open out of my peripheral vision. "Maybe I should now."

I nod. "I think now would be a good time."

He nods back slowly, then turns to Trish. "Baby, Steffen and Adele were still married when Christi . . . well, you know." Trish nods. "Steffen thought it would be good for me to get back out into circulation. I didn't really want to, but I figured it would be safe enough with the two of them."

"When was this?" I can see Trish trying to digest the

information.

"Let's see . . . When Christi left us, McKenna was about six months old. She came back about six months later, so McKenna would've been about a year old. She waited about a month until she . . . So McKenna just turned ten. Christi's been gone nine years. And that was about, what, Steffen, two years after?"

I nod. "Something like that."

"Steffen and Adele would scene at the club several times a week." He glances at me. "Hell, did you even have sex at home?"

I snort. "Not really. She liked an audience."

Clint purses his lips. "Yeah. She really did. Anyway, babe, he asked if I wanted to scene with them a few times."

Trish interrupts with, "What's 'a few?'"

Clint looks at me, and I respond with, "Oh, maybe a dozen?"

"And what did this 'scening' consist of?" Now we've got Trish's attention.

Clint forges ahead. "Three-ways. Sometimes we'd fuck her all night. She couldn't get enough. She was always like that." Then he stops. "There's something you don't know, Steffen, something I never told you."

I can feel my eyes widening and I'm pretty sure everything is about to make sense, if I know Adele. "Oh? What's that?"

"She called me once while you were on one of those bankers' trips you always took, said she was lonely and needed to be fucked. Asked me over, told me she'd cleared it with you. So I went to your place. It made sense; hell, we fucked each other all the time, but with you present, of course. Still, I didn't think much about it. I showed up, brought a pizza, we ate and laughed, and then she turned on the charm. Actually, she was all over me. I'd had a couple of beers and I was younger than I am now, and I was really, really hard and turned on. It didn't take much for her to get me into bed, and we did some pretty kinky shit that night. Damn kinky shit."

"Clint," I start, "I need to know something." He nods. "Did you by any chance fuck her without a condom?"

He's really scarlet now. "Yeah. I didn't realize it until later."

"How many times that night without a condom?"

With a shrug, he says, "I don't know. Maybe five? Six? Eight? I lost count. It was almost like she put something in my drink . . ." He stops. "Oh, god, she didn't put something in my drink, did she?"

The big breath I just sucked in comes out as a huge sigh. "Oh, yeah, she probably did. And buddy, I've got some bad news for you."

Every bit of redness drains from his face and he and Trish both go stark white. He manages to groan out, "Oh, god, please don't tell me she has AIDS."

"No, no. Nothing like that." I watch both of them relax, but only a little. "No. *Much* harder to treat than that."

"Wha????"

"Clint, she showed up here with a kid. And he's

yours. I knew his eyes looked familiar, and I finally figured it out. You got her pregnant. She's trying to convince me that he's mine, but I knew something had gone on there. He looks too much like you."

I hear Clint make a little sound, almost like he's choking, and his eyes go glassy. "Hey, buddy, stay with me!" I grab his shoulders and hold him upright, and I bark at Trish, "Go get him some water! Now!" She scurries off to the kitchen and I slap him hard enough to rock his head. "Wake up, Clint. Get it together, man, it's gonna be okay. We'll get through this." Trish reappears with a glass in her shaking hands and I put it to his lips. That seems to reanimate him, and he takes the glass and swallows a couple of huge gulps. "Better?"

"Oh my god," is all he manages to squeeze out of his throat. "Oh my god. How the hell? Oh my god." He turns and stares at Trish. "Baby, I swear, I didn't . . ."

And my faith in true love is completely restored by her next words as she takes his chin in her hand and looks straight into his dark eyes. "That was before me. It has nothing to do with us. I love you, Clint, and I'm right here. I'm not going anywhere. We'll face this together and do whatever we have to do." She turns to me. "What now?"

"Well, they let something important slip. I asked him – by the way, his name is Morris – if he likes school. He told me he doesn't go to school, that his mom says he's too smart for school."

"Oh my god." Clint stares at me. "She's not sending him to school?"

"Nope. And I'm wondering what else she's letting slip by in her insanity. The woman's crazy, you know that."

"Oh, yeah. Definitely. If he's not even going to school, he needs to be taken away from her and put in a home where that happens." Then I see a look pass over his face as he understands. "Oh shit. That would be our home. Oh, god, Trish." He props his elbows on his knees and drops his face into his hands, and she rubs his back between his shoulder blades.

"Yep. I've got to find out where they're holed up, and then get social services involved. And you'll need to do a DNA test right away so it's on file."

"Okay. I'll do that tomorrow." Clint raises his head and looks at me. "Steffen, I'm so sorry."

"No, it's okay. I'm sorry for you guys. I'm sorry you got dragged into this whole thing."

Then Trish turns and puts a hand on my knee. "Now, about you and Sheila. Steffen, what can we do? I want this fixed. You were so happy together. Sheila loves you."

I feel my eyes welling up. "I feel the same way about her. We talked about that last night and this morning, before . . . I can't live without her, Trish." And I can't hold it in anymore – I start to cry like a little kid, and Trish moves in beside me and puts an arm around my shoulders. "Damn Adele. She's kept me under a cloud for years. I finally thought that was all behind me, and . . ."

"Hey." With a soft hand, she pulls my face to meet

hers. "I'll talk to her. I'm sure it'll be okay when I explain. At least I'll do my best." She smiles at me. "Have faith, sweetie." Then she drops a soft little kiss on my forehead. Next thing I know, my arms are wrapped tight around her waist and I'm sobbing into her lap as she strokes my hair.

I feel Clint's firm hand on my back. "We're all going to make it through this, Steffen. I don't know how, but we will, I promise. We've got to stick together."

"Stuck like glue," I choke out.

Trish laughs. "Yep! Stuck like glue."

After they leave, I send Sheila a text.

Baby, please, I need to talk to you.

What I get back is short and sweet.

Don't text me again. Leave me alone. Stay away from me.

I send back another attempt.

Please, you just don't understand. We need to talk.

The next text is a valid question with a complicated answer.

Are you married?

I have to tell her sometime. Now would probably be a good time to be honest.

Legally, yes.

I wait for her next text, and it's the question that's

the most important.

Why didn't you tell me you were married?

I figure I should probably tell her the truth.

I forgot.

But her next text tears my heart right out of my chest.

And how long would it take you to forget me? I think you're about to find out.

A tear rolls down my cheek as I type with shaking fingers.

A million years. I wait, then try again. *Sheila, please talk to me. Please? I can explain.* Still nothing. *You know how I feel about you. Please?*

Twenty minutes later, I stop staring at my phone and lay it face down on the nightstand, then crawl into the bed and just lie there, staring at the ceiling. I don't know what else to do.

Chapter Nine

Trish calls me several times a day and assures me that, even though Sheila has vowed never to speak to me again, she's still working to get that to change. After two weeks, I'm starting to lose hope completely.

And then the bottom completely drops out. I stop by the club to pick up my things because I just don't have the heart to go back in, and I really don't want to work with another sub. When I get there, Dave meets me in the hallway before I can even get all the way into the building. "Steffen, we need to talk."

"I've just come to clean out my locker," I say as I try to press past him. Then I catch the look on his face. "What?" I don't like what I see, and I push on past.

"Steffen! Steffen, please! Wait! Steffen . . ."

It's too late. I step into the big room and my eyes hit the one thing I never wanted to see.

It's Lord Algernon, this crazy-ass Dominant that I've pushed to have removed from the membership about a dozen times. He's working with a sub who's strapped to a spanking horse, and he's working her over, the chain on her nipple clamps dangling. She moans loudly as he brings the cat o' nine down on her ass again, and my heart sinks.

It's Sheila.

I wish I could relate all the things that go through my mind in that instant, but I can't. It's so hideously, horrifyingly painful that there are no words to describe it. The room starts to spin and my stomach starts to turn, and I feel hands on me. Next thing I know, I'm in Dave's office, lying on the floor with my feet up the wall. He looks down at me. "You okay?"

"No. I'm not okay." I struggle to sit up, but I can't. I'm too damn dizzy.

"Just lie there for awhile until you get your feet under you."

My eyes close and I sigh. "How long?"

"About a week now. Bought her own membership. And by the way, I know everything that happened."

"Oh, I feel so much better just from knowing *that*."

"Aha! Still spitting out the sarcasm. You're in better shape than you think. Come on, let me help you up." He gives me a hand and helps me up to sitting.

"Thanks." I just sit there in the floor. I can't go back through there, can't stand the thought of seeing that again. My Sheila. My angel. I don't think my heart can take it. "Mind if I go out the back?"

"I'd rather that you sit here for a few more minutes until you get your feet under you." As the words drift from his lips, I hear a shriek, and I'm pretty sure it's Sheila.

"Nope. Gotta go. But thanks. I'll get Clint to bring

home my stuff." Throwing the back door open, I run to the front of the building and climb into my car. My phone rings almost immediately. Before I can even make a sound, I hear Clint's voice.

"Steffen, come over here. I don't want you to be alone." I try to respond, but all I can do is choke and cry. "We're headed that way. I'll drive your car to our house. Please, please, don't try to drive. I don't want you getting hurt. Promise me?"

"Okay," I manage to sputter out. Then I wait until they get there and go to their house.

Three days later, I'm still there. I simply can't take care of myself. I'm numb all over and I can't seem to function on any level. This is it. I've lost her. And I don't think I can face that idea.

"You sure you're ready?" Trish and Clint watch me packing what few things I have there. "Because you can stay as long as you need to," Clint adds.

"Nope. I've got to get back to some kind of life. Three weeks is long enough." Their faces are lined with concern as I turn to smile at them. "You have no idea how much I appreciate your help and friendship. Really. I don't know what I would've done without you two."

Trish plants a tiny, soft kiss on my cheek. "We're here if you need us. It'll get better, I promise. Have faith."

"You still talking to her?"

"Yes. Every day. But she's not budging. She still says

she doesn't want anything to do with you."

I give her a cheek-peck back. "Yeah. I know. Can't say as I blame her. My fault; entirely my fault. What about Morris? What are you guys going to do?"

Clint smiles. "I've got your Mr. Riley working on that. We're going after her. Well, as soon as we can find her. But I don't think that's going to be too hard. They'll be able to follow her around now because she's started showing up at the club, believe it or not."

"At the club? Are you kidding me?" I just can't believe Adele would do that, insert herself back into the one place she knows I'd be. And she has to know how much Dave hates her.

"Nope. Not kidding. And all decked out too, trying to get a Dom to play with her. They all know what she's been up to with you, so they're staying away from her, but I know there's one who's decided he's going to play with her if it'll help your case – *our* case."

"Who?" Now I'm curious.

He grins. "Reggie."

"Ah! That should be interesting!" Reggie is a world-class sadist. I'd *love* to see that. "Could you . . ."

"Absolutely. If she walks in and he's free, I'll ask him to stall and call you immediately. You wouldn't want to miss that show."

"Nope. Not at all! By the way . . ."

"Yes. Before you ask, yes. She's coming in and out. She's been scening every time she's there. She's trying to kill off the hurt, and she's not doing a very good job of it. It's always the hardcore sadists she looks for, so she's using the pain to get through it, and it's even worse when she and Adele show up at the same time. Honestly, I'm afraid Sheila's going to actually be physically hurt. It's kinda scary sometimes. I'm sorry, bud. I wish I had something better to tell you, but I just don't."

"Aw, it's okay. Not your problem. Mine entirely." I sling my bag over my shoulder. "I'll let you two get back to your own lives and get out of your hair." They walk me to the door and both of them hug me before I leave. "Tell the girls I'll miss them. You guys are so lucky." Trish turns away from me and I know she's crying, so I use my best brave voice. "It'll all be okay. Thanks again."

My car roars to life and I head home. When I get there, I carry everything to my room and look around. The whole house seems so empty and barren, just like my heart. If she'd just give me ten minutes – I know she still loves me. And I love her more than ever.

That's bound to count for something.

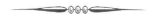

I've decided I'm going to go back to the club. I don't really want to scene with another sub, and I'm certainly not going to fuck one, but I need to be around people, and those are my people. It's a crowded night when I walk through the door and into the main room. Several of the male members stop and shake my hand, and the ladies hug me and kiss me on the cheek. Sometimes it's nice to know you've been missed.

But my heart sinks thirty minutes later when I look up from my seat at the bar and see Sheila stroll in. She's got this angry, defiant look on her face and when she sees me, she ducks into the locker room. My heart almost stops when she comes out.

A thong and stilettos. That's it. And that's not all. She's had her nipples pierced. I take a deep, painful breath and try to let go, but I can't. Everything inside me tips and I feel my heart spilling out onto the floor. She struts out without even looking at me and walks straight up to the bar. "Can I have a light beer, please? Don't care what kind."

Dave glances at me and I respond with, "I'll pay for the lady's drink."

"Thanks, but not necessary." She reaches for the glass, but I lay my hand on her arm. There's a hard, dangerous edge to her voice as she snarls out, "Don't touch me."

I draw my hand back, but I simply say, "Sheila, can't we at least be friends?"

Her eyes are cold when she turns them to me. "My friends don't lie to me. So fuck off." Beer in hand, she stalks away and finds a seat on a sofa. In no time at all, she's joined by a Dom I've known for years. I see them chatting away, and I realize I'm going to be treated to her scening again. Great. In minutes, they head toward a performance area, and I wince as she takes off the thong and shoes and climbs up onto the bondage table. I can't hear what's being said, but she lies down on her back and he straps her down, wrists and ankles. In agony, I watch him take out a three-way clamp and clamp both nipples, then the hood of her clit, and tighten everything so that it's pulled up and out of the way of that tiny little spot on her body that I called mine. He leans down, sucks it into his mouth a dozen times, and laughs as she squirms and cries out. Then he opens a drawer and pulls out a Hitachi Magic Wand.

He tortures her through at least eight orgasms. It's almost impossible for me to watch, but, like a bad traffic accident, I can't look away. She shrieks and strains against her bindings, and I remember the feel of her body under my hands, that satiny skin and dripping cunt, and I start to shake.

But that's all forgotten when I watch him climb up onto the table, unzip his leathers, and fuck her. And that's it. My heart is officially broken. There's nothing more I can do except to watch the only woman I've ever really loved be royally fucked by someone who's not me. Every jab of his cock into her is like a nail being driven into my chest. To my own surprise, I push my way up through the crowd until I'm standing right in the front, even with her head. Watching his dick pounding into her makes mine go completely limp, but I can't turn away. It's like it doesn't matter anymore as long as I'm somewhere near her. When he finally comes, she's a limp, worn-out mess, and all I really want to do is to go to her and hold her. And that's when it happens.

She turns and looks directly at me. There's a splitting sound in my head, like a tree branch cracking away from the trunk, and everything in my body goes still. Her eyes bore into me, empty and hollow, dead from the inside out. I really don't know what to do anymore, so I just look into her eyes and mouth, *I miss you.* And she turns away.

The crowd around me is chattering quietly as I spin and walk to the front. When I get into my car, I just turn the key and drive away. There's no emotion left. I'm just a shell. I don't hate her. I don't love her. I don't feel anything.

Down deep in my chest, there's no one home.

"Mr. Cothran?"

"Yes?"

"There's a Mr. Riley on the phone for you."

"Thanks, Bridget." I grab the phone. "Mr. Riley! I hope you have some good news for me."

"Yes, sir, I do. I just got off the phone with Mr. Winstead. We found her. I've got my guys on her, and they're watching her twenty-four seven, have been since yesterday when we confirmed that it's her. And I thought I'd ask: Do you know where she's going at night?"

"Oh, I absolutely do." I'd been seeing her at the club, and I always gave her a wide berth, so I tell him exactly what she's up to. "And we can't use that against her, because Clint, Trish, and I all frequent the club."

"Oh, no, that's not it. She's leaving him alone."

"What?" My voice goes up at least an octave. "You're kidding! Seriously? What the hell?"

"She's got some kind of point she wants to make, Mr. Cothran, and I think she's picked the wrong way to make it."

"Grounds for social services to . . ."

"Oh, absolutely. We'll nail her. A week of documentation is all it'll take. Hang in there."

"I'm hanging, but I'm concerned about Morris. Poor little guy."

"As long as my guys are watching, he's in no danger. They'd blow their cover before they'd let him be hurt."

I breathe a big sigh of relief. "Good. I hope you told Clint that."

"I did. It's just a matter of time, Mr. Cothran. But I thought you'd be glad to hear it."

"Absolutely. Thanks so much." Feeling better than I have in weeks, I don't even have time to call Clint before he calls me.

"I guess you heard?"

I chuckle. "Yeah. Bitch is toast. It's just a matter of time, Riley says. By the way, you guys doing okay with this?"

"Yeah. We're looking at bigger houses. Trish may have to get a part-time job, but we'll just do what we have to do. Steffen, man, I'm the luckiest guy in the world. She hasn't even blinked. The universe smiled on me when I found that woman."

I wish he could see my smile. "I agree. You're a lucky son of a bitch."

He laughs loudly. "Hey, watch talking about my mama like that!"

"Oh, shut up, Winstead! But I'm glad it's all working out."

There's silence, and then he asks, "How are you doing?"

"I'm fine. Just fine."

"I don't see how you can be fine if . . ."

"I said I'm fine. Let it go." I'm trying not to sound angry, but I really don't want to talk about it.

"Okay. It's let go. Let me know if you hear something before I do, and I'll do the same for you."

"You got it. Later." I hang up and sit there for a minute or two, just thinking. It's been four months and I still don't feel anything. Good, bad, nothing. It's time to play with a sub, I think. Maybe that'll get me out of my funk.

The first person I see when I step through the doorway into the club is Dominique. I've scened with her so many times during the years that I think she's got a plaque down there that says, "Regular fuckings courtesy of Steffen Cothran." Her eyes light up when she sees me – well, at least there's one woman who's glad I'm around.

"Hey, Master Steffen! You're looking handsome, as always." She bats those eyelashes at me and I think about how hot and wet that pussy of hers is. "What's up?"

I turn on the charm. "Up for scening with me?"

"Sure! Negotiate something?"

"Absolutely." We sit down and work it all out. She sucks me off, then she's bound ass-out to the St. Andrew's and a flogger is applied, after which I give her a manual orgasm. There's only a moment's hesitation before I add, "And then I fuck you."

"You'd better! I've been missing that cock of yours!" she grins.

Aw, yeah. Let the games begin.

I dress out, then take to the floor. There's a performance alcove waiting for us, and we do exactly as we've negotiated. Once she's had that promised orgasm, and I've given her a true screamer, I move in behind her and slide into her wet and waiting pussy. And that's when I feel it.

Sheila's out there watching. It's like I can sense her close by, but it doesn't faze me. I have every right to fuck someone if she does. As my cock hits home in Dominique's cunt over and over, I ask myself if I still love Sheila. And I do, but I can't feel it. I don't know what would happen if she knocked on my door and told me she wanted me back. I'm just not sure anymore.

But I do know one thing for sure. This pussy feels good, and it's been too long. Dominique is moaning and crying out, and I pour it on. I just want to fuck her until I can't fuck her anymore, until my cock is sore and her pussy is raw and I can't even remember my own name. She comes around me, her channel milking me, but I can't come; I'm just not ready. When I lean into her ear and ask her for the one thing I hadn't considered doing with anyone else, she nods in eagerness.

So I roll on a new condom, lube up, and fuck her ass. The sounds of her crying out fill the room as I slam into her with everything I have. It's hard, but I manage to clear my mind and think only of how it feels to grind in and out of her, and ten minutes later I come with a roar, balls-deep in her ass and thrusting away.

Master Steffen is back. It doesn't really feel good, but it's better than nothing.

Once I'm completely spent, I withdraw and slap Dominique on the ass. "Very good job, sub. You're a fine fuck, as always."

"Thank you, Sir," she manages to pant.

"You're welcome. Let's get you out of these bindings." I get her arms, legs, and waist loose, then pick her up and head toward a private room. And there, right by the alcove, is Sheila. There's a look on her face that I can't define, but I'm pretty sure mine is blank, as blank as the feelings I'm no longer capable of feeling. I just glide past her, Dominique in my arms, and stride out of the room, down the hallway, and into a private room, shoving the door closed with my boot. I drop her onto the bed and cuddle her close to me. It feels good to have a woman in my arms again. She's soft and warm and compliant, and I kiss her forehead. "You doing okay, little one?"

"Yes, Sir." Her breathing is soft and she smells damn good. "Thank you, Sir."

"No, thank you. Your body was as amazing as ever. Did you enjoy yourself?"

"Yes, Sir. Always with you. I love being used by a skilled Dominant." She reaches up, puts a hand on either of my cheeks, and kisses me. It's the first time a woman has kissed me since, well, in months, and she tastes like my cum and peppermint. What a combination, but it is what it is. "Your cock is amazing, Sir,"

"Thank you. You need to rest. Quit talking and rest, okay?"

"Yes, Sir." She stops, then says, "Sir?"

"Yes?"

"I'm so sorry."

There's nothing for me to say. "Don't be. It's all okay." But it's not. And it never will be.

Once I've gotten her settled down and back to the locker room, I head back into the performance area. I get a couple of slaps on the back and "attaboys," and I look around to see that Sheila's nowhere in sight. But there's something more interesting going on.

It's Adele.

She's strapped down to the spanking bench, and a wicked grin spreads across my face. I want to see this, but there's something else I have to do. I jet down the hallway and call Michael Riley. "Hey, Mr. Riley, it's Steffen Cothran. I just wanted you to know that Adele is here at the club."

"Just getting started or finishing?"

"Just getting started."

"Okay. We'll make our move now. Thanks for keeping me posted. And can you call Mr. Winstead?"

"Oh, it would be my pleasure!" I hang up and call Clint, tell him what's going on, then end the call and go out to watch the show.

And what a show it is, Adele and three Doms, one of whom is Reggie. I have to remember to thank him. The one under her fucks up into her pussy, Reggie behind her into her ass, and, after they've given her two orgasms, the third moves up and shoves his meaty cock down her throat. I love it. For the first time in weeks, I feel something, and it's total and complete hatred. Watching those cocks tear into her gives me some kind of sick, perverse sense of satisfaction, but I'm unprepared for what happens next.

They finish with her and one of them leaves the scene, then comes back rolling some kind of apparatus, and when they get it up into the performance area, I realize what it is.

It's a fucking machine. Yeah, I've seen them in porn videos, and I've even seen one in a store, but I've never seen one used before. And I'm thinking this may be the most entertaining thing I've ever watched. The crowd around me whispers as they unstrap her from the whipping horse, then carry her to the bondage table and place her on her back. One of them produces something I can't make out, and I push closer so I can see.

They're locking pliers. He sets the jaws, clamps them onto her nipples, and starts to tighten them down. We're treated to the sound of her shrieks as the biting ends of the pliers tighten on her hard nubs. When she settles down, he tightens them another bit to hear her scream again. This process takes place at least five more times, and the pliers are getting tighter and tighter and she's swearing and crying out. Just when I'm wondering where this is going, I get it as I hear Reggie, the oldest of the three Doms, the one in charge, growl, "Knees and forearms, sub. Immediately."

When she moves, she screams as the pliers shift, but

he uses his crop and slaps her ass several times, and she complies. They've placed a wide foam block in front of her, and her forearms rest on that. Once they're flat, the straps on the block are placed around her forearms to keep her in place; her ankles and calves right below the knees are already secured. It's painfully clear what they're doing, no pun intended. When she drops onto her knees and forearms, the pliers are dangling. All that metal has to be fairly heavy, and the stretching of her nipples is exaggerated by it. As she positions herself, they swing, and with every sway, she cries out. And then it's the moment we've all been waiting for.

Up rolls the machine. It's a Tornado R95, the one I've been hearing murmurings about for weeks now. Something new, they say, but I'm not sure how. According to Clint, it's something Dave had wanted for a long time, and he finally talked the club's board of directors into buying it. The dildo mounted on the end is extended as far as possible from the machine and then unceremoniously shoved into her cunt as far as it will go. Another little cry breaks from her lips, and then I hold my breath as they hit the switch and start to dial it up.

The damn thing is fucking her so hard and fast that I don't know how she's taking it, not to mention those heavy pliers cutting into her nipples and pulling them down at the same time. She's crying out and screaming, and they just turn the machine up. They're chuckling as they watch until one of them pulls out one of the large wand vibrators and cranks it up. The minute they touch it to her clit, she starts to scream in earnest. Reggie growls out, "Do you want to safeword?"

Over the cries and screams she yells, "Hell no! Turn it up!"

So they do. I've never seen anything like this before in my whole life, not even in porn movies. The thing is fucking her so fast that I can barely see it move, and those pliers are swinging painfully. I go looking for Dave and, when I find him, I blurt out, "Do you know what's going on out there?"

He nods and for the first time ever, I see Dave Adams do something that I don't think is entirely honorable but, by damn, I agree with him. "Oh, I know full well. And I've never let anyone do this before, but it's fucking Adele. As long as they don't permanently injure her, I'll let them stay and torture her for the next twenty-four hours. That bitch deserves whatever she gets. Problem is, I think she's enjoying it." With that, he turns and heads back to his office, as furious as I think I've ever seen someone without them completely coming unhinged.

Wow. It's been a long time since I've been that shocked. Usually, Dave would go out and tell them enough's enough, but I don't think he cares – at all. She's shrieking, rocking with spasms, and obviously loving every minute of it. Her pussy and ass are so open that you could drive a damn tour bus into them.

And I don't know how long this is going to go on, but I'm going to enjoy every minute of it. Every. Damn. Minute.

An hour later, the three Doms are sitting by the performance area, and the machine's still going. She's gone from screaming and swearing to muttering something that's unintelligible. Every so often, one of them goes back, turns on the vibrator, and holds it on her clit long enough for her to come, plus another five minutes to drive her crazy, followed by leaving and going back to sit down with a beer. She's still going after two hours with no sign of slowing, that dildo on that machine pounding into her. That's not all they've got in store for her. The younger of the three Doms goes to her head, whispers something to her, and then stands back to watch her open her mouth. When she does, he rams his cock down her throat and she doesn't even gag once. And it's a substantial cock too, not as big as mine, but big enough. This goes on for awhile, and then someone pulls out a video camera.

That's when something inside me goes dark with the knowledge that, regardless how I feel about her, this is a person, not some piece of meat that can be thrown in the garbage when they're finished with her. Now I go back to Dave because I can't help but believe this would be even too far out there for him with the way he feels about her right now, but when I stick my head in his office, he just waves me off. I'm kind of stunned. "Adams, you really need to . . ."

"Need to what?" He stands and gives me a steely look that really catches me completely off guard. I don't know what to say, and then I feel the vibration as my text notification goes off. It's Clint, and it's short and sweet.

Morris is with ss. It's done.

I go back to the bar, get another beer, settle down into a sofa, and watch every guy in the room but me fuck my soon-to-be ex-wife in some way. I'm now at the point where I'm not really sure how to feel. Between what's happened with Sheila, what Adele's put me through, put all of us through, actually, Dave's unbelievable apathy, and what's happening in front of me, I feel as though someone has just smashed me in the face with a skillet. Finally, just about the time I think I can't take any more, Dave strides out of his office.

"That's it, boys. Just cut it the hell out. I know she deserves it, but I've got some kind of reputation to maintain. Go home." He turns to the woman with the giant rubber cock up her kootch. "And that goes for you too, you miserable bitch. Get the hell out of my club and don't come back."

To my amazement, when they've drawn the machine away and removed Adele's restraints, she stands and leers at Dave. And the first thing out of her mouth?

"Where's my aftercare?"

He laughs right in her face and points toward the front door. "You don't get any. You get out of my club. Don't you ever show your face here again. Oh, wait – I won't have to worry about that. You won't be around anymore anyway." He smirks and starts walking away.

She's furious as she yells back, "What the hell is that supposed to mean? Hey! Get back here! I wanna know what the hell that's supposed to mean!" When he keeps walking, she looks around at the crowd, which has started to dwindle. She just stalks away to the locker room. I watch her with a measure of respect, because she's not even walking funny. Anybody who can take that kind of fucking is either a saint or numb from the waist down. About that time, she catches me watching her. "What the hell is your problem?"

"I don't have one." I drain my drink and stand. "Not anymore. I don't ever want to see you again. You're history." There's a smug look on her face that tells me she has no idea what kind of hell is about to rain down on her. Good. Maybe she'll get some idea what it felt like to me to find her standing at my door after all those years.

The purr of my car's engine is music to me and I sit there, as smug and satisfied as a guy with a broken heart can be. Another text pings in on my phone, and I pull it up: Clint.

Riley says 4 days on DNA. We get to visit in the meantime. Everybody agrees he looks just like me. Thanks, Steffen. I hear you were treated to a great show tonight.

I text back: *Never better.*

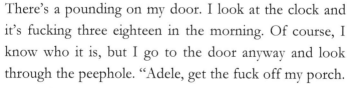

There's a pounding on my door. I look at the clock and it's fucking three eighteen in the morning. Of course, I know who it is, but I go to the door anyway and look through the peephole. "Adele, get the fuck off my porch. I mean it. Go away."

"Get out here, Cothran, you goddamn bastard! Where's my kid? Where is he? WHERE IS HE?" she's screaming at the top of her lungs.

"Where he needs to be. With his dad."

"You're his dad!"

That's it – I've just officially had enough. One of the lights in the door shatters as I sling it open and it hits the wall behind it. Before she can even gasp, my hand is around Adele's neck and I press her backward until she's teetering on the edge of the porch, held only by the pressure of my hand on the underside of her chin and jaw. She looks terrified. Good.

My teeth are clenched so tightly I can barely speak, but I manage. "You listen to me, you skanky, worn out, sluttified piece of trash, you know damn good and well I'm not that kid's father." In my peripheral vision I can see that the lights have come on at several of the houses around mine, and at least one neighbor is out on their porch, but I'm way past the point of caring about any of that shit. This is it – The End. And I'm going to end it all right here, right now. "You know *exactly* who his father is – we all do. That's where he is, with his father. And if you go over there and bother them, so help me, I'll kill you with my bare hands. You've *ruined* the best thing I ever had in my life and I have no pity for you, nor will I show you any mercy. If you ever, *ever*, come back here, god help you for what I'm going to do to you." I hear sirens and I'm beyond grateful because they just might save me from doing something that would put me in jail for a long time, and I certainly don't want any more of my life to go down the drain because of this miserable bitch. "Just tell me one thing, Adele, just one thing before the cops get here and sort out this whole fucked up mess. Why? Why did you do this to me? I never did *anything* to you, never. I treated you good; hell, I gave you way more respect than you deserved. I gave you anything you wanted, including other men. Why? Why are you hell bent on fucking up my life? What did I $EVER$ do to you?" I see red and blue lights coming up the street and I know I only have a minute or two, so I tighten my hold around her throat to encourage her to get it in gear. "Why Adele? I want to know!"

"Because," she stammers out, her voice reedy from the chokehold I've got on her, "because you wouldn't tell me that you loved me."

Her words hit me like a runaway train. There's a whirring sound as I speed flip through the pages in my mind, searching back over the years and thinking about our relationship. I *did* love her, had grown to love her despite the rocky start, loved her for years. How could I never have told her that? But I know in that instant that it's true: In all the years Adele and I were together, not once did I ever say those three words. And that's when I realize something tragically important.

I haven't said them to Sheila. And now it may be too late.

The cops stop at the bottom of the steps. "Sir, turn loose of the lady and step away or we'll have to Taser you, and we don't want to have to do that." But they needn't have even said it. I've already pulled her forward so her feet are solidly on the porch. I turn loose and put my hands up in the air, and I'm on my face on the porch floor in an instant.

"She's no lady. Her name is Adele Cothran. You guys need to check your information. There's a warrant out for her arrest."

"What? There is not!" I hear her shriek. "No one's looking for me! That's just nuts, Steffen. You're crazy, you know that?"

Then I hear the other officer say, "Adele Cothran?"

"Yes, sir?"

"Ms. Cothran, turn with your back to me and put your hands behind you, please." I hear the click of handcuffs locking. "You have the right to remain silent . . ."

"What the hell?" Adele is so loud now that the entire neighborhood can hear her, and every light that wasn't already on is suddenly ablaze. "Why am I being arrested? He's the one hurting *ME*! You should take *him* away!" she yells as the officer shoves her in the back of the cruiser and finishes his Miranda speech.

"Sir, I'm going to let you up slowly. Please don't make me take any action against you," the police officer says as he starts to release the pressure on my hands and back.

"No worries, officer. I'm not going to do anything but sit up. What I wanted most is done now. So everything's good." He turns loose of me and I push myself up to my hands and feet, then stand. "I'm sorry for the racket and that you guys had to come over here like this."

"We started getting calls about a disturbance. I don't

know if she'll want to file charges against you or not, but I'm betting what happened here is going to be the least of her problems." He takes out his little pad and starts asking me questions. When he's finished, he just says, "Glad we could be of assistance, sir. We'll be in touch if we have any more questions."

"Yes, please, officer, anytime. I'd be happy to help." I watch as the first car drives away, and the officer who's dealt with me climbs in his car and drives away too.

When the front door closes behind me, I sag against it and think back. Adele was right. I never once, in all those years, told her that I loved her. It was like I was waiting for that moment when she'd earned it, and she never did. But, in reality, she'd earned it over and over and over again, and I'd been too selfish and self-serving to give her that. Honestly, she'd done everything I'd ever asked her to do, almost eagerly, and I now know why.

That was all she wanted from me, and I'd withheld it. I've been doing the same with Sheila, dancing all around it but never really coming right out and saying it. It's time for that to stop. It's the only chance I have to salvage the relationship, if there's even a chance that it can be salvaged. But I have to try.

"Thirty-four times, Trish, thirty-four goddamn times." I'm pacing in their living room, running my hands through my hair and feeling more frantic with every passing moment. "Thirty-four times I've called, and she's hung up every one of them. Answers them, mind you, so

I know she's there, but hangs up without even letting me say a word. I don't know what else to do, I really don't."

"Sit down. You're making me a nervous wreck," Clint barks at me. I plop down on the sofa and drop my face into my hands.

"Steffen, there's a distinct possibility that this can't be fixed. I think you need to move on."

"NO!" I wish I could explain how I feel right now. I left the hospital with the doctors telling me that my mother has terminal cancer. She's not going to be around much longer. She's the last person I have. Yeah, there's my sister, but we really don't talk much and we've never been close. Once Mom is gone, it's just Trish and Clint, and Dave and the people at the club. I have no one else. No one. "I can't just move on. She loves me, I know it. If she'd just talk to me . . ." I stop for a minute, then ask, "She knows all about Morris and how he came to be, and all of that stuff. What does she think about that?"

"She thinks Adele is a reprehensible human being. She feels sorry for Morris, and for us. And for you too, in that respect. But she doesn't trust you anymore. You withheld a very important piece of information from her, and I don't blame her for not trusting you. If I were her, I wouldn't trust you either."

My stomach turns. "Oh, great. Thanks for that validation."

"Well, it's true! Clint didn't tell me about scening with Adele, but at the same time, he was never married to her. He's scened with a lot of subs over the years. I can't ask for the names of every one of them."

Clint sounds apologetic when he says, "Wouldn't matter. I couldn't remember them all anyway."

"Wow, don't you sound like a manwhore?" I sneer.

He growls back, "Just because you're in emotional pain doesn't mean you can be a huge dickwad."

"Boys, boys! Cut it out!" Trish moves over to where I'm sitting and takes my hand. "Steffen, let it go. You can find someone else. There are dozens of subs who come in and out of the club and want to scene with you. Start over. Take stock of them, see if one of them appeals to you. I'm sure you'll find that there's *someone* out there."

"Nope."

"Yes! There's bound to be someone."

"Nope." I know I'm exasperating, but I can't help it. I feel like I'm losing my mind, and everything is crashing down on me all at once. "There's only Sheila. No one else."

"Well, then, my friend, life is going to be very, very hard for you for a long, long time." Clint slaps me on the shoulder, then looks to Trish. "I've got a meeting at the board of education in about an hour and it takes forty-five minutes to get there. I've got to go. You can handle him, right?"

She wraps an arm around my shoulders. "We'll be fine. Just go. Call when you're on your way back to let me know you're coming so I can start dinner."

"Sure thing, baby." He leans down and gives her a peck on the cheek. "Bye."

"Bye. Love you, babe."

He grins and calls back, "Love you too, Vänaan," as the door closes behind him.

I just drop back into the sofa and sigh. "I hate you both. You're so lucky."

"No you don't. You love us. And we love you."

"Why do I have such a hard time saying that word?"

Trish shrugs. "I don't know. Why do you think?"

"I don't know."

She looks thoughtful. "Did everyone in your family say it?"

"Yeah. My mom told me all the time that she loved me. My dad didn't, but she did."

"Your dad didn't?"

"No. Never. I never heard him say it to my mom either. It was just assumed that he loved us because he worked hard to provide for us."

"Did you ever tell him that you loved him?"

I shake my head. "Once, but he told me not to ever say that to him. He made it clear early on that men didn't . . ." I stop.

"What, Steffen? Men didn't what?"

"Go. Around. Saying. I. Love. You. Oh my god." The pain I feel with the realization is almost unbearable. "My dad pretty much said that if you told someone you loved them, you weren't a real man. You were weak and feminine." I turn to look into her face, and there's love and sadness there. "Shelia would say things like, 'I love you, Steffen. I'm so glad to be here with you.' And I'd say back, 'I'm glad to be here with you too. There's no place I'd rather be.' But I just couldn't say those three little words." The tears come to my eyes and I can't stop them. "I couldn't bring myself to say them. And now look. Look at my life. It's broken. What do I do?"

A big tear rolls down her cheek. "I don't know, honey. I really don't."

"What did she say the last time you talked to her about me?"

Pink spreads across Trish's cheeks. "She said with your memory she figured you'd forgotten about her by now."

A knife-edged pain flashes in my chest and I can barely breathe. "I've got to go. I've got to think." I jump up and almost run to the door, then turn around and go back to hug Trish and give her a kiss on the cheek. "Thank you. Thank you for being my friend and loving me, you and Clint. I love you both so much. I hope you know that."

"Steffen, please stay for a few minutes and . . ."

"No. I've got to go." The walls are closing in on me and I've got to get out of that room, find a place where there's more air. "But thanks, honey. Thank you." I'm practically running by the time I get to my car.

I drive aimlessly for hours, thinking, running conversations back in my head, wishing I'd done things differently. I finally park down in one of the pay garages and walk down to the pier. There are gulls everywhere, and I think about the night that Sheila and I walked down here after dinner. Her hand had felt so good in mine, and I want that moment back, want to relive it, want to turn back the hands of time and reclaim what I gave away. But I can't.

After dark, I finally get up and go back to the car. Numb and dazed, I just drive home and crawl into bed in my clothes.

It's over. I know that now. I've lost her. And I've got no one but myself to blame.

Chapter Ten

"Have you ever seen needle and blade play?" Clint's obviously eating something while he's talking. "I really want to go and watch. Trish doesn't; she says it'll freak her out. But I want to see what it's all about. I mean, I've heard about it, but I've never really seen it done."

I shudder. "I've never seen it either, but it's never appealed to me."

"It doesn't really appeal to me either, but it's something I've never seen."

I hesitate before I ask, "Have you seen her?"

Clint sighs. "No one's seen her, and she and Trish don't talk much. She's afraid Trish will bring you up, and she just doesn't want to talk to or about you. I heard a rumor that she's going to another club here in town, but I don't know if it's this one or not."

"Why is it named The Catacombs?" The picture I have in my head is of old bones lying about.

"Because it's in a subterranean location. Under a bank."

"Great. I can't get away from banks even in the

BDSM world." I take another sip of my beer and wonder why there are banks everywhere. Why does the world need so damn many banks?

"So will you go with me?"

Now it's my turn to sigh. "Sure, I'll go out with you. I'm not dating anybody else." I hear him groan. "Yeah, yeah, I'll go. Sounds like fun."

Clint snorts. "Smartass."

"Yeah, that's me. When?"

"It starts at seven thirty tomorrow night. And they're expecting a big crowd, or so I hear. Want me to come and pick you up?"

"Sure. Tell Trish I said hi and we'll all have to get together soon."

"Sure thing. See you tomorrow night, Steffen."

Needle and blade play. That's not something I think I'll ever be interested in, but it might be interesting to watch. I finish my beer and drag myself to bed after the late night news.

When Clint picks me up the next night, I'm a little confused. "So how are we supposed to get into this club? We're not members."

"Bliss has reciprocal memberships with the other clubs in the area. If you're a member of one, you can get into the others. Encourages cross-play and stuff like that."

"We don't get many people from other clubs though."

Clint grins. "That's because Bliss is tightly-run and clean. We have too many rules for a lot of people. But the ones who come to Bliss come because they want a clean, safe place to play. You'd be surprised at the condition of some of these clubs."

Huh. I knew there were a couple of other clubs in the area, but I've never even seen them. Clint drives us up into the parking lot and we stride to the stairwell that leads down to the entrance. I look around at the other people either coming in or hanging around outside the door on the sunken patio-like area. The difference is night and day. Most of them are kind of sloppy-looking and unkempt, and here we are, just a hair away from being considered metrosexual, our hair neat, our clothes clean, and leathers that would be the envy of most of the people here. Yep, I'd say there aren't a lot of rules here.

The guy at the door takes one look at our IDs from Bliss and lets us right in. He doesn't even check them against our driver's licenses. We could be anybody and they'd never know. The place is crowded, and it's not nearly as comfortable as Bliss. The bar is just chipboard and Formica. Sad, really. The music is okay, but the lighting is terrible. It's too low in the general areas, and way too harsh in the performance areas. I hate to think what the private rooms might look like.

Two guys come out and start laying stuff out on a small table. I can't see what it is from where I am. In the performance alcove next to that one, there are another couple of guys laying things out, and I *can* see those – knives. One of them holds something up to look at it, and it flashes in the light. A scalpel. "So which are you most interested in?"

Clint looks back and forth. "I think the needle play."

"Yeah, me too. The knife thing scares the shit out of me."

That gets a shivering nod from Clint. "Good. I'm glad to hear that."

There are announcements made, and one of them is about the names of the Doms who'll be performing. Each man has a sub he'll be working with, and they'll all be up there scening at the same time. I'm looking around, checking out the subs. Trust me, I'd never scene with most of them. Too scary. Plus they're eyeing us like bears at a campground full of bacon lovers. But there's a lot of them there, and I'm just perusing when Clint says, "Come on. We need to leave."

"But we just got here!"

"Yeah, but we need to go." When I catch a look at his face, it's pale.

"What the hell?"

"Steffen, please, just . . ." I turn and the room starts to spin.

It's Sheila. She's completely naked, and she's being escorted by the biggest and scariest of the four Doms. The first thing I notice is the expression on her face: It's very odd, almost wooden-looking, like the muscles are paralyzed. I'm trying to figure it out as she walks up into the middle of the performance area. He says something to her and she drops in perfect presentation pose. Someone's been working with her, obviously. Plus he has her turned facing the crowd, so they can see everything with her knees as far apart as they'll go. I can feel Clint bristling beside me. He asks me, "What's up with the look on her face?"

"I noticed that and I don't know. I can't figure it out. It's like . . . it's familiar, but I don't . . ." I watch her carefully, and then I remember. She had a migraine one time and I took her to the emergency room. They gave her a pain pill. She looked just like that for about ten hours. Now it's clear – we're looking at someone who's drugged. "My god, Clint, they've given her something."

"Shit. I don't like this at all. Shit, shit, shit. What do we do?"

I shrug. "We do nothing. She's a grown woman and she signed on for this. But I don't know if I can watch."

The Dom unzips his leathers, whispers something to her, and when she opens her mouth, he shoves his cock down her throat. She chokes, and I almost throw up. He pumps into her about four more times, and she settles into it. But about the time she does, he stops, zips up, helps her up, and points to the cross.

It's a six-point restraint – both wrists, both ankles, waist, and neck. He immobilizes her head, too, with a strap across the head rest but, before he does, he blindfolds her. I look at that soft, curvy body that I held in my arms and I feel like I don't even know its owner anymore. Maybe I never really knew her. Once he's got her strapped in, he starts to flog her with a leather flogger. Not suede; leather. Her skin not only turns red, but there are lash marks on it. Occasionally she opens her mouth as though she's going to scream or cry out, but no sound comes out. That really scares me. I sneak a look at Clint, and his face is drawn and chalky. I probably look the same way.

She takes at least fifty lashes, mostly on her breasts. They're beet red, and they're bound to hurt. I watch as he pulls the little table closer and picks up a package of some kind.

They're hypodermic needles, the little plastic fittings with the metal needles on them. I've seen some pictures on the internet of this kind of thing, so I figure I know what he's going to do, but there seems to be an awful lot of them. He pulls the first one from the package and I notice two things: He isn't wearing gloves, and he doesn't have anything to prep her skin with. And then, without any further preparation, he goes to work.

I watch in abject horror as he takes the first needle and presses it into her flesh at the edge of her areola. Once again, she opens her mouth, but she doesn't make a sound. I assume he's going to run it just under the skin and back out, a secant – that's what they've done in all the pics I've seen on the internet. But no, he runs it in at an angle, and the needles look to be an inch and a half long. He does that all the way around her right areola, and from what I can tell, it's about sixteen needles. He starts the same process on the other nipple, and I cringe with every stick. I'm watching her face, but it's hard to tell what she's thinking or feeling with the blindfold in place. I count this time – yes, sixteen needles, all perfect-ly symmetrical.

When he's done with those, I assume he's finished, but he's far from it. I hear Clint murmur, "Oh my fucking god, I don't believe what I'm seeing." The Dom, if you could call the son of a bitch one, begins again, doing the exact same thing, this time where the nipple joins the areola. He again runs the needles all the way in and at an angle, and I realize that they're long enough that their tips have to meet under the skin; hell, their shanks may even crisscross each other. This time, he uses eight needles on one nipple, then turns to the other to repeat the process.

Now, every time he runs a needle in, she makes a little whimpering sound and her knees buckle a little. I don't know how she's tolerating it. I'd be screaming like a little bitch, but she's taking it. I think back to what Clint told me that day: *It's always the hardcore sadists she looks for, so she's using the pain to get through it.* My stomach churns to think that what happened between us could cause her to do something this drastic and, quite frankly, dangerous. A few trickles of blood have started to run down her breasts, and I'm more than alarmed. With every additional needle, she whimpers and her knees give way just slightly, but she's spread-eagle and bound in tight, so she's not going anywhere. She can't fall. And it almost looks like she can't cry or scream for some reason.

"Steffen, we should go. I don't know if I can watch any more of this." Clint's shaking, and I can honestly say I've never seen him looking like this.

"I can't. I can't leave. I have to know that she's okay." The guy finishes with her left nipple, and then he picks up another package, a different colored one. I can't figure out what he's planning to do.

Until he holds up one of the needles. The thing is at least two inches long and a big enough gauge that I can see it really well from where I'm standing. There's a cheer that starts in the crowd, and I can't figure it out. He walks toward her, places the tip of the needle on the tip of her nipple, and shoves it straight in until the plastic is seated on her skin.

This time, there's no doubt in my mind about the expression on her face. It's excruciating pain. Features contorted and mouth open in a silent scream, her knees buckle again. I want to do something, anything, but she had to know what she was getting into and it's none of my business. He runs the second needle into her left nipple and she finally does get something out – it's a groan that sounds like someone's squeezed all the life out of her. This time, her knees sag and they don't straighten again. She's practically hanging there, limp, unable to move.

And my stomach lurches when he takes his hand and swipes it up and down over the protruding ends of the needles. I see Sheila shudder, her skin turning a pasty white, and she's panting in an odd fashion. I'm getting really scared. I turn to Clint and I see that he's not looking too well at all. "What do you think is happening to her, Clint? I'm scared."

"I'm scared too. Something's not right. I don't know if she's going into shock or what, but it's just not right." Every time the guy runs his hands up and down, back and forth, over the needle tops, the crowd cheers. Can't they see how much pain she's in? I've watched subs be striped until blood was running down their backs, but this is something I've never seen before. It's barbaric in its follow-through. And just when I think he's done and maybe he'll start backing everything out, my heart freezes.

I'm not sure I'm going to make it out of the club standing when he takes up another needle and kneels in front of her. I hear Clint groan out, "Okay, somebody needs to stop this. It's just too much. Why doesn't somebody stop this?" I watch in terror as he retracts the hood of her clit and, with great flair, takes the needle in his hand and runs it directly into the spot on her body with more than eight thousand nerve endings.

The scream that comes from those beautiful lips is something I'll never forget as long as I live. It's like all of the screams she wanted to utter prior have all joined together and come thundering out, the screams of a thousand tortured souls, a sound that makes my blood turn icy and my extremities go numb. He flicks the end of the needle and she shrieks, an ungodly sound that rattles the light fixtures, and the crowd roars their approval. I catch a glimpse of Clint's face and I see something that chills my heart – tears. His face is coated in them, and I reach up and touch my cheeks to realize my face is soaked too. What I'm seeing there is going to scar me for the rest of my life, I'm sure, and I double over with the overload of what's happening to a woman I'd give my life for, even more so for the fact that what's happened between us makes her want to hurt this way.

That's when I hear Clint say, "What's she doing?"

When I manage to straighten, I take a look. "What? What are you talking about?"

"Look at her hands."

I watch for a few seconds. But what I see next sets me on fire. Because the "dom" in front of her glances up, sees what she's doing, and he does something that ignites a dangerous fury inside of me.

He laughs.

And that's when I realize – it's her hand signal. The one she showed me. The one I told her to use if she couldn't speak for some reason. And that chuckle? It means she told him, she showed him.

And he's chosen to ignore it.

She has no idea that I'm here, but somewhere in her heart, that signal means she's begging me to do something, to help her some way, not knowing I'm here but hoping, hoping someone will figure it out. What comes out of my mouth is a roar. "THAT SON OF A BITCH!"

Clint's eyes go wide. "What? What is it?"

"THAT'S HER FUCKING HAND SIGNAL AND HE JUST LAUGHED IT OFF!" I'm already on the move, Clint right behind me, and I know he's figured out what I'm talking about. When I take the stage in the performance area, I'm sure I look like a mad man, but I don't care. I thunder up to the asshole, grab him by the neck, and slam him against the back wall. "I know exactly what you're doing, you no good fuckstick! I saw you laugh."

A half dozen guys are coming toward the stage and I hear a telltale "click" followed by Clint growling toward them, "Back the fuck off." And they do. That's Clint – packing. I can always count on him.

The smarmy guy looks me in the eye and says, "Fuck off."

"I'm gonna show you fuck off. You tell me you don't know what that hand signal means and I'll tell you you're a lying son of a bitch. You touch her again and you'll die by my hand right here in front of everyone in this room. You got that? Huh? GOT IT?"

I guess I look just crazy enough to make a believer out of him because he takes a look at Clint and the crowd and says, "Take the crazy bitch. She can't handle the pain anyway." That finishes shoving me across the line in the pissed off department, and I double up a fist and knock him to the floor before I turn to Sheila.

She's twisted in the bindings in her efforts to get away from the pain, and I lean into her ear and whisper, "Baby, it's me. It's Steffen. You're going to be okay. I've got you. Clint's here too – we're going to take care of you. Just give me a minute. I want to do this so I don't hurt you any worse, okay? We're getting you out of here." I start loosening one ankle while Clint does the other, and then he undoes the restraints on her wrists, taking an arm down at a time. As soon as her arms and legs are free, I sweep my arm behind her knees and lift them to a sitting position. He unbinds her head and neck, and then I hold her tightly under her knees and ass in my doubled arms when he unbuckles her waist. He pins her shoulders back until I can get an arm behind her back to lift her without her upper body falling forward, not wanting to drive the needles farther into her flesh. Once she's in my arms, I run down the back hallway with her, Clint right on my heels, and grab the first empty private room I see.

"What do you need?" he shouts at me.

"Something with lidocaine in it, a wash or something. And something with alcohol. It'll hurt, but we've got to do something to minimize the risk of infection."

I hear him out in the hallway. "Where's your goddamn first aid kit?" There's mumbling, and an older man bursts into the room.

I'm sure my eyes are glowing red when I spit at him, "Who the fuck are you?"

"I'm the general manager. I had no idea what was going on, I swear. I just . . ."

"Shut up and help us. I need something with some kind of numbing agent in it."

For a few seconds he rummages around in a drawer of a cabinet there in the room. "Here." It's some store brand version of Solarcaine. "This should work."

Clint thrusts a bottle in front of me. "Bactine wash. It'll work as an antiseptic."

"Thanks. Help me keep her still." I pull the blindfold off and look down into her face. "Baby, can you hear me? Sheila? Talk to me, sweetheart."

"Should we call an ambulance?" the older guy asks.

"No. Hang on for a few minutes. Let me see what I can do before we do that." My first thought is the humiliation she'll feel if it comes to that, but I'll have them called before I'll let her suffer more or undergo more damage. I watch as her eyes roll around in her head, and then they swivel and catch mine. "Baby, you with me?"

"Steffen?" Her voice is thin and wispy, and I can barely hear her.

"Yeah, angel, it's me. I'm going to try to help you here, but you've got to be still for me. Can you do that?"

Her voice is a breathy whine. "Steffen, it hurts. Please help me. It hurts."

"I know, baby, I know. Here we go. You've got to stay still, okay?" She nods. "Okay, I'm taking out the one in your clit first. Hang in there with me." My hands are shaking and I feel hands on my shoulders: Clint. I've never been so grateful to have a friend in my entire life. "Take her hands, pull them up over her head, and hold them there." Without having to tell him, the manager guy mercifully presses a hand to the top of each of her thighs. When they've got her restrained, I grasp the end of the needle tightly and pull straight out in one quick movement. She shrieks, then quiets. Clint hands me a cotton ball with the antiseptic wash on it, and I wipe and clean as best I can.

I spray both breasts with the numbing agent and set about to systematically remove the needles from the right one. I'm trying to remove them in the order they were put in, but I really can't remember. I do know to take the one in the tip of her nipple out first, and then the ones closest to it, followed by the outer ones. One by one I pull them out, and she cries out a little each time. There's some bleeding, but not a lot. As I pull them out, Clint works to wipe each needle mark with the antiseptic. I manage to get all of them out of her right breast, then start on the left one, and it appears that the numbing agent has already gone to work, because by the time I get all of the needles out, she's quieted. She'll hurt in the morning, but right now, she's okay. When she rolls her eyes back toward me, I smile. "I got them all out, precious. They'll hurt in the morning, but I think you'll be okay." She gives me a tiny smile. "Honey, what did you take? What did he give you?"

"Muscle relaxant."

Clint grimaces. I know exactly what he's thinking, and I'm thinking the same thing, but I don't have time to go out front and kill some scum-sucking motherfucker right now. It's way more important to get her out of here. "Give me a blanket and get the hell out of my way," I snarl at the older guy, then turn to Clint. "Can we stay at your place tonight?"

"Absolutely." Clint holds the door for me as I carry her out the back and around the building to the car. "I'll call Trish on the way home and tell her what's going on." We manage to get her into the backseat, and I ride back there with her, her head in my lap. I stroke her hair and talk to her the whole way there. I can hear Clint talking to Trish on the phone, can hear Trish crying, and I wonder when I'll stop doing the same. My tears are dripping off my jaw and into Sheila's hair, and I break down and cry like I've never cried before.

Trish is waiting for us. She's got their bedroom ready, and I carry Sheila in and put her in the middle of the bed, then crawl in with her. "Can you get her some Tylenol or something?"

"Sure." Trish disappears and comes back with two Tylenol and a glass of water.

"Pumpkin, can you sit up and takes these?"

She mumbles, "More muscle relaxant?"

"No, baby, Tylenol to help with the pain." She opens her mouth, I shove them in, and she takes a big drink and lies back down.

Trish strokes her hair for a minute before she leaves the room. "I'm sorry, honey. I'm so sorry," she keeps whispering over and over, but I'm not sure Sheila can hear her.

She turns to leave and Clint bends down over the drugged, lifeless woman lying there with me. "Get some rest, honey. We'll see you in the morning." He drops a little kiss on her forehead, then reaches for me and hugs me. I start to cry again. I can't help it. Even with her lying here, those images keep playing in my mind and my brain is screaming in misery.

I settle down in the bed and she shifts in my arms, then snuggles into me. I'm guessing Clint and Trish are either sleeping on the couch, or can't sleep so they'll just sit there and keep vigil all night. Two hours later, a hand on my face wakes me, and I look down to see her looking up at me. "Steffen?"

"Hey, baby! Yeah, it's me. I'm right here. How do you feel?"

"Hurts." She closes her eyes and grimaces, then looks back up at me. "How did you find me?"

"A total fluke. I guess something or someone made sure I was there tonight because you'd need me. And I'm glad I was."

"Me too." She stopped for a second. "I was calling your name. Did you hear me?"

I start to cry again. I don't care that she sees; that doesn't matter anymore. "No, baby, you weren't. But I didn't have to hear you. I saw your hand signal."

She nods. "But I was screaming your name."

"No, sweetie. You were screaming in your head, but it wasn't coming out. The drugs he gave you kept you from being able to talk or scream, but I understood. I knew."

"I didn't think you were coming." When I kiss her forehead, I hear her whisper, "I thought you'd forgotten me."

That's it. Every aching, broken, jagged, raw, bleeding corner of my heart is torn apart with those five little words. I bury my face in her neck and turn loose with big, crazed sobs that shake the whole bed. I cry like that for ten minutes. I can't stop. When I finally do, I look into those blue eyes that are looking back into mine. "Baby, I love you so much. I didn't tell you that before, but I'm telling you now. I love you more than I've ever loved anyone else in the whole world. You're everything to me. There's no one who's more important to me than you." Her eyes search my face. "Girl, I could never, ever forget you in a million years, even if I tried. You're in my heart forever, little one. You're part of my soul. I could never forget you. Never."

Her voice is innocent and pure. "You love me?"

"Yes, angel, I love you. I think I've loved you since the first time I laid eyes on you, at Clint and Trish's wedding. I'll love you forever."

"I love you too, Steffen." The muscle relaxant is still working because she says, "I love you and I want to marry you and have your babies."

"Oh, is that right?" I laugh through my tears.

"Yes, that's right. Tomorrow," she slurs.

"I don't know about that, but I'll see what I can do. Won't change your mind, will you?"

"Nope. Marry me, Steffen, right now."

"I can't. It's the middle of the night and we've got to sleep, and then I want to take you to someone to have you checked out tomorrow. But we'll talk about it then, okay?"

"Okay." She sighs, closes her eyes, and burrows into my chest. "But I need a ring."

Oh, baby girl, you're *definitely* getting one of those.

"Ouch!"

"I'm sorry." The physician's assistant is poking around down below, and Sheila's making all kinds of faces. "Does it hurt much?"

"Yeah. Well, no, not a lot, but it's in a bad place to hurt."

"Uh-huh, I would think so." She snaps off her

gloves, then puts on two more. As she starts pressing around on Sheila's nipples, my baby makes another face.

"Ouch." When the woman looks up at her, Sheila reassures her. "Just sore."

I'll admit it: I'm terrified. "She's going to be okay, right?"

"Oh, yeah." The woman pats Sheila on the shoulder. "You're going to be fine. But I'm going to prescribe an antibiotic just in case. Keep doing what you're doing, and when you're home, try going without a bra and panties for a few days. It'll help all of that heal better." She looks at Sheila and then back to me. "Did you . . ."

"No. It wasn't me. Don't ask. It's complicated. Let's just say this won't happen again, right, babe?"

"Oh hell no! Never again." Sheila's shaking her head vigorously and I almost laugh. I don't think I ever have to worry about this again.

"Okay, well, just keep the wounds clean and dry. You can use antibiotic cream if you want; they make some with a numbing agent in it that might help. Take Tylenol if you need it. And call to come back in if there's any problem at all." She snaps off her gloves again. "You can get dressed and they'll take care of you out front."

We both call out our thanks as she closes the door behind her, and I take a look at my baby. "You okay?"

"Yeah. I'm just sorry for everything. That was so stupid of me . . ."

I take her chin in my hand and put a finger to her lips. "Stop it. We both got hurt. We both learned a lot of lessons. We accept them, deal with it, and go on. I love you and you love me. That's all that matters."

"Do you want me to get rid of the piercings? Because I will if you want. I'm not sure why I did them."

I look at them and feel a clenching in my stomach. "That's up to you. If you want to keep them, you can, but frankly, they just remind me of all of this and I want us to move forward."

"Then consider them gone as soon as I can get somewhere to have the rings cut." She stands to get dressed and weaves a little, then catches herself with a hand on the examining table. "Oh, god, I think I'm still a little hung over from that muscle relaxant."

"Sit down. Let me help you." She sits on the table and I help her get her panties on, then hook her bra, and help her with her jeans and her tee shirt. When all of that is done, she puts on her athletic shoes and I tie them for her.

"Thanks." She slides down off the table and takes my arm. "I'm kind of lightheaded. Can we get something to eat?"

"We'll go wherever you want to go."

"Can we go to the German place?"

"If that's what you want, we're there." When she's paid her copay and gotten her prescription, we head to the car for lunch downtown. As we walk in the sunlight from the building to the car, I turn my face up to the sunshine and I can't remember a more beautiful day.

Over lunch, I can't help but ask her, "Do you remember what you said to me last night?"

"When?"

"When you were really out of it."

Her face goes pink. "Oh, god, what did I say?"

I try not to laugh. "You said you loved me and wanted to marry me and have my babies. And that you wanted to do it right then. I assume you meant the marrying part, not the babies part, because they take a while."

Now she's flaming red, and it's spreading from her face down her neck. "Oh, god, please tell me I didn't say that."

"What would be wrong with it if you did?" She doesn't answer me. "You told me you need a ring. Is that what you want?"

"Steffen, I . . ."

"Look, I'm not trying to trap you with something you said under the influence. I just want to know if you meant any of it, that's all."

"Well, I mean, I was just . . ."

"Because if you didn't, that's okay. I mean, I'll be disappointed, but that's okay."

"Wait." Her jaw goes slack. "You mean that's what *you* want?"

"More than anything."

Her eyes go round. "You want to marry me? Really?"

She catches the scowl on my face. "Is that so hard to believe?"

"Wow." Those baby blues are staring at me like I've just sprouted an ear out of my forehead. "Wow. Would you really want to?"

I purse my lips. "If I didn't want to, I would've just

made like you hadn't said anything and hoped you wouldn't remember. No, I'm not proposing. I would do that more formally. But I need to know if I need to be looking at jewelry, that's all."

"If you asked me, I would say yes."

"Then there's something you need to know." She waits to see what I'm going to say. "My mom has terminal cancer. Her doctor has said probably about four months. I'm just asking because if we're going to do anything like that, I'd like to do it while my mom is still around to be there."

"In that case, you ask me anytime you want and I'll say yes. And I don't have to have any kind of fancy get-together, as long as the family and friends who want to be there can be."

I close my eyes and try to pull myself together. I just got a fiancée. And I'm about to lose my mother. I really don't know how to process all of this except that I know making these plans with Sheila is right. I finally manage to come out with, "Good."

We eat in thoughtful silence for about five minutes and then she takes my hand. "Can I ask you a couple of things?"

I nod. "Sure. Anything."

She thinks for a few seconds, then says, "Why weren't you honest with me? About Adele, I mean?"

The sigh I let out is painful and long overdue. "At first, I forgot – I really did. We'd started building our relationship before Clint mentioned it and reminded me. Then I didn't want to tell you because I hate talking about it. It's been years and it still hurts. Frankly, if I'd been able to, I would've had the marriage annulled. I didn't really consider us married after everything that happened. I wanted to finalize it and then tell you later when I'd had a chance to find a way to explain it all." I drop my eyes to the tablecloth. "Because by most people's standards, it's inexplicable."

One eyebrow shoots up. "You guys keep talking about the awful things Adele did. What were they? What did she do to you? I'd just like to know. I don't want to accidentally do the same thing."

I close my eyes, take a deep breath, and sigh it out. I knew this would come up sooner or later, and I should probably go ahead and get it out of the way. It makes me so sad to talk about it that I can barely breathe, but I need to do it. And there's no delicate way to say it. "You could never 'accidentally' do what she did, Sheila. She tricked me into marrying her. She said she was pregnant, and she wasn't, but I did care for her, so I just stayed in the relationship."

Sheila grimaces. "Well, at least you were honorable."

Then I cap it off with the rest of the story. "And while we were married, she had four abortions."

Her brow shoots down into a deep "V." "What?" I just nod. "First she tricked you by telling you she was pregnant so you'd marry her, and then she had four abortions? What the hell? Why on earth did she do that? I mean, did you want her to? Had you told her you never wanted kids?"

"No! I never said that to her, and I never knew about

them. I don't know why she did it. I guess she just didn't want them. And when she showed up with Morris, that was like plunging in a knife and drawing it out, only to plunge it in again. She'd aborted four fetuses that I assumed were mine, and yet when she decides to not abort one, she runs away and doesn't come back for all these years. And the kid she comes back with and tries to stick me with isn't even mine. I have no idea what was going on in her head."

"Oh my god, Steffen, now I see why you were so upset with her."

"Yeah." My fingers rub tight little circles on my temples because my head feels so tight that I think my brain's going to explode just from talking about it all. "When I said I forgot about her, I think what I was trying to say was that it was all too painful for me to remember. I tried to block it out because it hurt so much. She dumped all of that delightful info on me and then disappeared the next week. And I had no idea when she left that she was pregnant. None."

"Honey, I'm so sorry." She takes my hand and holds it tight, and I want to just hug her to me and never let go. "Why do you think she came back?"

"She said because she found out that I was happy and she wanted to ruin it for me. I still don't understand that, why she'd even care after all that time. Or why she'd hate me that much, for that matter. I was always good to her."

"How long is she in for?"

I shake my head. "I think eighteen months. I'm not

225

sure. It's not a long time, but it'll buy Clint time to sue for custody and win." Our eyes meet and I say something I don't want to say, but I have to. "I think I need to go to the detention facility and talk to her." Sheila's eyes question. "I have to at least go and try to make things right with her as far as my behavior was concerned. We were married for all those years and I never once told her that I loved her. That had to be a real personality-bending mindfuck for her, and I do regret that. I just feel the need to own up to my portion of the disaster."

"I can appreciate that." She looks around for the server, and I'm guessing she wants our check. "I need to go home. My head is splitting from that damn drug and I'm worn out. Why don't you take me home and then go to the facility?"

I nod. "Like bad medicine – just swallow it down and get it over with. Yeah, I already took the day off from work and today's as good a time as any." Right now, clearing up anything left over before we start a life together is my number one goal.

Chapter Eleven

"It'll just take a few minutes and the guard will bring her in. You can go ahead and have a seat."

"Thanks." I sit down in a chair by the window. It's a comfortable room, more like a den than a visitation room in a detention facility, cheerful even. There are pictures taped to the walls that I assume are drawings or pages torn from coloring books and sent in by inmates' children. It's a nice touch to an already nice room.

The door opens and as soon as she sees me, Adele glares at me from the corner of her eye. "What the hell are *you* doing here?"

Keeping my face passive and my voice calm, I give her a tiny smile. "I just came to talk to you, that's all. I have some things I need to say to you."

She sits down across from me warily, and I understand her hesitation. With no idea what I want, she probably thinks I want to blast her again. "What could you possibly want to say to me except to give me a hard time? Don't you think I've got enough of that around here?" She just continues to stare at me, then drops her gaze to her hands in her lap.

"Adele." She just sits there, eyes down. "Adele, please look at me." Her eyes finally rotate upward, and I say, "I'm sorry."

The glare she gives me is wild-eyed and she snorts out, "For what?"

"For all the years we were married and I never told you I loved you. And I did, you know."

Now her eyes are sad, and it pains me to know I'm the reason. "No, I didn't know. You never told me."

"I know." I move to sit beside her on the sofa, and she doesn't make a move to get up and move away. "That was wrong of me. In my defense, I'd never told anyone that I loved them. When I was growing up, my dad made me believe that real men didn't say that, so I just bit it back, even though I wanted to tell you, I really did."

"You did?" I see her tremble slightly, and I know she's wondering what I'm going to say next.

"Yes, I did. I did love you, and I wanted to tell you, I really did. But I just couldn't."

I can tell she doesn't believe me. "So what changed?"

I close my eyes; it hurts to even think about it. "Losing Sheila. I had to really think about what had happened and my role in all of it. And then when you said that at my house that morning, about why you did what you did, I had to admit to myself that you were right. You needed to hear those three words, and I'd withheld them the whole time we were together. But please, can you tell me, why did you do what you did?"

"You mean with the abortions?" My heart breaks

when I see that tear roll down her cheek.

"Yeah, why? I just don't understand."

"Because you didn't love me. And I couldn't have a child with someone who didn't love me."

Now I'm really confused. "But then why did you run away and have Morris when you found out you were pregnant again?"

"Because." She takes a deep breath and lets out a long, harsh sigh. "Because I wanted a child so badly, and I decided that I'd be better off to raise it by myself than to raise it in a home with someone who didn't love me, us."

The ache of grief in my chest doubles. "But I still don't understand. If that was the case, why did you come back?"

I've never seen a face as sad as hers when she answers me, her eyes lonely and haunted. "I'd been raising him alone all that time. I was tired and lonely and broke. I lost my job and I'd run out of money. I sold my house and I'd been spending what I had from it just to have a place to stay. I'm not sure what I thought would happen when I showed up here, but when I found out that you were seeing someone and you were happy, I was furious. I wanted it to be me, but I was so stuck that I just couldn't even hope for any happiness. I wanted someone else to be as miserable as I was." She looks back down at her lap. "I know what you think of me. I know you think I'm trash, that I'm a slut, but I don't care. I like sex. And I like a lot of variety. But I never meant to hurt you, Steffen, honestly, I didn't. But when you just wouldn't, well, you know . . . oh, I'm so confused." For reasons I can't understand, the sound of her despair really gets to me. It may be the culmination of all of the things that have been and are going on with me, but I'm truly sad for her.

It's quiet for a few minutes before I say, "Adele, I really am sorry. And I hope you get all of this worked out for your own good. I'm sorry you've been separated from Morris too, but you had to know what you were doing and weren't doing for and with him was wrong."

"I swear, Steffen, I didn't know he was Clint's." I have a really hard time believing that. Then she adds, "He looks a lot like my father, so I thought he just favored after that part of the family." Her dad's face flashes in my mind and she's right – Morris *does* look a good deal like her dad. I can definitely see how she'd think that.

"Doesn't matter. He's Clint's child, and now he's with Clint and Trish and he's fine."

"Is his wife a nice lady?"

"She's an angel. His girls love her. She's really good to them." The muscles in her face relax just a little. "Morris is in very good hands."

"Good." Her voice gets very small. "I always liked Clint. He was a good guy. I took advantage of the fact that he was hurting and alone, and I'm not proud of that."

"I'm glad to hear you say that and to know you're willing to take some responsibility for the things you've done. Truthfully, Adele, I don't wish anything bad on you. I hope you can get your life together. And I can tell you that I believe Clint will ask to have something worked out so you can come and see Morris. He doesn't want to keep you from your son. He just wants to make sure his son is taken care of properly. They enrolled him in school and he loves it. He's a little behind, but his sisters are helping him get caught up. He's a good kid. You did a great job of raising him alone."

She looks up at me and a tear trails down each cheek. "Wow. Thanks, Steffen. I appreciate that." After a pause, she says, "And thank you for coming here today to talk to me. I feel like we've made a little progress toward something other than being sworn enemies."

"Me too, Adele. Me too. Now I want you to concentrate on getting some help so you can get back on your feet. I don't want to see you down like this. I'll always be civil to you, but frankly, I really want you to just stay away from us. You've caused us enough grief. Sheila almost got herself hurt badly because of all of that, and it can't happen again. Now, I've gotta go – she's waiting for me at home – but if I can help you in some way, please let me know. No matter what you think, I'm not your enemy, but I can't ever be your best friend."

When I stand to go, I'm shocked when she stands too and hugs me, and I give her a firm squeeze back. "Thanks again. I appreciate you coming to see me." I nod and before I can say anything else, she adds, "Oh, and I signed the divorce papers."

Ah – I feel a huge burden float off of my shoulders. "Thanks, Adele. I appreciate that. Stay out of trouble and

I wish you the best." She waves at me until I'm out of sight, and I sigh and shake my head. I'll never understand that woman if I live to be one hundred and nineteen. Of course, if I could understand her, everyone would have reason to worry about *me*.

All the way home I think about the things we talked about, and I understand exactly why she did what she did; I don't agree with it, but I understand it. It's hard to know what to do when you feel like your options are so limited, and she didn't think I was an option as a father. That makes me wonder – am I an option as a father? I mean, what if Sheila accidentally got pregnant and we had a child? Would I be a decent father? Could I do a good job of raising a kid?

I drop my car keys in the bowl beside the front door and go looking for Sheila. She's not in the bed, and I can't find her, but I know she's here somewhere because her bag is by the front door. I find her in the back yard, sitting on the old metal glider I rescued from my grandmother's estate, and I sit down with her. "Well, that's done."

"How is she?"

"You won't believe it. She's very contrite. Explained to me why she did what she did and, honestly, I can understand it. I can't say I was all to blame, but I most definitely wasn't faultless. We both played our own roles in the breakdown. I told her she's done a great job of raising Morris alone, and that I'm pretty sure Clint's going to ask that she have some kind of visitation with him when she gets out. I almost feel sorry for her –

almost." I pat her knee. "But now it's over. I move forward. And I want that to be with you." Her eyes are red and tear-filled. "What, baby? What's wrong?"

"Steffen? Will you just hold me?"

God, I've missed this. "Come here, baby girl." She climbs into my lap, turned sideways, and I pull her into my body and clutch her tight. The fragrance of that beautiful hair fills the air around me, and I'm overwhelmed with her touch, her sigh, her very presence. I had no idea that I could love a woman this way, but she fills every empty place in my heart and soul. We sit there in the fresh air and sunshine for awhile, just enjoying being together. I think my upside-down, topsy-turvy world has righted itself, and I couldn't be happier.

Well, yeah, actually, I could. But that can wait. We've got some work to do first. After about ten minutes, I loosen my grip around her and push her back enough to be able to see her face. "You need to call in for a couple of days, and so do I. There are some things we need to work out up front." There's a look of dread on her face until I say, "No, no, no! It's good, really! I just think we need to talk about some stuff, you know, each of us come to an understanding about where the other one wants the relationship to go and what they expect, goals, wishes, fears, all of that. We need to talk about that at length. And we don't need to be disturbed. I've got plenty of sick leave."

"Me too."

"Then call in tomorrow morning. At least two days."

"I'll make it three. That'll give us the weekend too."

She gives me a soft smile that just turns everything inside me to mush.

"Three it is."

After the calls the next morning, we go to the café down the street for pancakes. When we get back, we sit down to talk about things I never thought I'd discuss with a woman. No, neither of us are interested in a total power exchange, and neither wants a full-time D/s relationship either, but we want to bring in the elements we like. She wants to be collared; I don't want to restrain the free spirit inside that beautiful body, so we agree on a pretty chain with a lock and a couple of charms that mean something to us. Then the conversation goes into territory I've never even considered.

Kids. Do we want kids? How many? How soon? The things she says surprise me. I was pretty sure I knew what she'd say, but I was completely wrong, and I discover she's far more in line with my thinking than I ever dreamed. Our ideas on parenting, education, activities, all of that, they're all so similar it's kind of frightening – and exciting. We talk about long-term birth control. We talk about mealtimes, combining our households, sharing a space, and what that will be like. Do we need to move? What will she do with her house – sell it or become a landlord? A yard? A dog?

In between, we eat takeout or cook. We take naps and, for three days, unless we go out, and we have to a couple of times briefly, we're in pajamas. For the first time ever, she lets me shower with her, and I decide right then it'll be the last time too. What a shower hog, and she must have fifteen elbows, all of which wind up in my midsection. The sex is fun, but not enough fun for the trouble we'd go to, so if it happens spontaneously, great, but otherwise, we won't plan it. After all, we don't have to be soaking wet to get off.

And we decide planning sex is important. Regularly scheduled date nights to have time to sit and talk, enjoy ourselves, with or without kids, are really important to us. We'll have one night a week when all we do is cuddle, no sex. I laugh and say that doesn't rule out mid-afternoon fucking sprints, and she laughs and hits me in the face with a throw pillow, so I'm not sure that's worked out, but whatever. Small beans compared to everything else we iron out in those three days.

Day four is Saturday, so we take the day to go out and walk along the shoreline at one of the state parks. We eat at the lodge, then drive to a secluded little area and make out in the car. I feel like a high school kid, and I love it. We role play that I'm the cool guy who bagged the cheerleader, and it's awesome. But I never realized how long my legs really are until the car. And they are. Really, really long.

Sunday we spend in bed, and I don't just mean screwing. We giggle and cuddle. We watch TV and eat popcorn. We talk about things we did when we were kids, insecurities we had, awards we won in grade school, first crushes that broke our hearts.

And with every passing minute, I'm more in love with this woman. She loves me, she really does. I'm overwhelmed with what I feel for her and how she responds to me. We're a couple.

I've found the love of my life. I saved her from the clutches of an evil Dom. And she saved me from myself.

"How are you feeling?" I ask as I lean down and give my mother a peck on the cheek.

"Oh, just tired, honey." She draws the fuzzy throw I gave her for Christmas one year a little tighter around her thin legs. "I'm just tired."

The chair adjacent to her sofa is my favorite spot, and I sit down and lean forward toward her, elbows on thighs. "So is there anything I can do to help?"

She chuckles. "You? The hand-tool-impaired son?" After a pause, she says, "Well, yeah, I could stand having a couple of the light bulbs in my bathroom replaced."

I have to laugh. "I think even your handyman-wannabe son can handle that." It seems unbelievable that in a few months, I won't have a mom. "Anything else I can do?"

"Can't think of a thing except to sit down and talk to me for awhile." I change the light bulbs she mentioned, and then I sit on the sofa next to her chair, and she reaches for my hand. "How are you doing, son?"

"I'm good, Mom, real good."

She waits, and I know what she's wondering about. After ten minutes of me sitting quietly and not being at all forthcoming, she finally asks, "So, what about Shei-la?"

"What about her?" I'm trying hard to keep a straight

face.

"Is she still around?"

"Yeah, Mom, she's still around. We had a little hiccup in the road, but we're back on track now."

"Good. She's a sweet girl. All couples have little hiccups. They move forward, go on with their relationships, work to make things better. Look at me and your father. We had plenty of hard years, but we had good years too."

"Speaking of which," I say, then stop for a few seconds before continuing. "Mom, did Dad *ever* tell you that he loved you?"

"What on earth would make you ask me that?" She's feigning indignation, but underneath it I see the hurt and humiliation.

I look into those eyes that have looked at me with love, patience, and pride all these years. "Mom, you don't have to pretend with me. I know. I know how he was. I just want to know: Did he ever give that to you?"

"Yes, son, he did." I sit quietly, wondering what she's going to say. "He told me about two hours before he died."

Two hours before he died. All those years together, and he had to be dying to finally tell his wife that he loved her? That's some kind of fucked up. She interrupts my thoughts with, "And he said, 'Maggie, I was wrong to keep this from you all these years. You earned my love and respect over and over, but I was afraid to show it. Guess I don't have anything to lose now, do I?' I never questioned if he loved me; it was obvious he did. But I'd waited all those years to hear that, Steffen." There's a sadness on her face that takes my breath away.

"He taught me the same thing, that real men don't go around telling people that they love them. It cost me one relationship, and it almost cost me another one."

"But you fixed it in time, right, son?" There's a little spark in her eyes that's been missing for awhile now.

"Yes. Finally. It was almost too late, but I fixed it. And that's why I wanted to come and talk to you." She's gazing intently at my face like she's going to miss something if she blinks. "Mom, I'm going to ask Sheila to marry me."

She claps her hands together and starts to laugh. "Well, thank goodness! You certainly work slow, Steffen! I thought you'd never get around to it. Do you think she'll say yes?"

"Oh, I'm certain of it. She told me she will."

My mother reaches for my hands and takes them in hers, her tiny fingers thin and cool against my skin. "I'm so happy for you, for both of you. You may be my son, but you're a fine man, Steffen, and pretty damn handsome too." Her smile is a mile wide. "So when do you think you'll be doing this?"

"Probably in the next couple of weeks. Think you'd like to come?"

I'm unprepared when my mother starts to weep. She cries harder and harder and I don't know what to do. What would I do if it were Sheila? I just lean over, pull her out of her chair, and draw her into my lap. The little boy she once held is now holding her, trying to take away the pain and fear, and my heart tells me in that intimate moment how much I'm going to miss her. I wonder if I'll ever be able to have some kind of relationship with my sister, or if that's just too far gone. Almost as though she can read my mind, she says, "You could call Cecilia, talk to her. I'd really like it if the two of you could spend some time together. She's all you've got left, Steffen."

"I have you," I blurt out. I know what she's trying to say, but I don't really want to acknowledge it.

"You know exactly what I mean. Will you try, Steffen? Please?"

I nod. "Yes, Mom, I promise – I'll try."

"Good. Want something to drink? I've got some stuff in the kitchen."

"No, no, that's okay. I need to go. I just wanted you to know what was going on. So we'll plan on you being there, right?"

"Wouldn't miss it for the world! I love you, son."

I hug her close to me. "I love you too, Mom. I love you so much."

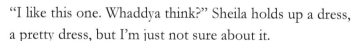

"I like this one. Whaddya think?" Sheila holds up a dress, a pretty dress, but I'm just not sure about it.

I shake my head. "It's just not 'you,' if you know what I mean."

"Yeah. I know." She puts it back on the rack and keeps looking.

"Look at this one." I hold up a royal blue that's just too lovely to leave on the rack.

She shakes her head. "I don't know about that."

I hold it out to her. "Just go try it on." Standing and staring, hands on hips, she finally reaches out and takes it from me. "Good girl. Go on. I'll be waiting." I know there's a little smirk on my lips which she tries to kiss away, but it doesn't work. I'm still smirking as she disappears into the dressing room.

Two minutes later, I hear a feminine throat-clearing and turn. "Oh. My. God. Baby, you look amazing."

She's so excited that I can see it all over her. "I know, right? I mean, I didn't think it looked all that great on the hanger, but I put it on and turned around and, oh my god, it's beautiful!"

Every curve on that super-feminine body is accentuated by the cut, and the soft, clingy, shimmering fabric drapes perfectly. Give her a pair of black patent pumps and she'll look like a million bucks. Hell, she looks like a million bucks already. "Sweetheart, I didn't think you could possibly look any sexier, but I was dead wrong. Dead wrong." She turns so I can see her ass. "Wow. Was I ever wrong."

"You like it?" She's beaming.

"No. I love it. And I love you." After I let her kiss me sweetly, I step back. "I've got something for you."

"Oh, Steffen. Not here. Really? No, please . . ."

"Would you stop it? Just wait." Reaching into my pocket, I draw out something and I see her eyes glisten and tears well in the corners. "Hold out your arm."

I fasten the bracelet around her wrist and watch as she looks it over like it's the crown jewels, a faint smile spreading across her face. "You know, when I walked out without that bracelet, I felt like someone had stripped me bare and raped me. My arm felt so naked and raw. All that time, I'd look down and hope it was there, but it wasn't, and my heart would break again."

I reach out to her and she leans into my chest, my arms tightening around her protectively. "You never have to take it off again. Except while we're scening if we're doing restraints. I don't want it broken."

"No, Sir." She giggles a little when she says it.

"Now, go change. Oh, and do you want the dress?"

"Yes!"

I smile. "Give it to me and I'll go pay for it while you get dressed. Then it's on to the lingerie store." At that, she claps and jumps up and down, then kisses me and runs back to the dressing room. About forty-five seconds later, she calls out, "Here!" and the dress sails through the door and hits me in the face. Classy – very classy.

An hour and a half later, we leave the shoe store with new Louboutins after having cleaned out the lingerie store. Every panty in a medium and every bra in a 34D is now in a bag that hangs from my arm, and she's laughing and smiling and teasing me as we go to the car.

I can't remember a time when I've been this happy. But the day's not over yet.

"I love this place. Don't you love this place? I love this place." She's all grins as the maître d shows us to our table. She's so bubbly and excited to be here that she doesn't realize almost all of the tables are empty. If I didn't know better, I'd think she'd taken a hit of speed. Her eyes twinkle in the candlelight, and I think to myself that I've never seen a more beautiful woman in my entire life. Fuck those lingerie models; she's got them beat hands down.

"I do love this place. I love that this was the place where we had our very first actual date." I grin at her and she knows exactly what I'm thinking.

"We kinda did it backwards, didn't we?"

I shake my head. "Absolutely not. We did it the perfect way for us." The gentleman helps Sheila into her seat as I take mine, then promises that our waiter will be back in just a few minutes. "So, have any idea what you'd like tonight?"

"No! I want to try something new. Look – this dish has truffles in it. Do you like truffles?"

I look up and nod to a couple coming in as they're seated nearby. "I love truffles. What about pork?"

"Oooo, I like pork! What about this pork saltimbocca? That sounds good!" She's wandering through the menu.

"I think we should choose our wine first. That's what he'll be asking about next. Shall I order for us?"

"Oh, please!" As she keeps staring at the menu, I glance up and nod to two more people.

"She'd like a glass of pinot gris, and I'll take a glass of merlot," I tell the wine steward. Watching him walk away, I ask, "So what have you decided on for dinner?"

"Oh, I think it's the pork or this chicken dish. What about you?" Thankfully, she doesn't look up, because I'm looking at someone else who's come in just then.

"Um, I think I'm having the filet mignon, actually. Oh, yes," I tell the server as he returns, "We'll both have a fresh salad with the chardonnay vinaigrette, no onions, and grated parmesan on them, please." He nods as he retreats, and the wine promptly shows up. Sipping on it, we make our final selections from the menu and order, sit and chat while we wait, and just generally enjoy each other's company.

The food arrives, delicious as usual. And I've been looking around the room. The empty tables have all filled, and I'm stuffed. She looks like she is too. The table is cleared, and the server asks, "Would you like one of our famous desserts?" With the eye she can't see from where she sits, he winks at me.

"No, I don't think so, but thank you."

Sheila's eyes fly open wide. "What? What do you mean, no? I want dessert! Sir, I . . ." she calls after him, but he's gone. Her eyes turn back and fix on me. "I wanted dessert. Why couldn't you just let me order?"

"Because you don't need it."

"Oh? And what the hell is that supposed to mean exactly?"

"It means this." I stand and go to her side of the table. Her back is to the rest of the room, so I take her hand, help her stand, then turn her sideways to face me. When she's turned, I drop to one knee right there in front of her. The look on her face is pure shock as I look up at her. "Sheila, I love you. I'm going to love you until I die. And if you should go before me, I'll make you a promise." I choke back the sob that's threatening to spill from my throat. "I'll never, never forget you. Never. I couldn't. I wouldn't. Being without you would be like being without the best part of myself." Hesitating for just a second as I watch the tears rolling down her face, I simply ask, "Will you be my wife?"

Barely above a whisper, she answers, "Oh, god, Steffen. Oh, yes. Yes, I want to marry you." With those words, I reach into my pocket and produce a ring that I chose, one with a stone large enough to let her know with just its presence that she's the most precious thing in my life. As I slip it onto her hand, she feels a touch on her shoulder and turns.

"Welcome to my family, daughter," my mother says in a tiny, shy voice, and kisses Sheila on the cheek. I hear someone begin to clap and, sure enough, it's Clint. He rises and Trish joins him, followed by Dave, Marta, and Angela, most of my employees from the bank and their spouses, and all of Sheila's research colleagues. To her shock and delight, the last group to rise is her parents, sister, brothers, and all of their families. But the most surprised person in the room is me: Cecilia and her husband and kids are there, and I decide right then that getting to know her is worth the time I'd spend. Everyone applauds as I take my gorgeous girl in my arms and kiss her, and as our lips touch, I feel every gram of doubt and uncertainty that might possibly have still existed evaporate and disappear into the ether like vapor.

"This! This is what the dress was all about! And the shoes!" She rests her forearms on my shoulders and looks up into my eyes. "And the underwear?"

Leaning into her ear, I reply, "Nah. That was just for me. But if you've got some of it on right now, hey, that's great!" Before I have a chance to say anything else, she takes the neckline of her dress in her hand and pulls out so I can look down her torso to see the bra underneath. Yep – it's the two-tone blue number with the iridescent lace that I bought for her. "Nice. Very nice. I can't wait to take that off."

"Oh, you'll get your chance, Mr. Cothran, believe me." She kisses me again as the servers roll out a banquet buffet serving line full of the most gorgeous desserts I've ever seen. "This is why you wouldn't let me order dessert!"

Laughter is just bubbling out of me. "Yep! I didn't want you eating some run-of-the-mill crème brûlée when I had this waiting in the wings! But hey, watch that dress. Don't spill anything on it, hear me?"

She shoots me an odd look. "Well, okay. Hadn't planned to anyway."

"It's important." I give her a stern glare.

"Okay then." She gets her dessert and takes a seat at the table with one of her coworkers, and I join them after I've gotten my plateful.

Another gentleman comes in, and when a server tells me who he is, I excuse myself, go and greet him, and ask him to accompany me back to the table. "Sheila, I'd like you to meet someone. This is Father O'Brien. Father, this is my fiancée, Sheila Brewster."

"Miss Brewster, it's a pleasure to meet you." He waits expectantly.

"So were you Steffen's priest growing up?"

Before he can answer, I shake my head. "Do you remember when I told you what you said to me at the club that night?"

Brow wrinkled in confusion, she said, "About being in pain?"

"Nope." I grin from ear to ear. "About wanting to marry me right then?"

"Yeah?"

"Well, here's your chance. Marry me right here, Sheila, right this minute. Everyone's here. They're all willing to stay. Hell, we've already had the reception." Then I remember and turn. "Sorry, Father." Sheila starts to laugh. "So please? Let's not waste another second. Whaddya say?"

Now she's laughing right out loud. "I'd say you're crazy, Steffen Cothran! And I'd also say you're smart and sexy and very, very clever. Plus I'd say you're about to get yourself a wife." She turns to the priest. "Don't mind us, Father O'Brien. Just get out your piece of paper or whatever it is and let's get to it. I want to marry this man before he forgets that he asked me," she says and winks at me.

"Never happen, babe. Never happen." We all sober as Father O'Brien begins the vows, and we answer appropriately. When we get to the "richer and poorer" thing, I finish with "I do" and then I say directly to

Sheila, "You are my wife and I will love you forever as sure as the sun rises in the morning and sets in the evening." She smiles up at me and I know what happiness looks like.

The priest goes on with the repeating of the vows, and Sheila parrots him word for word until she says, "I do," and then looks up into my face. Her face is all sweetness and light as she says, "Steffen, you're the only man I've ever truly trusted. On this day, every slate is wiped clean and we start fresh in every way. There'll be no secrets and no regrets." I nod, and she whispers to me in a voice coarse with emotion, "You are my everything. If you truly love me, and I believe you do, then only you can make my life complete. I give you everything I am and everything I have, my husband."

In the most precious gesture anyone's every directed toward me, she takes my hand and kisses the back of it. Out of the blue, I start to weep. I can't help it. When I turn my face away from her, her soft hand turns it back toward her and she smiles up at me. In a choked, raspy wheeze, I let out, "I thought I'd lost you."

"I'll promise you something right now, Steffen Gunnar Cothran. If you lose me, I'll always find my way back to you. And if I lose you, I trust that you'll always find your way back to me. Deal?"

I wipe one eye with the back of my free hand and smile. "Deal. God, I'm sorry, baby. I'm a real mess."

A smile widens her lips as she shakes her head. "Never, never apologize to me for being a real man. That emotional honesty? That's what I need from you.

Always."

"Do the two of you have rings you'd like to ex-change?" I hear the priest ask.

I smile and nod, still sniffling, but Sheila gasps. "Oh, no! I didn't know this was going to happen so I don't have his!"

There's a soft chuckle and Trish appears next to Sheila and there, in her palm, is a ring box. "Good thing you told me where you hid it. And good thing you have a spare key hidden outside too." That makes Sheila giggle. She hands Sheila the tiny box, and I watch my new wife reach for her friend and hug her before taking the little treasure and turning back to me.

As she opens the box, takes out the ring, and hands the box back to Trish, Clint hands me Sheila's ring; he'd had it since I picked it up from the jewelry store. As it passes from his hand into mine, he leans into me and growls, "For the love of god, Cothran, marry this woman and stop blubbering."

"Shut up, Winstead."

"No, you shut up, Cothran. And have a happy life. I love you, brother, and I'm happy for you. Put that ring on her finger and seal the deal before she can change her mind. I know if I were her, I'd be looking for a way to skip town as fast as I could."

"Lucky for me I'm not marrying you."

"Lucky for *both* of us."

In that moment, I can't help it; I reach for Clint and hug him tight, and he hugs me back. "Thanks for being a true friend, Winstead. You have no idea what your friendship means to me."

He whispers back, "What are you trying to do, get *me* to blubber? Not happening, man. But thanks. Your friendship means the world to me too." He pats my back and turns loose, and his eyes are red and teary too.

In that moment, I realize that it doesn't matter that I won't have any family here when my mother is gone. I have family, a family that I've chosen and made, and that bond is strong. Across the room I can see Dave smiling, and Marta and Angela are there too. I know when I need a dad or a mom, the three of them will be there for me. Bridget is near them, and it's clear to me that I hired a remarkable young woman when I hired her. She's been there for me to do anything I asked, and to do so cheerfully. I look around and see that the whole restaurant is filled with love, from Hailee and McKenna, who were excited to be able to have new dresses for the occasion, and Morris, who looks hideously uncomfortable in his little suit and tie, to the servers, people I've seen over and over through the years whose names I don't even know but who are standing and watching, their faces stretched in smiles, happy for both of us. And Sheila's family seems genuinely happy to know that I'm part of them now, a thing I'll be eternally grateful for. I've never known love like this, but it's this remarkable woman standing here with me who awoke me to the possibilities for happiness and love all around me. I owe her everything. I owe her my very life.

My hand trembles as I slip the ring onto her finger. "Second thoughts?" she giggles.

"No. Afraid you'll jerk your hand away before I can get it on your finger!"

"Not happening." She takes my hand and, before she slips the band on my finger, she holds it up and turns it slightly so I can see the inscription. I can't read it, but she quietly says as a tear slips down her cheek, "It says, 'Never forget me.'"

I take her face in my hands and look deep into her eyes. "You can count on that. I'll never, never forget you." Pulling her face to mine, I kiss her. In that kiss I feel the promise of a future I never thought I'd have, and suddenly I'm excited to be going on this journey with this amazing woman.

Master Steffen is officially out of circulation and, surprisingly, he's thrilled about it.

Chapter Twelve

"Are you nervous?" Sheila's voice is sort of shaky as she asks.

"Nervous as hell. You?"

She nods. "Almost unbearably." She's straightening the flowers in the vase, then straightening the throw on the back of the sofa, then straightening the pictures on the walls.

"Baby, nobody cares about that stuff. Come over here and sit down." When she sits down beside me on the sofa, I wrap an arm around her and pull her up against me. "It's going to be fine. Remember, if this doesn't work out, we'll just look for another way, okay? Don't get all freaked out if it doesn't fly."

"I know, I know. But I want it to, I really do." About that time, the doorbell rings. "Oh, god, do I look okay?"

I kiss her nose as I rise to answer the door. "You look spectacular. She'll love you, I promise."

I sling open the door and flash that famous Cothran smile, then realize it won't do me any good. This woman has to be the manliest woman I've ever seen. There's no doubt in my mind that femdom has just arrived on my front porch. "Ms. Abernathy?"

"Yes! Mr. Cothran?"

"Yes, ma'am! It's so nice to meet you." I extend a hand and she shakes it heartily. "Won't you please come in? Make yourself at home. This is my wife, Sheila." Sheila extends a hand and the woman takes it in hers and smiles. "Honey, this is Ms. Abernathy."

"It's a pleasure to meet you." Sheila smiles warmly at her, and the woman responds. For all her masculinity, she's very gentle and personable, and I feel comfortable with her immediately. "Would you like something to drink? I've got a fresh pot of coffee on, and we have juice and soda and bottled water . . ."

"Oh, a nice hot cup of coffee would be wonderful!" Before Sheila can ask, Ms. Abernathy responds, "And just black. I don't want to be any bother."

"No bother at all." Sheila disappears into the kitchen, and I motion to Ms. Abernathy to have a seat. Once she's in the chair, Sheila appears with her coffee. She takes a sip. "Wow. This is a nice roast. You must've paid a fortune for it."

I can tell Sheila's under her spell. "No, not at all. It came from Publix. Isn't it wonderful?"

"It really is." She pulls some things out of the bag she brought in with her and spreads them out on the coffee table. "Okay, first things first. I'm not Ms. Abernathy; I'm Amy. May I call you Steffen and Sheila?"

"Please," I nod.

"Great! Remember, I'm your ally here, not your adversary. I'll be the first one to point out if I think a situation is poorly suited for you, but it won't be to hurt you or anyone else; it'll be to spare everyone some grief. I've been around long enough to be able to spot a bad situation in a heartbeat, and I want the best possible outcome for everyone."

"We understand that," I reply.

"Good. Now, you both got all of your paperwork filled out and it all looks good. You also turned in your compatibility sheets, so I know what you think will work. So tell me, what provisions have you made?"

"We have a room ready. I mean, we don't know how to decorate it yet, but it has new furniture and bedding, the walls are freshly painted, there's new flooring down, and some plain curtains that can be replaced easily. We didn't know whether to buy a changing table and a rocking chair, or a desk and chair to go with it, because we don't know an age or anything, but . . ."

"Slow down, Steffen! It's okay. As long as there's somewhere for a child to sleep, everything else can be done later. I noticed that you said you'd rather not have a baby. Is that correct?"

"Yes, ma'am. That's correct," Sheila echoes back.

"Well, I have to tell you, that increases your chances by about ninety percent. You won't have any trouble there. I also noticed that you have no race restrictions."

"No, ma'am. That doesn't make one bit of difference to us."

"Well, you just increased that ninety percent by about ninety percent. Better all the time. Now, let's talk about the elephant in the room."

Sheila and I look at each other nervously. "Okay," I manage to squeak out.

Amy chuckles. "I know you're not stupid; it's pretty obvious I'm a lesbian." When we both nod, she starts to laugh right out loud. "We've got that out of the way! And as such, you've got a real advantage in having me as your adoption agent. I know all about gender and sexual discrimination in the adoption community. I'm here to help you circumvent that, and there are ways. So tell me about your particular situation so I know what we're dealing with." She looks directly at me. "I somehow get the impression that I should be directing that statement to you, am I correct?"

I nod. "Yes. I'm the Dominant in this relationship."

"Yeah. I got that vibe. So are we talking about a TPE, a Master/slave arrangement, a D/s relationship, what?"

"D/s. And I wouldn't say we 'live the lifestyle,' but elements of it permeate our relationship, and we do scene regularly in a private club where we do so in the public areas."

"Full-blown sex acts?"

"Yes, ma'am."

She shrugs. "I don't see that as a problem. It's not like you're scening in front of children, and I have no reason to believe you'd do that. Do you have some references from the club who can vouch for your character?"

I nod. "Oh, yes, absolutely."

"My husband's been a well-respected Dom there for

years," Sheila adds with obvious pride.

Amy smiles. "To watch you respond in that manner, I know it must be true for the community as well as in this household."

"Yes, ma'am, it is," Sheila beams. Instantly I'm so proud that I feel like my chest is going to burst open.

"Good, good. Now, here at home, what kind of D/s activity do you engage in?"

"We're pretty subtle about it. Once we close the bedroom door, it's no holds barred, but otherwise, we're pretty careful. I mean, we don't just do it in the bedroom, but, well, you know, oh . . ."

Amy laughs loudly. "Steffen, I'm not here to judge. I just need reassurance that you're not going to intentionally or negligently engage in any sexual activity in the presence of a child, that's all. If you want to fuck each other's brains out on the kitchen table, as long as there's no kid there watching and you wipe it down with an antibacterial agent afterward, I really don't give a shit."

Damn, I like this woman.

"So here's what I'd suggest. Don't volunteer any information, but if you're asked outright, be truthful but give as little in the way of details as you can possibly give. For instance, if asked if you engage in, oh, let's say BDSM, you could just say something like, 'We do enjoy variety in our sexual relationship, but I wouldn't exactly call it BDSM.' Because, frankly, you can call it anything you like. I mean, a Leatherman could say, 'I like puppies,' and no one would have to know that he meant puppy play."

I nod. "I see what you're saying. Semantics."

"Exactly. So we do the placements, but the state comes in and does both a home study and a six-week monitoring, since it's more or less private, even though you're going through the state register. And you can do anything if you have to for six weeks, correct?"

We both nod and I say, "Yes, ma'am."

"Very good. Okay, let's see what we've got." She drags out three large binders and we start looking at pictures and profiles. As we flip through, she suddenly stops. "How many bedrooms do you have?"

"Three, but one's a home office." I look up at her. "Why?"

"Oh, nothing. I thought this would be a great fit, but you'd need a three-bedroom house." She keeps flipping pages, but my mind is running ninety to nothing. It's just a little home office, and I do have a desk in the living room. Plus Sheila and I had been talking about selling her house and buying something else, something that was ours instead of hers or mine.

"We could convert the home office back to a bedroom. And we've been talking about buying a different place. So could you tell us about your prospect there?"

"Not prospect. Prospects – plural." She flips back and places the book open on the table. There, staring back at us, are two little faces. The boy looks to be about eight, and the girl about six. Under their pictures are the names Joseph and Rachel. "These two are half brother and sister. Fathers have never been in the picture, and mom is in and out of jail. She finally agreed to sign them over to the state, worst part of which is that they've had to be separated. We didn't have a foster home for them together, and the only spaces we had were in gender-specific group homes. And it's killing them to not be together." I study the little faces, and Sheila leans in with me. "Mom's white, and Joey's dad is Hispanic. Mom's not sure about Rachel's dad, but looking at her, I'd say it's a pretty sure thing that he's black. Two issues with them: Rachel's got asthma, and Joey's got a learning disability, but he's done very well with a tutor." She stops to let it all soak in. I pick up the book and lay it in my lap so Sheila and I can look it over more closely.

Then I let out a sniggle. "Joey and Rachel. Is somebody a *Friends* fan?"

Sheila lets out a little giggle, then sobers. "It says her favorite color is purple," Sheila says with a small smile. "She wants an American Girl doll. And she likes ponies." Her eyes are sad. "What little girl doesn't like ponies?"

"And he wants to be an astronaut when he grows up." I can't help but grin. "You know, I wanted to be an astronaut when I was that age. And he likes basketball; I can forgive him for that!" I laugh. I'm a football fan. "He wants a bicycle because he's never had one." That makes me sad. Every kid should have a bike. Then I see something that brings tears to my eyes. "Oh my god. It says here that if he could have anything he wanted, it would be his own bed, a toilet that flushes right, and clean clothes." Something catches in my chest and I have trouble drawing in a breath. When I lift my head and level my gaze with Amy's, I blurt out, "How many kids like these are out there waiting for families?"

The corners of her mouth turn down and her eyes are suddenly tired. "Thousands. Tens of thousands. More than we'll ever find homes for. Thousands of people get on social media and in cars every day and do hours of volunteer work to save animals, but there are only a handful of people on this planet helping these kids. They'll get on a plane and go to China to adopt a child when there's a whole houseful twenty blocks away who don't have homes. Hell, the state pays for almost everything related to the adoptions and offers a huge stipend, plus pays for their college educations. Right now, the stipend is," she says, looking at a paper in the back of her notebook, "eleven thousand eight hundred and fifty dollars per child. The idea is to give you the money so you can do whatever you need to do to offer them a suitable home. Buy another place, knock out a wall and enlarge your home, whatever you need to do. Those numbers change constantly, based on inflation and cost of living per government standards, but they hover in that range."

I turn to my wife. "Putting both places on the market tomorrow?"

She nods. "Absolutely. First thing. We'll get a realtor out here and over there and get the process started." Her eyes lock with mine. "Steffen, is this what you want to do?"

"There's something about their little faces. I feel like I've connected with them somehow. I didn't get that from the other pictures, but these two, yeah. What about you?"

She nods. "I feel the same way."

"I've spent time with both of them," Amy offers. "They're adorable kids. Smart, funny, polite. We've almost decided Joey's learning disability is due to some vision problems, and he needs a good ophthalmologist to look into that. As for Rachel, she's doing well in school, makes friends easily, and she's a very affectionate child." She closes the binder. "What about childcare?"

"I can drop them off at school, and Sheila's employer has made it clear that her hours are flexible, so she can go in earlier and leave earlier to pick them up from school. And once we can find a babysitter, that won't be an issue anymore anyway."

Amy sits with her head down for about twenty seconds as Sheila and I glance back and forth at each other. Then she sighs, raises her head, and turns to us. "I can make arrangements for you to meet them tomorrow. Is that what you want?"

Sheila smiles at me, and I turn and smile at Amy. "Yes. Absolutely. We'd love that. We'll talk about it for the rest of the evening and if we change our minds or have any misgivings, I'll give you a call, but I'm sure this is the direction we want to go in."

"Well then, that's that." She closes the binder and loads all three of the thick vinyl tomes back into her bag. "I have every reason to believe that you'll make fine parents, and I have no qualms whatsoever about recommending you as adopters. I will warn you, however, that until we get absolute dissolution of parental rights, consider them your foster children who may be removed from your home at any time. That will be best for everyone involved."

"We understand. How long will the dissolution take?"

"Hard to say, but I'm guessing under six weeks. If I'm not mistaken, this time the mother was involved in a bank robbery and she's not getting out until after they're grown, so she has no reason to hang onto custody. And so far, none of the relatives have shown any interest at all in them. So I don't foresee a problem." She stands, and we both rise too. "All right then – tomorrow, if nothing goes wrong, we'll set up a meeting for the four of you at about four thirty at the child protective services office downtown. You're welcome to bring small gifts with you, nothing elaborate, maybe a comic book or coloring book and crayons, some cute little barrettes for her hair, maybe an inexpensive watch for him, something like that. This is not about giving them something to win them over. Trust me, if they could come home with you tomorrow night, they would; they'd jump at the chance. In the meantime, I'd suggest you do whatever you need to do to get two bedrooms ready, because social services will not let you adopt them unless they have a bedroom apiece."

"Got it. I'll get on that tomorrow," I promise her.

"Good. Listen, it's been great meeting the two of you. I wish you a lot of luck and I'll be with you every step of the way. And call me if you have any questions or concerns. I'll do whatever I can to make sure this goes smoothly."

I shake her hand as she stands in the open doorway. "Thank you, Amy. Thanks so much. We'll be looking forward to your call tomorrow."

Sheila echoes with, "Yes, thanks, Amy. We really appreciate it."

To my surprise and delight, Amy reaches to hug Sheila. "I'm a mom too. I know how anxious you must be. Trust me, it's all going to work out. Big smiles and fingers crossed," she grins as she heads down the steps. "Talk to you tomorrow."

"Yes, ma'am! Thanks again!" I call out as she gets into her car. When I close the door, I lean against it and blow out a ragged breath. "Oh my god, I was nervous, but she's so nice."

"She sure is. I like her a lot." Sheila sits back down on the sofa, perching on the front edge with her elbows on her thighs, leaning forward and rocking to and fro. "Oh, god, Steffen, we're about to get two kids."

"Yeah, but Winstead's been doing it alone for years, so how hard can it be?" I snicker.

"You're awful!" she giggles.

"I know. I give him so much shit." About that time her phone rings, and I recognize the ringtone. "Yep, Trish. She wants a blow-by-blow. Talk to her. And no squealing. You know how I hate that," I grin.

"Hello? Yeah! It went great!" I watch her walk down the hallway toward the bedroom, and I know what she's doing. When she and Trish get on the phone, she lies down across the bed on her stomach, props up on her elbows, and kicks her legs up and down, ankles crossed. They're like a pair of teenagers gushing over a boy in the latest edition of a fashion magazine. I do the smart thing and just go into the kitchen to order Chinese delivery. That'll keep us from starving. She won't be able to concentrate long enough to cook tonight without catching the house on fire anyway.

By about nine we've both calmed down. I'm sitting on the sofa reading an article in an architectural magazine when she saunters into the room. Kneeling in front of me, she unbuttons and unzips my chinos, and I lift my hips enough for her to pull down my slacks and my boxer briefs to free my cock. Not a word is said as she leans in and pulls the head of my manhood into her lips, and I take a deep breath and blow it out as she begins to suck. Five minutes in, she stands, slips off her panties, and mounts me, her dress fanning out and over my lap as she slides down over my shaft with that hot, slick cunt that somehow always makes me insane with need. Leaning in, she kisses the hollow at the base of my neck, and I breathe in the scent of her hair. I'm the first to speak when I groan out, "Damn, girl, you turn me on. I'd rather fuck you than breathe."

"Yeah, but if you stop breathing, you won't be able to fuck me. So breathe, wouldja?" There's mirth in her voice, and her encore is a trailing of her tongue up the side of my neck until she reaches my ear and promptly rims it, then nips my earlobe. I grab her face and pull it to mine. I spend the next five minutes devouring her mouth, then maneuver us both until she's lying on the sofa with me above her. I gaze down into those warm, gorgeous, blue eyes looking back up at me, and I'm overwhelmed by the love I feel for her. It fills me; it fills the room. It fills everything in my whole world.

Instead of remaining inside her, I slip down until my lips can touch her chest, and I travel downward, suck first one nipple and then the other into my mouth, then kiss down her ribcage and belly until I reach her mound. There I stop, pull back, and thrust my tongue into her channel just to hear her gasp. She grabs my hair, not pulling, just for the connection, and I slip the tip of my tongue up and between her pussy lips until I find that tiny, swollen pearl. First I suck it in between my teeth, then give it a tiny nip. She yelps and I snort under my breath. Then I settle down to work, my tongue circling her bud, sucking it into my lips several times, then going back to the circling motion. She's moaning and crying out, her back arching and hips thrusting, and she asks in a desperate whisper, "Sir, may I come?"

I whisper back to her, "Anytime you want, sub. Anytime at all." I grab her hips and hold on, and in just a few seconds her pelvis starts to buck as the pitch and volume of her voice travels upward in a long, frantic cry. At the apex of the onslaught she screams out, "Oh, god, Steffen, I want your cock in me. Fuck me, please, fuck me?"

Now what fool would say no to that? Not this one, uh-uh.

She's hot and wet and ready, like always, and I rise up and take her with one fierce thrust just to hear her cry out and feel her claw at my shoulders. I'm hammering away at her until I suddenly just stop, buried up to my ball sack in that tight pussy, and stare down at her. "Whaaa? Why did you stop?" I almost start laughing as I feel her trying to thrust her hips upward.

"Nah-ah-ah, little subbie. You forget who's in charge here." I pull back so slowly that it takes me what seems like forever, and I burrow back into her at the same languorous pace while she frets and twitches. She wants me. Yeah. I like this – I like it a lot. Stretching the length of my body out on top of her to pin her to the sofa cushions, I wrap my hands down and around her hips and grasp her ass cheeks in my hands, continuing to withdraw and recommit every stroke an inch at a time, relishing the feel of her channel pulsing around my shaft, listening to her moan and cry out. I savor it, deliberate in my movements, working the angle in which the head of my cock is stroking her g-spot, and waiting for the right moment. My mind spirals in wicked little bursts of erotic musings until I tip my face to her neck, suck on the tender spot just above her shoulder, and then let my teeth dig in just slightly but quickly, like a flash fire in a forest.

As she explodes around me, I ramp up the pace of my thrusts until she's crying out and begging me for more, and I give her what she wants, maybe more than she expected. Her body's trembling and I know what's about to happen, even if she doesn't. My angle is intentional, and she finally begins the pleading that I knew was coming. "Oh, Steffen, oh god, oh, god. Oh, god, please, oh, god. Steffen, please? Please? Oh, god, oh, jesus, oh jesus, oh, oh, oh . . ." Her voice drops and in a deep growl, she cries out, "Oh, god, OH, GOD, STEF-FEN, NOOOOO . . ."

That's when it happens. There's a sudden gush of wetness that shoots down between us, soaking us and the sofa thoroughly. Now she's screaming, "Shit! Fuck me! Oh, god, baby, stop, STOP! I can't take any more, I can't! I CAN'T! Oh, god . . ." I let her go on like that for, oh, about five more minutes, until she's frantic and practically pummeling my chest to get me to cease fire. Her mound, my abs, and our thighs are wet and slick, and I drop onto her and drag my fingers up her back and into the hair at the nape of her neck, fisting a handful in both palms and pulling her head back to force her view to my face.

I grin. "Good?"

Her eyes go wide. "Steffen! What the hell?"

That makes me snicker. "What? What's wrong, ba-by?"

"Are you trying to kill me?" She's glaring up at me and I'm trying hard not to laugh. But the smirk I'm wearing is going to get me into a world of trouble, I'm pretty sure.

"What? You didn't like it?"

She rolls her eyes. "I didn't *say* that!" I give her a sweet little peck on the lips, and when I pull back again, she's grinning.

"Put you through your paces, huh, little subbie?"

"Is that what you call it? Geez. Well, Sir, I hope

you're happy. Now I've got to clean everything up. What the hell am I going to do about this sofa?"

"I'm very, very happy. My little girl's a squirter!" With that, I unwind my hands from her hair and trail them down her sides until I can tickle her ribs. "And call the carpet cleaning guys tomorrow to come and clean the sofa. Or we'll buy a new one."

"Quit! Quit! I swear, Steffen . . . cut it out!" She's laughing and I'm laughing and we're rolling around and she's squealing. And then I just stop. "What? Why'd you stop? What's wrong?"

I look into that lovely face and I see a future that's bright and promising. "I'm just looking at the love of my life, my wife, the mother of my children." She smiles at me and I watch as big tears escape the outer corners of both eyes and roll down her temples into her hair. "Oh, sweetie, why are you crying?"

"I love you, Steffen. I love you more than I thought it was possible to love somebody. I've never been as happy in my whole life as I am right now."

"Good." I roll us to our sides so we're more comfortable and stroke her soft cheek with my fingers. "I'm so excited about our life together. We're going to have a home and a family and fun and laughter and people who'll stand by us through thick and thin. And each other. Don't forget each other."

She just stares at me.

"Oh, yeah, right, sorry. I love you, Sheila. I love you to infinity and beyond. To the moon and back. Deep as the ocean, high as the sky. Until the end of time. Wait,

I'm thinking – there's got to be another cheesy, corny one in there, I'm sure." She giggles. "But I really do, baby. I love you and I'll love you forever."

"I like the last one best."

I smile. "Me too." Without warning, she puts both hands on my sternum and gives me a push.

I hit the floor in front of the sofa and all the breath is knocked right out of my lungs. But before I can gasp or sit up, she's on top of me, tickling me and nibbling on my neck. My gasping turns to howls of laughter, and she has me screaming, "Stop! Stop! Woman, stop it!" Eventually she just slumps on top of me, shaking with laughter, and I ignore the pain in my back from the hard floor and the headache I'm about to get from where my skull smacked the hardwood. Her weight on top of me feels right, and I tighten my arms around her and kiss her forehead.

I can't imagine what life without her would be like. And I hope I never have to find out.

The drive is torture. We're both as nervous as a new dad in a maternity ward. "So, was the realtor positive?"

I nod. "Yeah. She said she thought both places would move pretty quickly and if they don't, she'll help us with a bridge loan as soon as we find something we like."

"Is she going to start looking for something for us?"

I nod again. "Yeah, and right now too. I told her living room, dining room, eat in kitchen, den, four bedrooms, three and a half baths, laundry room, and a good-sized yard. And preferably in the Hanover school district."

She nods vigorously. "That sounds perfect. Do I look okay?"

That makes me chuckle. "Why do women always ask that in instances where their appearance has absolutely *nothing* to do with the outcome of things?"

"I have no idea. We just do," she says with a shrug.

"Well, if it's any consolation, you look amazing. But then you always do." I can't help but beam as I'm watching the traffic. I have a beautiful wife and I don't mind saying so, especially to her.

"You look amazing too, you know. You're probably the most gorgeous guy I've ever met."

One eyebrow shoots up and I stare at her as best I can while I drive. "Me? I'm gorgeous? Seriously?"

The sarcasm is rolling when she says, "Yes, you. You have to know that. Women are slobbering messes when you're around." I know I'm looking at her like she's crazy, but I can't help it. "Really, Steffen. I'm not kidding. Remember when we went to the Italian restaurant last week?" I nod. "I went to the restroom. While I was in there, these two women came in. One of them said, 'Did you see that hunky blond Viking over there across the room? Oh my god, he's gorgeous.' And the other one said, 'Yeah, and he's with a ginger. I swear, I don't get what men see in those pasty little red-haired girls.'"

"They said that?" Now I just don't believe her. She's

making this up.

"They sure did." Then she laughs. "The first one said, 'She's got an amazing rack. It's gotta be the boobs.'"

That makes *me* laugh. "You've got to be kidding. They were talking about your boobs?"

"No, silly, they were talking about *you*. My boobs just happened to get mentioned. They are pretty amazing, if I do say so myself." She slips her hands underneath her tits and hoists them up, and I start laughing right out loud. "What? They are! When you go into the restroom, aren't the other guys talking about my boobs?"

Now I'm gasping for breath. "No!"

She fakes indignation. "Well. I'm disappointed. The women notice my husband, the blond Viking, but the men don't even notice my boobs? That's ridiculous." I've gone from laughing to outright wheezing. "Maybe next time you should start the discussion. You know, 'Hey, did you guys see the redhead out there with the amazing boobs?'"

"Tits. Guys say tits." I'm still laughing so hard that I'm shaking all over.

"Ick. Tits. I don't like that word. I'm sticking with boobs." She turns and grins at me as soon as I've finished parking the car, and she's still smiling but her face is serious. "I love you, Steffen."

"I love you too, Sheila Ann Cothran. Always and forever. Let's go see a couple of kids who need parents, shall we?"

We walk hand in hand into the office where we meet

Amy and, and after they've verified our identities with our drivers' licenses, they escort us to a good-sized room full of toys and books and things kids would love. The carpet has alphabet characters printed on it with a little animal incorporated into each one, and there's a big window where the sun streams in and makes the whole place cheery and bright. The door opens and two small, anxious faces peer around until they find us. Bless their hearts, they're holding hands. They've got to be terrified. "Mr. and Mrs. Cothran, meet Joey and Rachel." The social worker pushes the children forward but they both try to hang back. I pull out one of the teeny-tiny chairs at the teeny-tiny table and drop all six feet and three inches of me into it. Maybe I won't look so imposing if I'm sitting down. Beside me, Sheila does the same. "I'll leave you four alone to get acquainted. Have fun." With that, she heads out the door and closes it behind her and, glancing back at her, I see Amy standing there. I suppose she's going to observe too. Both kids watch her go, then turn back to us, trepidation all over their faces. Bless her heart, Sheila gets the ball rolling.

"So, I'm Sheila, and this is my husband, Steffen. And you're Joey and Rachel, right?"

The little boy squeezes his sister's hand even tighter before he answers. "Yes, ma'am."

"So, Joey, what's your favorite thing to eat?"

He thinks for a minute. "Hot dogs."

I grin. "Mine too! Especially at the ball park. I love hot dogs from the ball park, with relish and mustard and ketchup."

He nods. "I've never been to a ball park."

For me, that's hard to believe, but I'm sure, in his instance, it's true. "Would you like to go sometime?"

"Yes, sir." He's still not smiling, but he doesn't seem quite so frightened.

"So, missy," I say, directing my question to Rachel, "what kind of animals do you like?"

Very quietly, so quietly that I can barely hear her, she replies, "I. Like. Ponies. And. Dogs."

Sheila pipes up. "I do too. I had a dog when I was about your age. Her name was Princess. She was my best friend." There's a sadness in Sheila's smile, and I wonder: Does she still miss that dog after all these years? Yeah, it's pretty obvious she does. I make a mental note: Dog for her birthday.

"What. Happened. To. Your. Dog?" She's so afraid that her speech is halting. Poor kid.

Sheila smiles. "She got old and she died. And I cried for a month."

"I would too," Rachel whispers out. "Do you have a dog now?"

"No, but I'd like one." Sheila turns and smiles at me.

I grin back at her. "Already duly noted." From that, I get a big return grin out of her. About that time, Joey speaks up.

"So how many kids do you have?"

I smile at him. "None. We just got married. We need some kids, and we're looking for some kids who need us."

My heart breaks when Rachel whispers, "I need a

mom." One glance tells me that Sheila's biting back tears.

"So if you could pick a mom, what would she look like?" I ask the child. She stands and thinks for a minute.

"I'd want her to be pretty."

"Yeah? That would be good, huh?"

She nods. "And have a nice smile. And nice hair."

"Oh yeah?" I decide to try something. "What color hair would you want her to have?"

She shrugs. "I don't know. Maybe orange?"

"Really? She sounds pretty already. What kinds of things would you like for her to do with you?"

"Drive me to school maybe. Make dinner. Hold my hand when we go to the store. Stuff like that. Mom stuff."

"Yeah, mom stuff," Joey repeats. "Maybe pop popcorn? And show me how to make my bed?"

This is tearing me apart. These kids are trying so hard to get us to like them. I'm trying to find a way to let them know that we already do when I decide to play another card. "Did you know we looked at a kid catalog?"

Rachel's little brow furrows. "A kid catalog?"

"Yeah. One of the adoption worker ladies brought a bunch of kid catalogs to our house. You know, kind of like a big book of kids that we could choose from."

Joey's eyes go wide. "Did you choose some kids?"

Sheila jumps in. "Actually, we did. Two."

Rachel's voice trembles when she asks, "What are their names?"

I hear Sheila almost let out a sob when she says, "Oh, you might know them. They're named Joey and Rachel."

Joey's eyes go wide. "You picked us from the catalog?"

I smile at the little boy. "Yes, we did. We looked at a lot of kids' pictures, but we just kept coming back to yours. But we were really, really worried."

His eyes widen again. "Why?"

I give him a little shrug. "We were afraid you wouldn't like us. Like maybe you'd looked in the parents catalog and found someone you'd like better. We were hoping you'd give us a chance."

I watch the small boy look down at his even smaller sister, then squeeze her hand. "We could talk about it, I guess. But there's no parents catalog. We don't get to choose."

"Yes you do. If you tell us you don't like us, we'll leave and let you choose someone else."

Bless her heart, the little one begins to cry and I feel horrible until she sputters out, "Please don't leave! We like you, honest! Don't leave." Then I feel like I've won the lottery.

"Hey, we brought you something. Come here." When Rachel steps toward me, I reach into my pocket and pull out the brightly-colored length of braided cord.

"What is it?"

"Hold your arm out." When she does, I take the cord, wrap it around her wrist twice, and then tie it. "It's a friendship bracelet. If something happens that we never see each other again, I want you to look down at it and remember that you have a friend. No matter what, I'll always be your friend."

She stares at the bracelet like I've just given her a piece from Tiffany's. "Thank you, Mr. Steffen. I'm your friend too."

"Good. Joey, I think Sheila has something for you."

"What? What is it?" Both of us can hear the excitement in his voice.

Sheila opens her bag and pulls something metal out. "They're dog tags, just like soldiers wear! And they've got your name on them, see?"

"I can't read good. What do they say?" he asks, standing beside her and trying to peek over at them in her hand without getting too close, like he's afraid she's going to grab him or something.

"Well, this one says, 'Joey is awesome!' And this one says, 'Always friends.'" She slips the chain over his head and the tags clink as they come to rest on his little chest. "If we don't see you again, at least you can remember us."

"We'd never forget you, right, Rachel?"

Those words. I feel Sheila tremble beside me and I know she's about to come undone, so I reach out, wrap an arm around her, and pull her up against me. When she turns her reddened eyes up to mine, I drop a soft little kiss on her forehead and smile at her. "We'd never forget you guys either. But I hope we don't have to worry about that. I hope we see a lot more of each other really soon."

Now Rachel gets bold. She comes over and leans up against my knees, puts her hands on my thighs, and stares up into my face. "Do you have a house?"

"Yes. But we're going to sell it and her house and buy a bigger house with more bedrooms and a big back yard."

"That's cool. Do you have a basketball goal?" Joey asks.

"No, but I want one. Would you like to play basketball with me?"

"Yeah! I wanna slam dunk. I need a shorter goal."

"And I know where they sell those. So," I start, venturing out into dark waters and hoping somebody throws me a line, "if we can work it out, would you like to come and visit our house? Look around, see if you like it there? I mean, we're getting a new one, but in the meantime, it's the only house we've got and it's pretty nice."

Rachel's still staring into my face. "So do you want more kids?"

"I don't know. All I know is that when we saw your pictures, we didn't look at any more. We knew you were the kids for us."

"That's good. Because I don't want to share a mama and daddy with a million billion kids. Just Joey." Rachel's scowling and she's pretending to be fearsome. It's the cutest thing I've ever seen.

"Oh, no. We wouldn't want that either," Sheila breaks in. "The first two kids wouldn't get enough attention that way. No, we just want enough kids that we can spend lots of time with them so they're really happy and we all really, really love each other."

Rachel's head snaps over to look at Sheila and she says in a very matter-of-factly, patronizing tone, "Don't worry. You're pretty enough to be my mom." I can tell my wife doesn't know whether to cry or laugh until I start to laugh, and she smiles a big, broad smile.

It's time. I just look from one little face to the other and I have to ask, "So, do the two of you think you could ever choose us out of all the other people who would be good parents? Do you think you might be interested in trying us out, giving us a chance?"

I watch as Joey looks down at his little sister and the little girl closes her eyes and gives him one tiny nod. He turns back to me. "Yeah. I think we'd like to give you a chance if you want. You seem pretty nice."

I let out a big, deep breath. "Well, okay then! Honey, how about you? Does that sound good to you?"

Sheila grins. "That sounds excellent! So you guys work on it from your end and we'll work on it from ours, and your people can talk to our people and maybe we can get it all worked out. Sound good?"

"Yep. And I'd like some cupcakes please. You do know how to make cupcakes, right?" Joey doesn't pull any punches. He knows what he wants and he doesn't mind asking, obviously.

"Oh, yes! I sure do!"

"Yeah, she's going to make someone an awesome mom because she makes really, really awesome cup-cakes!" I grin at both kids. "Really awesome. You won't believe it."

"I like chocolate!" Joey yells and starts to bounce up and down.

"And I like chocolate chip!" Rachel yells out, bouncing up and down just like Joey and clapping her hands together softly.

Joey frowns at her. "There's no such thing as chocolate chip cupcakes."

Sheila laughs. "I'll check on that and if I can find a recipe, I'll make some!"

Before we can say another word, the social worker comes through the door. "So, how's it going in here?" I know she's been watching us through the two-way mirror, and I'm sure there's a microphone to pick up our conversation.

"It's going GREAT!" Joey shouts out, his voice rising in timbre and volume far above an "inside" level. "They're nice! She's gonna make us cupcakes!" He points at her and grins. "Miss Sheila!"

"Miss! Sheila! Miss! Sheila!" Rachel chants and claps harder as she hops up and down.

The social worker is grinning like a kid on Christmas morning. "Well, looks like the four of you had a good time! It's time to go. Say goodbye to Mr. and Mrs. Cothran, kids."

"Goodbye, Mr. and Mrs. Coffin," Rachel calls out as she's led away. "Bye! Bye!"

"Bye, Mr. and Mrs. Coffin," Joey calls back, and then he breaks away and runs back to us. He leans in conspiratorially, pulls the dog tags out of his shirt, and whispers, "Thanks. I'll never lose them. I'm keeping them foorr-

EHHH-verrrrr." Then he skips back to the waiting social worker and heads out the door.

Sheila and I sit, shell-shocked, and try to pull our thoughts together. Finally, I manage, "Well? What do you think?"

Her eyes meet mine and they're filled with tears as she smiles. "I think we just said a temporary goodbye to our kids."

About that time, the social worker reenters the room with Amy in tow, and I take Sheila's hand and squeeze it. "So how do you feel it went?" She and Amy pull out one of the little chairs and sit down across the table from us, and it hits me how silly we all look on the tiny furniture.

"I feel like it went very, very well. They're great kids. And I think they liked us. Honey, don't you think so?"

Sheila sniffs hard and smiles. "Yeah, I think they did. I know I liked them a lot. They're adorable and so smart."

The social worker nods and grins at both of us. "We'll schedule a home study in one week. Before you leave today, I'll give you a sheet of what we'll be looking at so you can be in compliance. If that goes well, we'll arrange for some home visits, one a week for six weeks, and maybe even visits with them at the facilities where they're staying in between the home visits. After that, there'll be a couple of overnight stays and then we'll make a determination for fostering. In the meantime, get an attorney lined up and start the adoption process. Hopefully, by the time you're ready for the overnight stays, we'll have parental termination and if all goes well, you'll transition directly into the adoption process and it'll be short and sweet. And if at any time along the way you have any questions or concerns, just call your adoption agent or your assigned social worker and talk to one or both of them. Your social worker will be meeting with you in the next few days before the home study to make sure you understand the process and know what to expect along the way." She finally stops and takes a breath. "Any questions?"

I summon up my courage. "Yeah. How often does this go wrong? I don't mean with the kids; I mean with the process, a monkey wrench in the works, whatever?"

Amy smiles. "Most of the time, by the time a couple's decided to come in and meet a child or children, they pretty well know what they want. So rarely does anything go wrong. Usually if it does, it's something to do with the birth parents and has nothing to do with the kids or the potential adoptive parents. So take a deep breath, both of you – this should go through just fine."

They both see us out and we walk hand in hand to the car. Once we're in and finally alone, I turn to Sheila. "And you're sure this is what you want?"

She nods. "Absolutely. You?"

"No question in my mind."

"Moving forward?"

I finally let loose the tears I've been holding in for the last hour. "Yep. Moving forward."

With her hands wrapped around the back of my

neck, she pulls me into her and we press our foreheads together. Then that sweet voice I love so much whispers to me, "Congratulations, Mr. Cothran. I think we're parents."

My heart is so full that I think it'll burst. A home. A family. A woman by my side for the rest of my life. What more could I ever want?

Not one damn thing. Steffen Cothran's got it all.

Chapter Thirteen

"Hey! Every one of you! Get in here and get cleaned up for lunch!" All five of them rush the door. McKenna, Joey, and Morris try to come through at the same time and find themselves wedged in the doorway, and I can't help but laugh.

"Hey, I can't get in!" Rachel yells from outside. The three of them finally pop through the doorway and she yells in, "Finally! I don't wanna miss lunch!"

"You're not going to miss lunch. I'd never let that happen!" I grab her up and turn her upside down to hear her giggle, and she shrieks with laughter.

"Oh, no!" Joey walks straight up to me and looks up into my face, his new glasses cockeyed. "Auntie Trish made lima beans. Do I have to eat them?"

I'm trying to look serious. "No. You don't have to eat them, but you *do* have to try them."

"Oh, man! No fair!" He hangs his head and I laugh at him.

"Yes, fair. She cooked, you eat."

Sheila's wrangling everyone into their seats when Hailee asks, "Uncle Steffen, I'm supposed to do a class project on how math works in the real world. Could I come to the bank sometime and take a tour? Or just look around? Maybe talk to one of the tellers or something?"

"I'll do you one better than that. We're open on Saturday mornings until noon. I don't have to work then, but I can go in this Saturday and take you with me if you'd like. You can stay the whole time, sit at a window with one of the tellers, look at the computer system, all of that, and I'll show you how we balance the drawers at the end of the day and all of the reporting we do to the Federal Reserve. Interested?"

"Yes! Oh, thank you!" She pops up from her seat, runs around the table, and gives me a big hug.

I give her a kiss on the cheek. "Happy to help." And I laugh when she kisses me back, but it's almost shallow because of the storm that I'm sure is brewing.

We're almost finished with lunch when the doorbell rings. Clint takes a swipe at his face with his napkin and says, "I'll get it." I know what's about to happen; we've all been on pins and needles about this, and we're about to see how it works out. I hear voices in the front hallway, hear the door closing, and I look at Sheila and Trish. They both shoot me nervous smiles until I hear footsteps behind me. Then Morris looks up from his plate and cries out, "Mom!"

I turn and there's Adele. And she's not the Adele I knew. She's gaunt, her hair is scraggly, and her skin is an ashy color. She just generally looks unwell, not the sultry, sexy, voluptuous woman who tried to get every man in her area code to fuck her. When Morris runs into her arms, he almost knocks her down. I watch the two of them as she smiles and talks to him, his excited chatter drowning out her voice. She turns toward me and I just nod. "Adele."

"Steffen. Good to see you." Morris takes her by the hand and leads her toward the den, jabbering a mile a minute.

"She okay?" I ask Clint.

"She's had the flu for the past week, but they said she was well enough to come over. I don't know. She doesn't look too good."

"My thoughts exactly. But she seems to be behaving herself."

He drags a biscuit across his plate through some cheese sauce before he takes a bite. "She's been going to counseling at the detention facility and they say she's doing very well with that. The times I've talked to her she's been very civil and polite, almost friendly even. I think she's getting herself straightened out."

"'Bout time." One by one, the rest of the kids ask to be excused to go back outside, and their moms nod and send them out the door.

Morris reappears in the kitchen. "Dad, can I go back outside?"

Clint shoots him a surprised stare. "Don't you want to visit with your mom?"

He shrugs. "Uh, I've been visiting with her. I want to play with everybody else. Can I, please?"

Clint sighs and shrugs back. "That's 'may I.' Sure. Go on. And on your way out, ask her to come in here with us."

"Okay. Hey, Uncle Steffen, your back yard is awesome!"

"Thanks, buddy. I'm glad you're enjoying yourself." It's the first time we've had everyone to the new house, and I'm enjoying how everyone else is enjoying it. Morris scoots out of the room and in just a minute or two, Adele comes dragging in. She stops, looks at all of us, and asks, "May I sit down?"

Clint stands and holds a chair for her. I can see that shocks her, but she nods and sits, and he helps her scoot her chair up. "Would you like something, Adele? We've got plenty of food left, and there's sweet tea and soft drinks and all of that," Sheila offers.

"Oh, I don't want to be any bother." I can tell she's sincere, and it floors me.

"No bother at all! Ham, biscuits, lima beans, corn, and I think there's some broccoli and cheese sauce left. Anything on the list you don't want? Oh, and a small salad maybe?"

"No, that all sounds fine – great, in fact. And thanks for being so warm and welcoming."

"You're more than welcome." My gracious wife scurries about filling a plate, then sets it, the salad, and a variety of dressings on the table for Adele to choose from. "Drink?"

"Sweet tea?"

"Coming right up," Trish calls out and grabs a glass, fills it with ice, and pours it.

After the first couple of bites, Adele looks around

the table at us, and then her glance lands on me. "Steffen, you seem happy."

"I am."

"Good. You deserve to have a nice home and a good family. The kids are very cute, and so polite and well-behaved."

"I can thank Sheila for that. She's got way more patience with them than I do," I smile, then look across the table at my wife.

"Oh, don't let him fool you. He's an incredible dad. Just amazing."

Adele stares at her plate, her face sad. "I knew he would be. That's why I brought Morris to him." She looks up at Clint. "I'm so sorry for everything I've done and for what I've put you through, you and your wife." Then she looks at Trish and says, "You're a very nice person and you've been very good to my son. I want to thank you for doing a better job than I could ever do."

Trish smiles back, but her eyes are sad. "Thanks, but he's no trouble. He's a great little guy and a joy to be around. You obviously did something right while you were raising him."

"Thanks, but I don't deserve that." She stops, and I can tell there's something going on inside her head, some kind of battle being fought. Finally, she says, "Um, my therapist said I should talk to all of you the first chance I got. And I guess that's now." We all wait expectantly, unsure if we should stick it out or run for the hills. "So I've been thinking." She glances from Clint to Trish and back to Clint. "I've made a decision. Unless you don't want him, I'd like for Morris to stay with the two of you and his sisters. He seems happy with all of you and I don't want to disrupt that and set him back. He deserves to have a good home, and you guys seem to be able to give him that."

"Thanks." Clint nods but doesn't smile. "He's a great kid and we're going to love having him here permanently. But you'll be welcome to visit with him. We can set something up, no problem."

"That's very nice of you. You don't have to do that, but I'm thankful that you will. I love him and I'd like to stay in touch with him, but I want him to have a better life than I can offer him."

"Thank you for putting him first. I'm sure when he's grown he'll thank you," Trish offers.

"Thanks for trying to make me feel better." I think she's finished, but she turns her attention to me. "Steffen, I just want you to know that I'm sorry for what I put you through. I'm especially sorry for driving a wedge between the two of you." She turns to Sheila, and Sheila closes her eyes and nods. "And Sheila, I heard about what happened to you at that . . . well, what happened to you. That wouldn't have happened if I hadn't done what I did, so that's my fault. And I'm so, so sorry. You just have no idea."

"No, Adele. I'm a grown woman. I chose what I did, and it was my fault. If I hadn't . . ."

"No. If I hadn't come there and torn your lives apart, that never would've happened. So I'm sorry for it, so sorry. You're okay, right?"

"Oh, yes! I'm fine. No permanent harm done. So for whatever part you played in all of that, I forgive you. Steffen played a role in all of that too, and I've forgiven him. It's all behind us and we're just moving forward, not dwelling on the past. You should too."

"That's hard to do when thinking about the past is all you've got. It's not like I've got lots of fun activities or social options in there. But I made my bed, so I have to lie in it." To my surprise, she turns back to me. "Clint told me about Maggie. I'm so sorry. She was a very nice lady and I know you miss her. She was lucky to have you as a son. You were always so good to her."

That's a shocker. She always seemed to hate my mother, but then, she hated everybody. "Thanks, Adele. Yeah, it was an awful way to go, but in the end she had so much morphine in her that she didn't suffer. But thanks. I appreciate that."

"You're welcome." She looks up at the clock, then back around the table. "Well, I think I've only got about thirty more minutes before I have to go. I think I'll go out into the yard and try to spend some time with Morris. He's so excited to be here and enjoy himself that he's really not interested in me." The little smile she manages is fake, and I know she's hurt by his apathy, but he's a kid, trying to have fun and fit in with his new family and surroundings. Clint and I both stand as she rises and heads out the back door. Sitting back down, we both look at each other and at the two women there sharing our lives.

"I think she was sincere," Trish offers.

I nod gently. "As sincere as I've ever seen her. I actually feel sorry for her. I think she's broken."

We sit in silence for awhile, and I'm sure they're doing the same thing I'm doing – thanking my lucky stars for the other three people at this table with me, especially my sweet ginger girl sitting here beside me. The doorbell rings, and Clint goes out into the yard to escort Adele back inside to the waiting corrections officer. We all tell her goodbye but, as they start out the door, I can't stop myself. "Wait!" Everyone turns to look at me. "Can I have just a minute alone with her?" I ask, pointing at Adele.

"I'll be waiting in the car," the officer says with a nod, and I feel Clint shepherding the women back into the den. When they're gone, I turn to Adele.

"You know, for the first time, I feel like there's some hope for you." I reach out and take both of her hands in mine.

"Doesn't feel that way to me. I've lost everything I ever had."

"And you've gained something. You've gained four friends. You've gained our respect, and the respect of your son. That's got to count for something, right?"

She gives me a tired smile. "Being good is hard work for me, Steffen."

How horribly sad. I know the smile I manage is a sad one. "Oh, I believe that, but you're doing a good job. Just keep doing it. It'll get easier when you realize how many more flies you can attract with honey than you can with vinegar." That makes the corners of her mouth turn up just the tiniest bit. I can't help it; I reach for her, hug her against me, and kiss the top of her head. At first, she's stiff as a board in my embrace, but then she softens and her hands find their way around my waist. "Adele, I'm so sorry, but I want you to know, I did love you. I loved you with my whole heart. And honestly, I guess there's a little tiny piece of it that will always love you. I just want to see you be happy and healthy and enjoy life. Please try, for your son's sake."

She looks up at me and a single tear rolls down her cheek. "I will. Thanks, Steffen. Thanks for forgiving me and giving me another chance to show you that I can be a good person. I'm trying, I really am."

"I know. Now get on out there to the car and behave yourself. I'm sure you'll see Morris again in a few weeks. It'll all be fine, you'll see."

She turns without another word and walks out the door, straight to the waiting cruiser, and I watch her go, head down and shoulders rounded. Once she's in the back seat, the officer climbs back in and the car pulls away.

I wish I could describe the way I feel standing here, watching her roll away. Part of me is very relieved, but another part is sad. Watching her so devastated, her life wasted, is hard, but she destroyed herself with her choices. I almost destroyed my life with mine. Sheila gave me another chance to redeem myself, and I want to give Adele another chance to redeem herself too.

A pair of soft arms wraps around my midsection from behind, and I feel her press her cheek into my spine. "You okay?"

I turn and sweep her into my arms. "I'm fine. I'm so, so fine. Thanks, babe. Thanks for letting me back into your life when I didn't deserve it, and for loving me when I wasn't very lovable."

"Thanks for saving my life. I can't imagine what would've happened to me if you hadn't walked into that club. Speaking of which, I think it's about time to let someone watch the kids for the evening and go in to play a bit, don't you?"

I give her a peck on the lips and shake my head. "Not until the adoption's finalized."

"Yeah, you're probably right. That's probably best. But I miss it."

"I do too, baby. Let's go spend some time with Clint and Trish until we have to go. Joey has that birthday party to go to, remember?"

We stroll back into the den, arms around each other's waists, to find Trish and Clint making out like a pair of middle schoolers on the sofa. About the time we start to do the same, five kids come thundering into the house asking for cupcakes.

A cupcake. That sounds good right about now.

⟩⟩◦◦◦⟨⟨

The phone wakes me. "Steffen?" I look at the clock; it's three twenty-five in the morning on a Sunday. "Steffen? You there?"

"Clint?" Now I'm confused. "What the hell's going on? You guys okay?"

"Yeah. No. I don't know what to do."

"What do you mean? What's wrong?"

There's a long pause and I feel dread wash over me, but I'm totally unprepared for what he says next. "The detention facility called about ten minutes ago. They found Adele in her cell. She hanged herself on the bars. She's dead, Steffen. Adele's dead. And I don't know what to do, what to say. Does she have family? You were married to her; you know more of this stuff than I do. Tell me what to do."

I stop and think, but there's not one soul I should call. Her family is mostly dead, and the ones that aren't are in jail, so there's really no one to notify. "There are no calls to make. Just make arrangements for the body. What's your gut tell you?"

"Cremation. And then find a way to tell Morris."

"I'll help you with that if you want."

"Would you? Oh, god, that would be great. I really don't know how to approach that."

"We'll figure it out. Go back to bed and try to relax. Fuck Trish. That'll do it."

"Jesus, Steffen, really?" Then he chuckles. "Hmmm. You're right. Talk to you later."

"Later, bud."

"And hey. Thanks."

I smile on my end. "That's what friends are for."

I think back to my days with Adele, and the years I'd spent wondering where she was and trying to get out from under her curse. In all that time, this was not what I'd ever wished for her. I don't know what had been wrong with her to make her be the kind of person she was – probably that fucked-up mess of a family of hers – but I'm sad for the time we'd had together and how I hurt her. I know what she did had nothing to do with me, and I feel okay with the way we left things. But now Morris will never again see the mother who raised him.

Fresh starts. I've gotten one. Sheila's gotten one, and Joey and Rachel, and Morris. And Clint and his girls have certainly had one, not to mention Trish. Dave could probably use one.

In some odd way, I guess this was Adele's. And even though I feel bad that Morris will probably be the only person in the whole world who mourns her, I can't shed a tear. I forgave her for what she did to me. But I'll never forget.

"What a day!" I help Sheila out of the car. "We start out at the courthouse finalizing the adoptions, spend the afternoon in closings on both of the old houses, and then dinner with my Aunt Sophie. My throat's gonna be sore for a week from yelling at her. She's so deaf she couldn't hear her own thoughts."

She giggles. "I'm pretty sure that's true. She kept saying she didn't know where she'd put her teeth, and they were in her mouth. I managed to not laugh, and believe it or not, that was the hardest thing I've done in years!"

"I know what you mean."

"Will they be . . ."

"I know what you're going to say, and yes, they'll be

fine. I think Clint and Trish know what to do with two kids."

"Two more kids. Our kids."

"Give it a rest, Mommy Dearest." We walk into the dimly lit area and I call out, "Hey, Dave! How've you been?"

"I've been great! God, it's so good to see you two! Sheila, lovely as ever."

"Awww, thanks, Dave. You're looking damn fine yourself."

"Well, you're looking pretty fine for a women who had two great big kids since the last time I saw her! Got that figure back quick, I see!"

"Hey, she never lost it!" I wrap my arms around her waist and kiss her. "Got openings in the performance areas tonight?"

"Oh, hell yeah. You can have three anytime you want it. Right now it's set up for nipple torture and a three-way, but that's easy to remedy."

"A three-way, huh?" I watch as Sheila's mouth drops open, but there's a sparkle in her eye. "Maybe someday, but I'm not ready for that yet." She pretend pouts. "But nipple torture? Yeah. I can get into that. Shall we negotiate, sub?"

"No, Sir. Do as you please with me."

"No safeword. Can you handle that?"

"To service you, Sir? I can handle anything." She grins up at me.

"You're going to regret saying that. Meet you over there on that sofa in ten minutes." I slap her ass as she strolls away toward the locker room, and Dave laughs at us both.

"I was hoping to scene with the two of you. You know you can trust me, and that woman of yours is fine, brother."

"Don't I know it. But the idea of your cock up her ass just doesn't sit well with me yet. Maybe in a year or so, but not now."

"Well, if you change your mind, let me know. I'm always up for it."

"You're always up, old perv."

Dave throws back his head and laughs. "I'm glad you realize that, young deviate!"

I'm still laughing as I go to the locker room. I see Gary and a few other guys there as I'm dressing out. My leathers still fit like a glove, and I look down to see the outline of my hard cock plainly visible through the front. Yeah, Master Steffen's in the house. Lock down your women and hide your treasures. No one's safe tonight.

Yeah, right. Who am I kidding? I pulled up in a minivan. I'm like a Rottweiler with all of its teeth missing. And I'm oddly happy about it.

Sheila joins me and I get the usual jolt as I apply a pair of clover clamps to those big, hard nips. Then I strap her down to the whipping horse and stroke her clit until she comes, followed by fucking her ass like I mean it. Listening to her whine and cry out brings back all of the primitive, raw feelings I always have when I'm scening, and I want to fuck my little slut until she remembers who her master is. Once I've finished fucking her ass, I run my fingers into her channel and torment her sweet spot until she gushes onto the floor, then ram that beautiful pussy with my iron rod until we're both shaking and weak. A crowd has watched the whole scene, and I'm full of myself and overflowing with pride that I'm there with this beautiful woman who's now mine.

When I unstrap her and pick her up to take her to the back, a pair of eyes meet mine, and I give them a gentle nod. Once we're on the bed, I take off my leathers and meet her skin to skin, her chest, breasts, neck, and belly still flushed with arousal. She responds to my kisses and shows me her hunger, but she stops when she feels movement behind her on the bed. "Who's there? Is someone there?"

A familiar voice answers, "It's just me, darlin'. I think your Master here wants to give you a special treat tonight. You listen to what he tells you and you'll enjoy this. I've done it enough times to know what I'm doing, so you're safe with us."

I'm worried about her response, but I needn't have been. The look she gives me is saturated with deep, strong lust, and I know I'm doing the right thing. A foil packet rips and the top of a lube bottle snaps open. I watch her mouth make an "O" as he works the lube into her tight little back door, and I slip my stiff, unsheathed dick into her pussy and wait. Dave whispers to me, "Okay, I'm ready."

"Babe, Dave's going to enter your ass. When he does, you'll be full, and it'll hurt this first time, but after this, you'll want it the next time. Don't be afraid. Are you ready?"

To my shock and delight, she glares at me from under her brows and growls, "Fuck me."

"You heard the woman, Dave. That beautiful ass is all yours." I watch as he bores his way into her, the looks of fear and pain on her face at first, then the bliss that follows as he fills her in a way she's never experienced before. The three of us lie there on our sides for a few minutes, letting her channels adjust to our length and girth, and then I nod to Dave. His breath puffs in time with the strokes he's laying into her ass and I draw back, my cock buried deep in her, to start the stroking of her clit. In just seconds she comes with a scream, and I let her rock with it for about two minutes before I still my finger. And that's when I start my stroking in and out of that super-tight, hot pussy my manhood calls home. I hear Dave groan behind her, and I watch her face, completely immersed in the act of being fucked by two large cocks of men who love and respect her, their first and most important goal being to see her more satisfied than she's ever been. His hands snake around her ribcage and cup her breasts, and I watch fingers that aren't mine pinch, pull, and twist my wife's nipples, hear her groan, feel her back arch, forcing her tits out to meet his hands.

Her eyes are closed, her lips slightly parted, her hands gripping my biceps, and I'm enthralled, watching her being satisfied this way. And just when I think she's flying and knows absolutely nothing that's going on, she groans out, "Oh, god, thank you, Sir. Thank you for this fucking, Sir. Oh, god, fuck me, Sir." In that moment, I know that this is my woman. Doesn't matter who's fucking her, who's touching her, she's going home with *me*. She belongs to *me*. She's handed her body over for my pleasure, and I'm giving it back to her. I'm the guy she wants. I'm the guy she needs.

I'm the guy she loves. I smile, then say, "Ready, Dave?"

"Hell yeah."

"Okay then." I give her lips a gentle kiss and call out, "Let's make her fly."

"Steffen?"

"Yeah, baby?"

"Did we pack Joey's toothbrush?"

I laugh right out loud. "You're lying here with two huge cocks in you and you're worried about Joey's toothbrush? Hey, Dave."

He snickers. "Yeah, bud?"

"You know we're real motherfuckers now, right?"

"How's that?"

"Because we just fucked a bona fide mother. So I guess that makes us . . ."

"Crazy. You're fucking crazy. Sheila, baby," he laughs and kisses her shoulder, "your ass is the tightest thing I've ever been in. Thanks for a great ride. I'd love to do this again sometime, precious."

"Thank you, Dave. That was incredible."

"You're welcome, baby. I'm going to clean up and

dress. Stay as long as you like. And girl, let me give you some advice."

"Yeah?"

"Quit worrying about a toothbrush and fuck your master. He's a guy and guys need that. Don't worry about the kids. Clint and Trish have everything under control."

"Okay, okay. Thanks."

I turn my head toward Dave as he opens the door. "Thanks, bud. It was fun."

"Anytime, man, anytime." He closes the door and I hear his boots walking away.

"Well? How was it?"

"Like I said, it was incredible. The only way it could've been more incredible would've been if there was a guy available to fuck my face."

I can't help the groan that shoots out of my mouth. "You're not serious!"

"Well, yeah, I am. We should try that sometime." While her soft fingers meander through the hair on my chest, she smiles. "But I wish I could clone you so every cock in me was yours. That would make me really happy."

"Aw, thanks. I think. How weird."

The sound of her laughter fills the room. "You're welcome. Steffen, why did you decide to do this? I thought you didn't share?"

I don't quite know how to explain it, so I think for a minute or two before I say, "I never shared before because I was afraid whoever I was with would be taken away from me by the other guy. But now? I know you're not leaving. It doesn't worry me. And I knew it was something you wanted to try, so why not? I trust Dave, and I was right to. And you got to experience something new." I stop for just a second before I ask, "And will you be wanting to do it again?"

Her fingers trail back and forth across my chest, pausing from side to side to ring a nipple before crossing over again. "Hmmmm. I'm not sure. Not anytime soon, I don't think. That'll do me for awhile!" She laughs when I pinch her nipple. "Now," she says, pushing me back into the bed and rolling me to face upward, "I plan to suck that cock of yours until you can't take it anymore." I close my eyes as she leans into my face to kiss me, and she grabs my hands and pulls them upward. When they meet above my head, she drops them and, quick as a flash, I realize she's just cuffed me to the headboard.

"What the hell?" I practically scream. "Sheila, what do you think you're doing?"

That grin and the way she licks her lips sends a red-hot jolt of sexual current through me. "I'm going to have you begging me to stop. But I won't. No safeword for you, Sir. Not tonight." I want to protest, but she trails her tongue down my chest, my abs, and down the inside of my right thigh, then circles back up and strokes straight up the length of my dick. Her mouth engulfs me. Before I can stop, I've filled her throat with cum and she's not stopping, not even slowing down.

It's too much, and I'm crazed and fighting the hand-cuffs. I manage to choke out, "Oh, god, baby, stop! I can't take it, please, stop! Sheila, oh, god, baby, no more! No more!" But she ignores me and keeps going, and the pressure and pain are just too much as everything in me readies to explode again. I think about throwing my legs around her and rolling her off of me, but then I think better of it. She wants to drive me crazy by sucking me off until I'm screaming.

Who on earth would turn that down?

Not this guy. Uh-uh. No way.

ABOUT THE AUTHOR

Deanndra Hall lives in far western Kentucky with her partner of 30+ years and three crazy little dogs. She spent years writing advertising copy, marketing materials, educational texts, and business correspondence, and designing business forms and doing graphics design. After reading a very popular erotic romance book, her partner said, "You can write better than this!" She decided to try her hand at a novel. In the process, she fell in love with her funny, smart, loving, sexy characters and the things they got into, and the novel became the Love Under Construction series.

Deanndra enjoys all kinds of music, kayaking, working out at the local gym, reading, and spending time with friends and family, as well as working in the fiber and textile arts. And chocolate's always high on her list of favorite things!

On the Web and blogging:
www.deanndrahall.com

Email:
DeanndraHall@gmail.com

Facebook:
facebook.com/deanndra.hall

Twitter:
twitter.com/DeanndraHall

Substance B:
substance-b.com/DeanndraHall

Mailing address:
P.O. Box 3722, Paducah, KY 42002-3722

Here's a sneak peek
from the next book
in the **Me, You, and Us** *series,*
Incredible Us

"Wow! What happened to you? You're almost glowing. Are you pregnant?" Ben's trying to be a smartass, and I know it.

"No. I just got spectacularly laid last night, that's all."

He laughs. "Happy birthday bang, huh?"

"You know it. Big, happy, awesome bang. Double bang. Man, I hurt all over. It's been a long time since I've gotten and given a fucking that was that aggressive."

Now Ben really laughs at me. "Getting too old?"

"Fuck you!" I throw a towel at him and he ducks and laughs at me. "You'd better find somebody before you're too old to cut the mustard!"

"I already said fuck you or I'd say fuck you," I play-snarl. Once he's finished with the beer delivery, I look around.

How pathetic. I live in a damn BDSM club. Why does everyone keep telling me, "when you find someone, when you find someone, when you find someone . . .?" Not gonna happen.

Then Melina walks in. God, that woman's something. "Hey, darlin', what brings you here?"

She grins. "Got anybody you think would like to be in a film?"

"Can old guys do that?"

She gives me the once-over. "That old guy standing in front of me right now? Hell yeah. I'll do him on camera anytime."

Oh, god, I want to do that. But Clint would kill me. I can hear him now: "Dad, what the hell are you thinking? Porn? Really?" And he'd be right. But it would be so much fun, I think. At least with Melina it would. "So, is this a bondage film, or punishment, or what?"

"Whatever it turns out to be. But you know me – I like it rough." With that, she licks her lips and all I can think about is undressing her with my teeth. Yum. Yes. I do know what she means. I've topped her about, hell, I don't know, eighty times? I remember watching her as I fucked her one night, watching the way she was taking it and playing into it. I wondered if she'd ever make this leap, and she did. She loves it, being in front of the camera, showing off her body, performing any and every sexual act she can think of. It just comes naturally to her. There was one night when she put a pair of clover clamps on herself and walked around out in the commons area. Any time a guy grabbed them and pulled the chain to him, she'd drop to her knees and suck him off right there. Porn is just second nature for her.

"Yes. I remember that you like it rough. Would you like it rough right now?" I just have to ask.

To my surprise, she says, "With you? Right now? Hell yeah, Amazing Adams. Let's get it on." And she drops her clothes right there. I mean, it's just a tiny little slip of a dress, but she's naked underneath, and now she's naked all over. By the time she makes the ten steps toward me, my cock is already popping my zipper. There's no foreplay; there's no warm-up. There's no fondling or kissing or any of that stuff. She just looks me right in the eye, throws one leg up and over my hip, and thrusts her pelvis toward me. That's all it takes. I slide in like a saber into its sheath, and in ten seconds we're fucking like rabbits.

I'm pretty sure I get more pussy than any other guy my age that I've ever known or heard of. Except maybe Hugh Hefner, even though I kinda think I probably get more action than he does. And, by damn, it's fun. My finger finds her control button and I pinch hard to initiate liftoff. And away she goes. When she does, she takes me with her, and we fly into our climaxes simultaneously. She takes my breath away, and apparently I do the same for her. "Damn, Dave, you fuck like a twenty year old."

"And when was the last time you fucked a twenty year old?" I laugh as I grip her waist, and I plant a kiss on her nose.

"Um, last week." Why did I even bother asking that question? I could've guessed the answer. I'm trying to tuck myself back into my jeans, but she says, "Here. Let me do that. I'll clean you up good." With that she drops to her knees.

Oh. My. God. "Girl, did you go to college to learn to do that? Because if you didn't graduate from BJU, you should have. You should get an honorary hummer doctorate. Fuck, girl." I didn't think I could get that hard again that fast, but apparently she knows the secret of the powerful erection. No little blue pills needed. To say she makes short work of me is an understatement. I don't think I've ever lost control that fast before, but I do – I really do. When she finishes licking up everything she might've missed the first time, she tucks my limp dick back into my jeans and zips me up carefully. Then she stands and cups my chin in her soft palm.

"Dave, if I were the marrying kind, I'd be all over you like lube on a strap-on, but you know that's never going to happen. I like fucking around way too much." Melina laughs about it, but I know she means every word she just said.

"I know, baby. You don't need to be tied down. Do your thing. Thanks for the fun and go have a good time." As she turns to leave, I swat her on the ass and she laughs again.

"Save that for next time. And get some good rope!"

"You got it!" I call out to her as she walks out the door. Wow. What a way to start the day. Well, yeah, it's four forty-five in the afternoon, but it's the start of the day at Bliss. And I have a feeling it's going to be a good one.

I hope you enjoyed this excerpt from the final book in the Me, You, and Us series. Check my website at www.deanndrahall.com for more information.

Connect with Deanndra on Substance B

Substance B is a new platform for independent authors to directly connect with their readers. Please visit Deanndra's Substance B page where you can:

- Sign up for Deanndra's newsletter
- Send a message to Deanndra
- See all platforms where Deanndra's books are sold
- Request autographed eBooks from Deanndra

Visit Substance B today to learn more about your favorite independent authors.

Printed in Poland
by Amazon Fulfillment
Poland Sp. z o.o., Wrocław